Capture the Moment

NOVELS BY SUZANNE WOODS FISHER

LANCASTER COUNTY SECRETS

The Choice
The Waiting
The Search

STONEY RIDGE SEASONS

The Keeper
The Haven
The Lesson

THE INN AT EAGLE HILL

The Letters
The Calling
The Revealing

AMISH BEGINNINGS

Anna's Crossing
The Newcomer
The Return

THE BISHOP'S FAMILY

The Imposter
The Quieting
The Devoted

NANTUCKET LEGACY

Phoebe's Light
Minding the Light
The Light Before Day

THE DEACON'S FAMILY

Mending Fences
Stitches in Time
Two Steps Forward

THREE SISTERS ISLAND

On a Summer Tide
On a Coastal Breeze
At Lighthouse Point

CAPE COD CREAMERY

The Sweet Life
The Secret to Happiness
Love on a Whim

———

The Moonlight School
A Season on the Wind
Anything but Plain
Lost and Found
A Healing Touch
A Year of Flowers

Capture the Moment

SUZANNE WOODS FISHER

Revell

a division of Baker Publishing Group
Grand Rapids, Michigan

© 2025 by Suzanne Woods Fisher

Published by Revell
a division of Baker Publishing Group
Grand Rapids, Michigan
RevellBooks.com

Printed in the United States of America

Library of Congress Cataloging-in-Publication Data
Names: Fisher, Suzanne Woods, author.
Title: Capture the moment / Suzanne Woods Fisher.
Description: Grand Rapids, Michigan : Revell, a division of Baker Publishing
    Group, 2025. | Series: 0 National Parks Summers
Identifiers: LCCN 2024035101 | ISBN 9780800745318 (paper) | ISBN 9780800747077
    (casebound) | ISBN 9781493450572 (ebook)
Subjects:
Classification: LCC PS3606.I78 C36 2025 | DDC 813/.6—dc23/eng/20240809
LC record available at https://lccn.loc.gov/2024035101

25   26   27   28   29   30   31   7   6   5   4   3   2   1

All the wilderness seems to be full of tricks and plans to drive and draw us up into God's light.

—John Muir

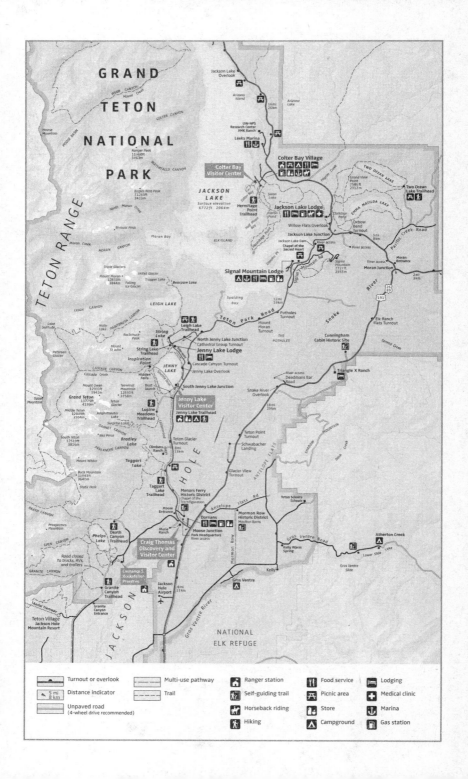

CAST OF CHARACTERS

Kate Cunningham (age mid 20s), aspiring wildlife photographer whose experience with animals has come from a zoo

Grant Cooper, known as "Coop" (age late 20s), high school biology teacher who works summers as a seasonal Jenny Lake Ranger

Tim Rivers (age 54), district ranger at Grand Teton National Park, grandfather to Maisie, friend to all

Maisie Mitchell (age 13), granddaughter of District Ranger Tim Rivers, a pint-sized rule follower with a zest for life

Frankie (age 16), summer intern assigned to Coop, borderline juvenile delinquent

Sally Janus (age 55), acting chief ranger at Grand Teton National Park, a Dolly Parton look-alike

Oliver (age mid 30s), Kate's heart-stoppingly handsome boyfriend

Thea (pronounced Tee-a) **Mitchell** (age late 30s), Maisie's mom, Tim Rivers's stepdaughter

Grizzly Bear 399 (age late 20s), dubbed the Queen of the Tetons, she's the most famous grizzly bear in the world

ONE

*In every walk with Nature one
receives far more than he seeks.*
—*John Muir, conservationist*

Kate Cunningham's eyes widened with awe as Grand Teton National Park unfolded before her, a sight so breathtaking that it forced her to pull over to the side of the road. No amount of research could have truly prepared her for the spectacle that lay ahead: a sweeping valley floor pushing right into the steep granite peaks of the Tetons, still covered with snow.

She sat in silence, mesmerized by those peaks, until the awe overwhelmed her and she had to look away. In the meadow in front of her, Kate spotted an elk grazing. The quiet beauty of the scene stirred something within her. Without a moment's hesitation, she leaped out of her car and popped the trunk to retrieve her prized possession—a brand-new Sony Alpha 1, heralded as the epitome of wildlife photography cameras. Working at a zoo to create a portfolio, padding her meager income with gigs from bar mitzvahs to weddings, and surviving on a diet of Top Ramen had led her to this moment. Kate was on a mission.

Just as she attached her zoom lens to the camera and focused in on the elk, her eyes widened in amazement as a black bear emerged from the tree line. Following behind her came two cubs.

A flare went off in her heart. She'd barely arrived in the park and she'd already seen more wildlife in two minutes than she'd hoped for in two days! With a mixture of excitement and trepidation, she aimed her lens at the sow and her cubs. As the black bear lumbered away, she looked at the images she'd taken. Good, really good, but not unique. Not noteworthy. Not for *National Geographic*, anyway.

With a vague promise from a *Nat Geo* editor dangling like a tantalizing carrot, Kate had set her sights on capturing a unique photograph of the world's most famous bear—Grizzly Bear 399. The editor, a woman she'd met at the zoo a few weeks ago, had said that if Kate could deliver *that* shot, she would take a serious look at it. But, she said, she would need to see the photograph by the end of May. She handed Kate a piece of paper with her email scribbled down. It was the closest Kate had ever been to a breakthrough opportunity, and she was de-termined to seize it. Within her grasp was her dream—to be a wildlife photographer.

Stopping at the Moose Entrance, Kate had learned that Griz-zly 399 hadn't emerged from hibernation yet. "Then again, she might be dead," the ranger said in a matter-of-fact way. "She's an old lady, you know."

Oh yeah, Kate knew. She had studied everything there was to know about 399. This bear was iconic, known particularly as a wise and vigilant mother.

The bear's age was the reason that the *Nat Geo* editor said she wanted a close-up picture—everyone assumed this could be the bear's last summer. From what Kate had read, and from the grim remark by the ranger, that was a reasonable assumption. No one expected Grizzly 399 to survive yet another winter.

Year after year, she kept surprising them. Kept emerging from her den, often with new cubs. A few years ago, she came out of hibernation with quadruplets—a rare occurrence for a sow. Keeping four cubs well-fed and well-protected was no small feat for a bear of any age.

This summer could be the start of Kate's wildlife photography career. She could sense it—something was coming her way. Something that could change everything.

And if she missed it, she'd be back to the zoo.

She reminded herself that it wouldn't be the worst thing to go back there. It was steady work. She shot pictures of the animals for exhibit signs, as well as for publicity and marketing. Locally, she'd been gaining a bit of recognition after adding quirky captions to the zoo photographs she posted on Instagram. One of her hits was a group of majestic giraffes all looking in unison, with a mischievous monkey photobombing in the background, hanging upside down and looking utterly ridiculous. Kate's caption for the shot: "The relative who never gets mentioned."

She took a few more photographs of the elk grazing in the meadow. Such a peaceful moment. She was tempted to stay longer, but she wanted to check in at Jackson Lake Lodge, get something to eat, and plan out her locations for the week. It was one thing to read a guidebook about the national park, it was another thing to be here, surrounded by its vastness. Its grandeur.

Thank you, thank you, thank you, God, for bringing me here.

She put the cap on her camera lens, satisfied. This, she thought, was a good note to end her first day on. A very good note.

Grant Cooper, known as Coop in Grand Teton National Park circles, stepped into park headquarters with a pretty strong suspicion as to why he'd been summoned. His boss wanted to chat. Coop couldn't help but find it ironic—District Ranger Tim Rivers, a man not known for his chatty nature, calling him in for a conversation. Then again, Coop wasn't much of a talker either, and that's one reason they got along so well.

Coop lived all year for summer months in the mountains. The rest of the year, he traded his seasonal ranger hat for the role of a high school biology teacher at a private high school in Salt Lake City, attempting to cram knowledge into the minds of bored teenagers until he ran out of words and patience by May, when the school year ended. Summers, however, were his escape, a time to protect grizzly and black bears and recharge his soul. Bears, especially, held a special place in his heart.

But this summer season, which kicked off recently, had started out on a bad foot. It was a record year for snowfall, with the park entirely socked in. In a regular year, most of the snow was gone by July and August, the heaviest tourist season. But this wasn't a regular year. It was mid-May, and there was still an enormous amount of snow and ice to melt from the mountains, creating dangerous conditions for inexperienced hikers—which, in Coop's eyes, were most of them.

A series of encounters with clueless tourists had left Coop frustrated much earlier in the season than usual. German backpackers disrupted a herd of elk for selfies, a day packer attempted to feed a granola bar to a bear cub, claiming he was "connecting with nature," and the grand finale—a camper had no clue how to put his borrowed-from-his-neighbor tent together. That was the clincher for Coop. It was a classic tip-off to rangers. When campers had no idea how to erect tents, they had no business hiking in the backcountry.

At that point, Coop's short fuse had heated to the point that these misguided campers complained to park management, which led to this moment in Tim Rivers's small office in the park's headquarters.

Tim sat across from Coop in his perfectly pressed uniform, with a badge gleaming on his chest. On a corner of the desk sat his wide-brimmed hat. He was a quintessential parkie and had been assigned to numerous parks, all over the country. Coop met Tim a few years ago, when he'd given a talk at Coop's high school about a career in the National Park Service. Afterward, Coop introduced himself, explaining that he had spent every summer of his life backpacking in the national parks. It was the main reason he had chosen teaching as a profession. Like everything in life, Coop took teaching seriously, he gave it everything he had, but he wanted his summers free for the wilderness.

Tim convinced Coop to work as a seasonal Jenny Lake Ranger at Grand Teton National Park, sealing the deal when he described the work of a backcountry ranger. Remote. Isolated. "You're already doing it," Tim had said. "You're a seasonal vagabond. Why not earn money and do a little good for the world while you're at it?"

So, for the last two summers, that's exactly what Coop ended up doing. Being a seasonal Jenny Lake Ranger was just the right fit for him, kind of like teaching but with even more passion poured into it. He was all in—maybe even more than that. The gig just clicked for him; his hair got all wild, shaving felt optional, and he took on a rugged, work-hardened look. It was like he turned into the opposite of Mr. Cooper, the biology teacher at the high school who rocked a tie every day. For him, being a seasonal ranger was like hitting the jackpot—a chance to hang out with nature all summer, far from the hustle and bustle of regular life. Far away from entitled teenagers, far away from most human beings. A certain female named Emma, in particular. The Emma Dilemma, he called it.

It had been a perfect job until now.

Sitting in Tim's office, Coop wondered if this was the way his students might feel when summoned to the principal's office.

Defensive. Indignant. Misunderstood. "Tim, I was only doing my job. Those tourists were deliberately ignoring rules of the park. Rules that are posted *everywhere.*"

"I don't disagree with you, but the park service is under fire to reexamine its training regarding insensitivity."

Coop slapped his palm against his chest. "Tim, how is it insensitive when I'm trying to stop some tourist from getting way too cozy with a wild animal she thinks is just 'the cutest thing'?"

Trying unsuccessfully to swallow a smile, Tim paused and dropped his chin. When he lifted his head, he was back to business. "Coop, you know as well as I do that the official policy of the NPS is to not make fun of tourists."

Yeah, yeah, yeah. Coop knew.

"Let me ask you a serious question." Tim leaned back in his chair and folded his hands behind his head. "What concerns you more? The people or the animals?"

Coop's eyes narrowed. "Is this a trick question?"

"The tourists reported that you called them idiots."

Did he? He might have. They *were* idiots.

"Clueless," Tim continued, leaning forward to read off the report. "Oblivious. Ignorant. Illiterate."

Yep. Coop might have added a few more adjectives. "Okay, okay. I get it. I'll be more careful." He started to rise from his seat, but Tim shook his head.

"Sally wants to reassign you."

Coop plopped back down in the seat. Great, just great.

If Tim Rivers was a true parkie, Sally Janus was a park lifer. She was acting chief ranger of Grand Teton National Park, but she sure wasn't acting.

Most likely, if you asked someone to describe a female chief ranger, they'd come up with a rather robust woman. Strong, big, fearless. Sally was petite, barely over five feet tall, bright bleached-blond hair, with a squeaky little-girl voice. She reminded Coop of Dolly Parton. Coop found her to be an interesting person. And Tim thought so too, far more so.

Coop knew from Tim that the National Park Service path to career advancement was full of bureaucratic red tape. Qualified rangers competed for the same top positions via a point system. So most of the high-ranking rangers Coop worked with, like Tim and Sally, had earned their points at less popular parks or historical parks, waiting to get appointed to a promotion at a popular park. Or they would take an acting role at a more popular park, like Grand Teton, and wait.

And that's what Sally was currently doing. As acting chief ranger, she was responsible for overseeing all aspects of the park, from law enforcement to resource management. Her word was law in the park.

Great, just great. So . . . he'd been yanked from the backcountry. His mind raced through the dreaded possibilities—visitor center duty, trail maintenance. Nope, he couldn't face it. "Tim, if I can't be in the backcountry, I'd rather not be a ranger. I'd rather just spend my summer with a backpack. I quit."

"Too bad. You signed a contract," Tim said, unfazed. "We're not about to lose that sixth sense you have. You're one of the best bear managers I've ever seen. Somehow you know the whereabouts of bears before anyone else. Including the full-time Jenny Lake Rangers. And even if you're not in the backcountry, you'll still be managing bears."

"What?" Coop squinted. "Please tell me you don't mean that I'll be directing traffic for bear jams."

"At times, yes. But Sally mostly wants you to manage the photographers who are angling for the best wildlife shot."

Worse than bear jams. Coop squeezed his eyes shut in frustration. "I don't get it," he said, opening his eyes. "How could it possibly help the park's insensitivity problem to assign me to babysit bear paparazzi?"

Tim pointed at him. "For that very reason. We're going to show the world that Grand Teton National Park encourages people and wildlife to coexist. We are going to help wildlife photographers do their work, but safely, from a distance." Growing serious, he leaned forward on his elbows. "Look, I agree with Sally on this. I'd feel better if you were down in the valley too. There's chatter about a poacher who thinks it's time to take 399 as a trophy."

"Is it a credible threat? Seems like every year we hear similar rumblings."

"Not sure." Tim seesawed his hand in the air. "And I'm not sure how many years the old girl has left."

"Then doesn't it make more sense to keep me in the backcountry? Keeping an eye on her?"

Tim shrugged. "If it makes you feel any better, Sally's replaced you with Gallagher, Baker, and Spencer. Three rangers."

Coop sighed. Three rangers who were more like the Three Stooges. But if Sally had made up her mind to reassign him, there was no way around it. And Tim wasn't going to intervene. Added to her authority was that Tim was sweet on her. His gruff voice got soft and gooey when he talked about Sally. Coop had warned him not to get involved with someone he worked with, especially not a boss, but did he listen? Nope.

Tim pushed an envelope across the desk. "Here's a plus. In that envelope is your key. I was able to get you in park housing near Jackson Lake Lodge. I tried to get you a trailer, but they were all spoken for."

"Those dorms?" Coop groaned. "Tim, I'm not a kid." That meant he would have a roommate. That meant sharing a communal bathroom. That meant the only time he'd be sleeping in the great outdoors was when he had time off. "Are you trying to punish me?"

"All ages live in those dorms. You know that. All genders too. Might end up being good for you. Who knows? Maybe you'll meet the woman of your dreams." He grinned. "My mother used to say there's a match for every flame."

Now Tim was pushing Coop's buttons. This was a touchy subject.

"There's a shoe for every foot." Tim's eyes danced with amusement. "A key for every lock."

With a huff, Coop scooped up the envelope with the key to his dorm room and stormed out to Tim's loud guffaws.

Twenty minutes later, Coop parked his truck in the massive parking lot at Jackson Lake Lodge, swung his backpack over one shoulder, and walked toward the dormitories, frustrated and annoyed. He slid the key into his room's lock, pushing the door wide open. The small room held two twin beds, a couple of desks, three built-in bureau drawers, and a window offering a view of the majestic Tetons.

That was a plus.

Then came the minus.

On the bed closest to the window was a scrawny kid with a mop of unruly long hair, a red bandana tied around his forehead. He had earbuds in, listening to something on his phone. He looked at Coop as curiously as Coop looked at him.

"Aww, man," the kid said, sounding disappointed. "Don't tell me I got stuck with a roommate after all. And they sent in Smokey the Bear? I bet my old man's behind this."

"Hello to you too." Coop unloaded his backpack on the empty bed.

"Sorry. I'm just bummed to have to share my space."

As was Coop. "Shouldn't you be at work?"

"Nope. Done for the day. I'm just sitting here contemplating the existential path of mankind."

In the middle of zipping his backpack, Coop stopped and turned. "How old are you?"

"Old enough." The kid sat up and slapped his hands on his knees. "Call me Frankie."

"I go by Coop." But if this kid were in Coop's biology class, it would be Mr. Cooper, the only teacher who wore a tie.

"Coop . . . like a chicken coop?"

"Like my last name is Cooper."

"Ah, like Alice Cooper," Frankie said, his tone an odd mix of enthusiasm and cynicism.

"Yeah, something like that," Coop said, suppressing a smile. "A little less makeup." He gave him a sideways glance. "Where are you working this summer?"

"I should be in the Wildlife Brigade."

"Why aren't you?"

"Apparently, you have to be eighteen years old or have *parental permission*." Frankie said it with a sneer. "But my old man decided I needed some"—he wiggled two fingers for air quotes—"character-building experience." His face contorted into an exaggerated frown. "So, here I am, serving time in the glorious Youth Conservation Program."

"So what exactly are you doing?"

"So far, I've been assigned to cleaning toilets and unclogging bear-proof trash bins." Frankie hopped off the bed with a lackadaisical stretch. "You seem pretty old for the Youth Conservation Program."

"That's because I am." This kid could use a filter on his mouth. "I'm a seasonal ranger. For the last few summers, I've been assigned to the backcountry."

"Now *that* sounds like a worthy and noble occupation." Frankie's eyebrows lifted, his expression serious. "So what happened to turn your luck for this summer?"

"Assigned to manage the valley's wildlife photography. Bears, mostly."

Frankie's eyes widened, then he burst out with a scoff. "Dude, what a comedown. You're the official bear photographers' manager." He couldn't stop chuckling. "Man, you must've done something really stupid."

Coop opened and shut the drawers, finding them full of Frankie's jumbled clothes. "Hey, I'm going to need some space."

"Yeah, yeah. Just empty one out."

"I'll empty two out." Coop scooped up Frankie's clothes and dumped them on the floor. He gave his obnoxious roommate a *look*. "Privileges of age."

Wade Schmidt tapped his fingers impatiently on the desk, glancing at the clock every few seconds. He expected punctuality, especially from those who worked under him. Finally, the phone rang, and he picked it up with a swift motion. "Feldmann, you're late."

"Apologies," came the response. "This case requires meticulous planning."

"Any sign of it?"

"Nothing yet."

"Good," Wade said, nodding. He glanced out the window, noting the overgrown grass, and made a mental note to speak to the gardener later. He prided himself on attention to detail, something he expected from everyone who worked for him. "I want a good hunt, Feldmann. Better than good."

"I assure you, sir, I'm doing everything in my power to ensure that."

"Timing is crucial. This needs to happen before it's seen. Within the next two weeks."

"Understood."

"And you're confident you've chosen the right person for the job?"

"Absolutely. As you said, a disgruntled insider makes the perfect turncoat."

Wade leaned back, running a hand over his face. Feldmann's reassurances were comforting, but he needed results. "Keep me updated on every development."

"You can rely on me, Mr. Schmidt."

"Can I?" Wade's skepticism rose a notch. "So far, your efforts seem more focused on negotiations than actual scouting."

"Well, it's this bear, sir. It's the prize everyone wants."

TWO

Grand Teton has it all.
—Matt and Karen Smith, travel writers

Thirteen-year-old Maisie Mitchell was jolted awake by odd scurrying sounds echoing in the small basement. As she blinked away sleep, she saw her mom hastily packing belongings into a worn-out duffel bag.

Maisie sat straight up, alarmed. "What's going on?"

Her mom darted around the basement, picking clothes up off the floor, with an unusual pep in her step. "I've been waiting for you to wake up, sleepyhead. We're going on a road trip."

"Why?" Maisie said, her voice flat. She knew this drill. "Why can't we stay with your friend? This basement is way nicer than the last place." That one was infested with roaches. When Maisie would flip the light switch on, she'd see them scurry along the walls. *Bleh.* Just thinking of those creepy bugs grossed her out.

Her mom spun around. "We're going on a trip to see your grandfather."

"Pops?" Maisie brightened at the mention of her grandfather. To everyone else, he was known as Ranger Tim Rivers. To

21

Maisie, he was Pops. She *adored* him. Pops looked like a cowboy, all weathered and sturdy. He wasn't her biological grandfather; he had married her mom's mom, whom Maisie had never met but heard countless stories about. Grandma had died when her mom was in college. Pops said that Mom's world broke apart and had never quite mended back together since then.

Maisie *adored* time with Pops, but visits were usually planned far in advance during summer breaks or holidays. "Why now?"

"Sometimes, honey, the stars align just right. This is one of those times." Her mom continued packing, but her voice held an excitement Maisie hadn't heard in ages.

Well, as long as Pops was involved, she wasn't going to slow this road trip down. She jumped out of bed and grabbed her jeans to change into from her pajamas.

Mom's art friend, an older woman named Rebecca Woodbine, poked her head over the stair railing, halfway down the basement steps. "I'm packing some sandwiches for you. Peanut butter and raspberry jam okay?"

Maisie nodded. "My favorite." Rebecca had been really nice to them. She'd met Mom at an art class Mom taught. When she found out Mom was getting kicked out of her apartment *and* that she had a daughter, she offered to let them stay for free in her basement. As long as they needed, she had said.

"I'll start loading the car. Can you strip the bed sheets for Rebecca? She wants to add them to a load in the washing machine." Mom picked up a laundry basket full of shoes and started up the stairs.

Wait a sec! That laundry basket full of shoes was a signal. Maisie turned in a circle. *Yep.* Mom was packing everything.

Something wasn't adding up. "Mom! Rebecca said we could stay as long as we needed. Why can't we come back here after visiting Pops?"

Her mom paused on the steps, her eyes lingering on the

shoes in the laundry basket. "Sweetheart, it's . . . complicated. Grown-up stuff, you know?"

Maisie tilted her head, confused. "No, Mom, I don't know. Why can't we stay at Rebecca's? I like it here."

"Don't sweat it so much, Maisie. Things are going to get better." And off she went.

Right. Band-Aid better. Maisie knew Mom's patterns.

She pulled the sheets off the bed and bundled them up in a pile, as Mom made trips back and forth to the car. Soon, the basement looked like it had when they'd first arrived.

"I'm going to miss this place," Maisie said, looking around the roach-free basement that had been home for the last few weeks.

Rebecca came down the stairs to get the sheets. "It's been nice to have you and your mom here. When my husband and I bought this house, we had a plan to create a spare room. We've been so blessed that we wanted to share our blessings. We wanted to create a place of respite. Provide a little extra help to someone we thought could use a helping hand or a fresh start. But somehow, we never got around to it. And then my husband passed away." She looked around. "That was when I realized that good intentions weren't enough. You have to turn them into reality. So, last year, I had the basement finished off. I added that little bathroom, had carpet installed, brought in some furniture. And then I prayed."

"You prayed?" Pops did a lot of that.

"That's right. I prayed for God to bring the right people into my life at just at the right time. So far, so good. You and your mom are my third guests."

All code, Maisie thought, *for your time is up. You're not coming back.*

Rebecca took the bundle of sheets out of Maisie's arms and went back up the stairs. Halfway up, she stopped to poke her head over the stair rail. "Why, it just occurred to me. You're the first kid who's stayed here." Then she disappeared up the stairs.

Maisie's smile faded. "I am *not* a kid."

Through the window, she heard Mom give a warning toot on the car's horn, so she dashed up the stairs. If she couldn't stay in Rebecca's cozy basement, then staying with Pops in the Grand Tetons was the next best place to be. Maybe the best place of all.

The day's forecast was full sun, no clouds. Kate was up early to head over to Oxbow Bend. Here, the Snake River widened, winding and curving in such a way that it formed the unique oxbow shape that gave the bend its name.

From what Kate had read, this was an ideal place to spot wildlife. Dawn and dusk were the hours of the day when most wildlife was active, out and about. The slow-flowing, reflective waters and the lush vegetation attracted birds and mammals. Moose might be wading through the shallows, and beavers might be busy constructing their lodges along the riverbanks. According to Kate's guidebook, anyway.

Being here, in person, beat the guidebook's enrapturing description. She could definitely see why Oxbow Bend, with its scenic beauty and reflective properties, was a prime location, the most photographed spot in the entire Grand Teton National Park. She knew it was the beginner's version to Grand Teton, but in many ways she was a beginner. To wildlife photography, anyway.

Down on the bank of the Snake River, Kate set up her tripod. She wasn't sure if she was going to use it to stabilize her camera but wanted it nearby just in case. Lifting the binoculars around her neck, she scoped the small island in the center of the river. She thought she saw something and squinted, but she couldn't see anything other than trees and bushes.

"You'll have to move."

Kate whirled around. A ranger stood behind her, hands on his hips. She couldn't make out his face under his hat brim in the dim light, but his tone struck her as someone who hadn't had his morning cup of coffee. "Why do I have to move?"

"Jackson Lake Dam is releasing water to manage snowmelt and runoff. Oxbow Bend is downstream of the lake. That means exceptionally high water levels in the Snake River today. Won't be long until the bank you're standing on will be submerged. You'll be ankle high in water. Maybe knee high."

She sighed. Okay. Sounded like this ranger knew what he was talking about.

"And a sow and her cub might be upriver. I'm not letting any shutterbugs get too close until I'm sure they've moved along."

Kate's eyes widened. "Could she be Grizzly Bear 399?"

The ranger shook his head. "She hasn't been seen yet. Besides, you're in the wrong area."

"I know. I've read. I should be staked out at Pilgrim Creek." She started to pack up her equipment.

"So why aren't you?"

"I couldn't find a spot to put my tripod." Countless other photographers had claimed their turf. They were shockingly territorial. Kate had not been welcomed.

He softened a little. "What time did you try?"

"Last night, before sunset." Kate had checked in at Jackson Lake Lodge and dropped her bags in her room. She was still practically buzzing with excitement over the animals she'd seen as she had arrived in the park, so she decided to head out again—three miles north to Pilgrim Creek. She had this picture in her head—she'd scout out the perfect little spot, set up her tripod, and just wait for the magic of the wilderness to unfold in front of her camera.

Turned out, she wasn't the only one with that brilliant idea. Dozens of other wildlife photographers had beaten her to Pilgrim

Creek. There she was, thinking she'd waltz right in, only to find it was more like elbowing her way through a rock concert to get to the front row. Talk about a reality check.

In that moment, Kate discovered wildlife photography in Grand Teton National Park was a competition. It felt like a silent contest where everyone was vying for the best spot and nobody was willing to share. She had eyed a small opening between two photographers, their lenses nearly as tall as she was, and made her move. Nope, that space slammed shut before she could even introduce herself. She tried again elsewhere, but each time she found a potential spot, the gap suddenly closed. It was as if everyone was on a mission to block her out.

Shouldn't there be a sense of community? Camaraderie? Professionalism? Disappointed and a bit irked, Kate realized the peaceful, serene photography experience she had enjoyed at the zoo was nowhere to be found here. Reluctantly, she packed up her gear and left, feeling ousted by a clique of tripod-toting rivals. So much for capturing the tranquil beauty of nature.

"You need to get there by dawn," the ranger said. "Actually, long before dawn."

"Before dawn?"

"Yep. At least in the last few years, 399 has made an appearance around Pilgrim Creek in mid-May, during the early hours of the morning."

"After living in a dark, cold den for months and months, I would think a bear would want to wait until the sun was high in the sky." She rubbed her arms. "You know, warm up those bones."

"You'd think so, but it's just the opposite. Bears are generally more active during the cooler hours of the day. Especially in the height of summer. They seek out food and explore their surroundings when temperatures are lower." He picked up the tripod as she set her camera in its case. "So I take it that you're new here?"

"New to the park. And . . . new to wildlife photography."

He stopped and turned. "And you've chosen 399 as your subject?"

Sure did. "That's the plan. I'm hoping to get a shot of her that hasn't been taken. An angle that tells an untold story."

He cleared his throat. "But you're new to shooting wildlife?"

"I, uh, well, yes and no." More no than yes. "I've been a photographer for a zoo."

He stopped and turned to her, his eyes wide. "A *zoo*?" A rustle in the bushes hinted at a presence nearby and Kate froze. The ranger squinted. Nothing emerged. "Probably a bird." His attention turned back to her. "So, let me get this straight. Your entire experience around wildlife is based on a *zoo*?"

"It's a pretty impressive zoo."

"Oh, like the San Diego Zoo? I've heard that's the top zoo in the country."

"It is. But that's not the zoo I've worked in." Not by a long shot. "Different coast."

Out of the bush came a small man, a large camera around his neck, to shush them. "Do. You. *Mind.*"

The ranger straightened his back. "Where'd you come from?"

"Take your party elsewhere," the man said in a loud whisper. "There's a bald eagle that should be feeding her young in that tree nest soon. I've been waiting an hour to snap a picture."

"Oooh, I'd love to see that," Kate said.

"You're going to have to see it from the road level." The ranger turned to the man. "Come on. Both of you. Away from the riverbank."

The man muttered an unmentionable word under his breath but gathered his equipment. Still carrying Kate's tripod, the ranger went up the steep embankment and waited until the small man staked out his new location. Then he started walking down the road to the turnout for cars. Kate followed behind, wondering if he was confiscating her equipment. He went a distance and then stopped to set up her tripod.

"Here," he said. "This spot will give you the best vantage point to see all the way up and down the river."

By now, the early morning sun had climbed high enough to paint the sky with its gentle glow, revealing the ranger in clear detail to Kate's eyes. He was young. Early thirties? Late twenties? Definitely much younger than she first thought him to be. He was handsome too—not in a *GQ* way like her boyfriend Oliver, but in a rugged, outdoorsy way. Square chin covered with stubble. Rich auburn hair that curled slightly over his collar. Roman nose. Nice lips. In his khaki uniform, weathered boots, and stern hat, he looked every inch like a park ranger. After testing the stability of the tripod, he lifted one hand to make the thumbs-up gesture. "You're good to go, miss, or um, missus. Or, uh, ma'am."

It was cute, how he stumbled over his words. "Kate," she said. "Call me Kate. I'm Kate Cunningham."

He glanced up for a moment, and their eyes met. Met and held. His gray eyes—the color of seawater—had smile crinkles at the edges. In those eyes she saw kindness and a hint of vulnerability. It surprised her, because his deep voice resonated a kind of grouchy authority.

He looked away, as if he could read her mind and was slightly embarrassed. "Since today's supposed to be sunny, come back at dusk and you'll see Mount Moran reflected in the river like a mirror." He tipped his hat. "Have a good day, Kate Cunningham."

He started to walk away but stopped and turned when she called out, "Hey! Hey, Ranger! What's your name?"

"Grant Cooper."

"Thank you, Ranger Cooper."

He cleared his throat. "I go by Coop."

"Thank you, Coop."

The small man popped out from behind a parked car to shush them. "Do. You. *Mind.*"

Kate's eyes went wide. Where did he come from? He must have followed them! Ranger Cooper—Coop—exchanged an amused glance with Kate.

"I'll leave you both," he whispered, "to your photographs." And off he went up the road.

Kate watched him for a while. She couldn't say why, but he intrigued her. The morning sun created a silhouette shadow of him, his ranger hat clearly delineated. Intuitively, she lifted her camera to take a few shots of him. In her mind popped the perfect caption for this photograph: "Morning rays and ranger ways."

Kate never planned to become known as "the zoo photographer with a twist" but that's exactly what happened after she started sharing her quirky captions on Instagram. She stumbled onto her own niche without even realizing it. One of her favorites was a close-up of a mule deer, in which she captured its head in a curious tilt. Her caption: "I'm all ears." Then there was the rare Soay sheep, staring directly at the camera with a knowing gaze, captioned "I like ewe." Her snowy owl, featuring the bird's perpetually annoyed facial expression (as all owls seemed to have, in Kate's opinion), was captioned with a cheeky "When you don't give a hoot." These little captions brought her photographs to life, giving each animal a unique voice and personality. The zoo loved it.

Her boyfriend, Oliver, kept insisting that she should launch a line of greeting cards, that she could make a fortune. Nice thought, but Kate's ambition had nothing to do with money. She was driven by the desire to capture extraordinary moments. And this week, she had her sights set on capturing the iconic 399 in a photograph that would truly stand out. Touch people's hearts. Make them realize why wildlife was such a treasure, so worth protecting.

Somehow, someway, she was determined to get *that* shot.

She glanced up the road at Ranger Cooper, wondering if he might return to Oxbow Bend at dusk later today. She thought she might come back to see that mirrorlike reflection of Mount Moran in the river. Shifting her focus to the river, she waited for the morning's wildlife to appear.

The sun continued its ascent, casting a warm glow over Oxbow Bend. After leaving that amber-haired zoo photographer—*man*, she was cute, really cute—Coop strolled along the riverbank, keeping a watchful eye on the photographers scattered around. The bald eagle had arrived at its nest with a fish in its talons, no doubt making the day for that photographer hiding in the bush. Two otters floated along the river on their backs. He thought he saw some movement upriver and lifted his binoculars. A coyote was traversing the sandy beach, slipping in and out of the willows, looking for breakfast. It wasn't common to see coyotes here, and it crossed his mind to tip Kate Cunningham off to its appearance. He shook off that thought. Don't be a sucker for a pretty girl, he told himself. It wasn't his responsibility to help a photographer nail a shot. His job was to protect them from getting eaten by unpredictable wildlife. Better still, to protect the wildlife from overly enthusiastic shutterbugs.

As he rounded a bend, he spotted a face he recognized—a lanky kid with an unruly mop of hair tied by a red bandana and a perpetual look of cynicism etched on his face. Frankie, his roommate. Sent by his government-employed father to enjoy a free summer in the park.

"Frankie," Coop called, waving him over. "What are you doing here?"

Frankie ambled toward Coop. "The drill sergeant told me to shadow you."

Drill sergeant? "Oh, you mean Tim Rivers? He's supervising the YCP? I thought there was a designated ranger to oversee it."

"Apparently, there's been budget cuts this year, so Ranger Rivers volunteered to pull double duty."

That sounded like Tim Rivers. It also sounded like the NPS. Despite skyrocketing visitations to many of the parks, it hadn't translated into much of an increase in federal funding to maintain and staff them.

Still, it might've been nice to know that Tim was assigning this kid to shadow Coop. "Did Tim say if you're assigned to me just for today? Or every day?"

"Dunno." Frankie shrugged. "Ranger Rivers said you're on the lookout for rogue photographers."

"More like wildlife enthusiasts who turn rogue."

The kid rubbed his hands together. "Now that sounds more like it! What's on the agenda?"

For the first time, Coop saw a spark of interest in Frankie's eyes. He explained his tasks for the day, which included monitoring wildlife activity, checking designated trails, and ensuring photographers maintained a safe distance. Frankie listened with a mix of skepticism and genuine interest, occasionally interjecting sarcastic remarks. Their banter continued until they reached a high vantage point overlooking Oxbow Bend. Coop pointed out key spots for monitoring wildlife and ensuring the safety of the photographers.

As they walked, Coop shared some insights about wildlife behavior and the delicate balance between allowing visitors to appreciate nature and ensuring the safety of both humans and animals. "Take this morning," he said, turning back to where Kate Cunningham stood behind her tripod. "That woman over there is new to wildlife photography, and she thinks she's going to get a winning shot of Grizzly 399."

Frankie's eyes almost bugged out of his head. Then he whistled two notes, one up, one down. "Aww. Yeah!"

Coop frowned. So maybe he had noticed Kate's attractiveness. "Her looks aren't important."

"Dude." Frankie snorted. "There's *nothing* more important than how a girl looks."

Coop shot him a look of disdain. "The point I was trying to make is that she might be unaware of danger. Her entire experience with wildlife is based on photographing animals in a zoo. Yet she's convinced she's going to get a shot of 399 that's new. Something different than any other photographer has gotten." Sorta sweet. Naive, but sweet.

Frankie hadn't stopped gawking at Kate Cunningham. "I think I might be in love with her."

Coop ignored him. "So our job is to keep people like her from getting maimed or killed."

"The drill sergeant described our role very differently."

Our role. That sounded like Frankie would be shadowing Coop for more than one day. "How so?"

"He said—and I quote—you and Coop are to help provide a positive, enriching experience for those photographers who seek out the wonder of the wilderness." He smiled, ear to ear. "Perhaps I should go introduce myself to the Zoo Girl."

As Frankie took a step in Kate's direction, Coop grabbed his shoulder and turned him around. *The raging hormones of a teenaged boy*, he thought, rolling his eyes. Their brains went south. As soon as Coop crossed paths with Tim, he was going to see about getting Frankie reassigned. Maybe to laundry duty. Something to clean up his mind.

"First," Coop said, "you need to head downriver and get a couple of shutterbugs off the bank. But don't call them shutterbugs. They'll take offense and complain to the visitor center. Politely ask them to move up to the road."

"What do I say if they ask me why they have to move?"

"Tell them that the water level will start rising soon. The Jackson Dam is releasing water this morning."

"Where are you going?"

"Upriver. A sow and her cub were spotted last evening, and I want to see if they've returned."

"I'd rather go with you. A bear sounds a lot more interesting than chasing off photographers."

Coop chuckled. "You know the routine, kid. Glamorous jobs are reserved for the senior rangers."

Frankie scowled. "Yeah, yeah. I know all about the privileges of senior rangers."

Coop pointed in the opposite direction of Kate. "You go that way. Meet me back here when the sun is completely visible."

Just then, a distinctive sound echoed through the air—an elk bugle. The two turned toward the source, spotting a majestic elk far downriver, its antlers silhouetted against the morning sky.

Frankie raised an eyebrow. "That'll wake up any and all campers."

"Nature's alarm clock." Coop chuckled. "That reminds me. Starting tomorrow, Ranger Rivers has put me on duty at Pilgrim Creek's overpass. That means an early start to our day."

Frankie's brow furrowed. "How early?"

"Super early. Four a.m. early. And it'll keep on starting at four o'clock until Grizzly Bear 399 emerges."

"What if the bear didn't make it through the winter? What if she's dead?"

"She's not dead." Coop sure hoped not. "We're going to be there waiting for as long as it takes her to emerge. Up at four a.m., every single day."

As the elk's bugle resonated once more, Coop couldn't help but feel a sense of delight at the horrified look on Frankie's face.

He neatly folded his camo clothing—hat, trousers, shirt—and packed them into his suitcase. These were his lucky garments, though he'd never considered himself superstitious until he realized they always seemed to accompany his success. He also packed his favorite disguises, the ones that never failed him.

Tomorrow morning, he had a flight to Jackson. If time allowed, he always preferred to drive. But time was short. As he finished his packing, his phone buzzed with a text notification. He checked it.

Getting things organized.

Wade texted back:

> Good. I want everything to be in place before the sow shows herself.

Finalizing things with the turncoat. Is there a $$$ limit?

Wade smiled. Of course there was no limit. He would spare no expense for this particular living room rug. It was priceless.

> No limit.

THREE

We all look at Nature too much, and live with her too little.
—Oscar Wilde, Irish poet

Tim Rivers leaned against his truck, squinting up at the cloudless sky as he listened to the chatter over the radio. On such a beautiful day like this one, tourists were starting to fill the park after a long, cold winter. Tim loved seeing their enthusiasm, but he also knew it meant summer was coming, and that meant traffic congestion, parking problems, overcrowded facilities, lost or injured hikers, and potentially dangerous wildlife encounters.

He heard his name crackle over the radio and reached inside the open jeep window to unclip the microphone. "Rivers, here."

"Where are you?"

He smiled. Sally was looking for him. He wondered why she didn't just text him. "I'm over by Jenny Lake Lodge, directing people to parking spots."

"There's a family in the visitor center who said you caused their children to cry."

"What?" Oh, now he remembered. "They wanted to go wading in the Snake River but—"

"The parents said their kids had their heart set on it and you told them they might drown."

"Yes, I did." Because those two little girls didn't know how to swim. And because the river level was supposed to rise all day as the Jackson Dam released water. Keeping people safe was a top priority for Tim. "Sally—"

Sally, clearly, wasn't interested in an explanation. "Rivers, you know better. A ranger's job is not to parent other people's children."

Tim looked at the microphone in his hand. Was she serious? And why "Rivers"? What happened to "Tim"?

"Find Coop and tell him to get over to Moose-Wilson Road to manage a bear jam."

Another crackling voice interrupted them. "This is Coop. I'm at Moose-Wilson Road. Bear jam is covered."

Good grief. Was everyone on the radio right now? Had they all heard Sally scold Tim?

"Which bear?" Sally said.

"793," Coop said.

"That bear," Sally said, "likes to hang near people. Cooper, do you have it covered or do you need help?"

"We're here too," another voice chimed in.

"Who's we?" Sally said.

"Shepard and Teale."

"All good," Coop said. "The bear is moving beyond the tree line."

"Fine," Sally barked. "Over and out."

Slowly, Tim clipped the microphone back onto the jeep's radio system. Sally's sharp tone stung.

Ever since she had returned from the Chief Ranger conference, held at nearby Yellowstone, something had changed between them, and Tim couldn't quite put his finger on it. Up until then, things had been going so well. In fact, this winter had been a significant turning point in their relationship. They'd even talked a bit about a future together.

He shook off Sally's brusqueness and focused on the task at hand. Cars had pulled over and people were standing along the road, watching a herd of elk, their cameras clicking away. Tim could see the elk had become aware of their audience. A few males were lifting their heads, which meant, to him, that people were too close for his comfort. When a wild animal was feeding peacefully, Tim wanted them to be left alone, not interfered with. He hurried over to the visitors, flashing his ranger badge, and politely asked them to give the animals some space. Most complied, but a few grumbled, muttering about their rights to get the perfect shot.

As the day wore on, Tim dealt with one wildlife-tourist conflict after another. A family had a close encounter with a moose because they ignored warning signs, and a group of hikers ventured off-trail, disturbing nesting birds. Another couple had brought their grandmother's remains to scatter, without a permit, without any idea of where or how to release ashes. They were just about to shake out the container into the Snake River—where wildlife fed and watered—when Tim stopped them. He escorted them straight to the Jenny Lake Visitor Center and into a ranger-on-duty's capable hands to fully instruct them about the dispersal process.

In between radio calls and park patrols, Tim couldn't shake off that radio call with Sally. Had he done or said something to offend her? Had he forgotten a birthday? An anniversary? It seemed a little soon in their relationship for celebrating anniversaries, but what did he know about romance? His late wife, Mary, wasn't the romantic type. She'd always said she'd rather have a year of being treated with kindness than a day of expensive gifts. So that's what he did—showed her kindness every day.

Mary was easier for Tim to understand than Sally. It might've had something to do with the faith they had in common. Sally had faith, he knew she did, but she wasn't a churchgoer. She said that she'd had too much church as a child, that it was crammed down her throat. Tim didn't push the issue. He attended a church in Jackson each Sunday morning, but alone.

He didn't pressure Sally to attend church because of his experience with his stepdaughter, Thea. The harder he pushed for her to find a church, the more she shut down on the topic. On everything. When had he last heard from her? He couldn't remember. He'd never quite decided if silence from Thea was a good thing or not. Did it mean she was managing life well, with steady employment? Or it could mean that she was struggling, financially and personally, and felt too much shame to call him for help.

Thankfully, faith came easily for Maisie, Thea's daughter. Tim had always had a special connection with his stepgranddaughter. He didn't even consider her a step. She was his. Unlike Thea, whom he'd first met when she was a boy-crazy thirteen-year-old, he'd known Maisie from her first day of life. How old was Maisie on her last birthday? Just ten or eleven, he was pretty sure.

But then a troubling thought occurred to him. Maybe they got along so well because she was still a little girl.

～

Maisie alternated between reading her guidebook about Grand Teton National Park and looking out the window at the stretch of highway guiding their journey from Denver to Jackson. Parts of it were familiar to her, and the prospect of spending the summer with Pops filled her with happiness. Well—as much of the summer as her mom would let her. As the car hummed along the road, Maisie had been reading aloud from the guidebook. "Fun fact. The name Jackson

Hole means a valley. It was named after a trapper named Davey Jackson."

Her mom murmured, "Interesting."

"Mom, are you listening to me?"

"Of course. You said Jackson Hole was named after Davey Jackson."

Good. She was listening. Sometimes it was hard to tell with Mom. "I can't wait to see Pops! It's been too long. I have so many things to tell him."

Her mom smiled. "Remember, he does have a full-time job."

"I won't get in his way." Maisie wiggled on her seat. "I hope he has Sundays off. He usually does, for church."

Mom's expression shifted slightly, her gaze thoughtful. "Well, you know, you don't have to go with him. I can have a chat with him."

Maisie furrowed her brow, puzzled. "Why would I do that? I like going to church with Pops. It's part of our thing."

Her mother sighed. "It's good to have traditions and rituals, I suppose. Just remember, church doesn't have to be a building. It can be wherever you find meaning."

Maisie tilted her head, considering her mother's words. "You mean . . . like nature?"

"Exactly. You can connect with the divine by appreciating the beauty all around you."

Maisie wrinkled her nose. "Pops calls that pantheism."

"It's *what*?"

"Pantheism is like, believing God is in everything, alive or not. Pops believes creation was made by God."

Mom cast a glance at her, shrugging. "Same thing. God is everywhere."

"Huge difference, Mom. Huge. Pops can explain it way better than I can."

"Pops has his way of thinking about God, and I have mine."

"Do you, Mom? Do you think much about God?"

Mom's back stiffened. "Why are we on such a heavy topic, anyway?" She breathed out an uncomfortable huff. "We're almost to the park. Let's talk about something a little lighter."

"Okay. What did Pops say when you told him I was coming?"

Her mother looked out the window at a passing motorcycle. "Well, you see, I thought we could surprise him."

Maisie's jaw dropped, and her eyes widened in disbelief. "What? You didn't tell Pops I'm coming? How could you? What if he has plans or something? What if he has a girlfriend?"

"Pops? A girlfriend?" Mom scoffed. "I highly doubt that." She glanced at her. "Surprises are fun, Maisie. The super heavy tourist season hasn't started yet. Besides, Pops is always thrilled to spend time with you."

Maisie slumped back in her seat. "I can't believe you didn't tell him."

Her mother waved that off. "Trust me, he will drop everything for you."

On the left side of the road was a small airport. Maisie opened her mouth to spout off a fun fact—this was the only airport in a national park in the entire United States—but then she closed her mouth. She was too bothered with her mother for springing her on Pops without warning. It wasn't fair.

And all because her mother wanted to go on a retreat to find herself. As far as Maisie could tell, her mom was on a permanent hunt.

After dinner, Kate returned to Oxbow Bend. The sun cast long shadows across the water as she adjusted the focus on her camera. She crouched behind a cluster of bushes, trying to capture the perfect shot of a moose grazing near the water's edge. The symphony of the wild surrounded her—birdsong, rustling leaves, and the babble of the Snake River.

Click. Click. Click.

As she lowered her camera to look at the tilt screen—an incredible feature of the Sony Alpha because it allowed her to shoot from different angles—she realized a clump of photographers were watching her. When she looked up, she saw them exchange amused glances. She gave them a half-hearted smile. "I've never seen a moose before."

"Don't they have moose in zoos?"

The snarky comment came from a lanky man with a telephoto lens slung over his shoulder. Kate recognized him from earlier this morning. He had commented on her expensive camera, and she had let him look at it. But she hadn't mentioned anything about her zoo experience. The only one she'd told was that handsome ranger. Apparently, he had told this photographer.

A woman with pigtails full of grizzled hair said, "Getting some good animal portraits?"

Rude! Kate raised an eyebrow, feeling the need to defend herself. "You can learn a lot about animals in a zoo."

At that, the other photographers started smirking, jabbing each other with elbows. "Like what?" one said.

"Like timing, patience, and how to read subjects. How they look through a variety of lenses. Different poses. Especially in a variety of lighting. It's not that different from being here."

They burst into laughter. "Not that different, she says!"

The pigtailed woman chuckled. "Now, now, guys. Don't make fun. There's nothing wrong with a photographer who's content with caged critters."

Critters?! "Hardly that," Kate said. "The zoo has all kinds of wild animals in their natural habitat. Lots of exotic species."

The woman smirked. "The wild doesn't have feeding times and scheduled performances. It's unpredictable. We spend weeks in the field, tracking animals, facing dangers."

"Zoos offer their own challenges."

"Like Photoshopping out the chain-link fence." She burst out with a laugh and looked back at the clump of photographers. "Hey, guys, what do we call Zoo Girl's profession?"

"Cheating!" a lanky man shouted out. "Better watch out, Zoo Girl. The BBC got in some hot water for not admitting that they'd used zoo footage in wildlife documentaries."

Kate's mouth dropped open. "I'm not cheating! I have never claimed that my pictures were taken in the wild."

"Here's an idea," the lanky man said. "Let's call it domesticated photography."

"Animals in a zoo are not domesticated," Kate said, frowning. "They're not pets. A wild animal is still wild, whether its roaming free or held captive."

"That's debatable," the pigtailed woman said. "They're captive. They're living in a man-made environment. It's not wildlife photography when you take a shot of an animal in a cage."

"You make it sound like a prison. Zoos are doing so much to enrich animals' experience. Like, keepers hide food so an animal needs to seek it."

The woman sneered. "But it's still delivered to them."

"If food and water are available," Kate said, "I doubt any animal in the wild would travel the distances they do."

"That's exactly my point. It's not available. They have to seek out nourishment. Animals lose those natural instincts in a zoo."

Kate glanced away, trying very hard to brush off the digs. "Okay. I get it. None of you like zoos."

"Look, don't get me wrong," the pigtailed woman said. "I'm not against zoos. Good ones, that is. Their breeding programs are great. People get to see a lot of rare species that they normally couldn't. But wildlife photography is a completely different thing. A zoo can't compete with wilderness. Out here,

42

it's a different game." She returned to her tripod, and the other photographers went back to their stakeout positions.

As Kate changed the zoom lens on her camera, she tried not to let herself go down that awful rabbit hole of feeling minimized. It was a recurring theme in her life. She knew she didn't look the part of the career she was pursuing—she was a young woman, small and light framed. She once overheard someone describe her as on the meek side of meek. A portrayal she hated but couldn't deny that it fit her. No one would ever describe her as brave or bold. Definitely not fearless.

As she clicked the zoom lens into place, she gave herself a pep talk. *I have every right to be here. Why should I let strangers make me feel foolish and insecure? Like I should run home with my tail between my legs? I've worked hard to be prepared for this experience. I've learned valuable skills, and I'm ready.*

She had the zoo to thank for her proficiency as a photographer. Each animal had its own behavior. She had spent hours getting to know her subjects. Lots and lots of pictures had to be taken in hopes of that perfect shot. She'd been able to further her skill set. She'd learned how and when to increase her camera's shutter speed. And patience. Photographing animals took some serious patience.

Feeling a little boost of self-assurance, she turned her focus back to the river. Several otters floated on their backs, letting the current take them down the river. Kate grinned. Her mood lightened.

Her phone rang, and she scrambled to answer quickly and stop the ringing. *Argh!* She should have remembered to silence it. She didn't dare look up; she could practically feel the disdain from the clump of nearby photographers.

"Hey, Katie-Kat," Oliver's voice echoed in the quiet.

Scowling, the pigtailed woman made a sweeping motion, as if to say, *Go elsewhere to talk! We're doing serious stuff here.*

Kate walked up the bank to the road. "It's not really a good time to talk, Oliver," she said, her voice hushed.

He passed right over that. "Has your bear made its appearance yet?"

"No. Not that I've heard."

"Really? No one's seen it yet?"

"No one has seen *her* yet."

"So . . . think you'll be home by Memorial Day weekend? I thought we'd head to the beach."

She just got here! She hadn't even unpacked her suitcase. "Too soon to say."

"I thought that *Nat Geo* editor said she had a deadline for the picture. You said that was why you chose this time of year."

"She did. And yes, that's why I chose this week. But what can I do? The bear's calling the shots." *Literally.*

"Do the rangers think the bear could be dead?"

"There's been some talk of that. Mostly, they talk about how cold a winter it's been and how late spring has been in coming. Everyone hopes she's just taking her time to emerge."

"Katie-Kat, you can't stay there indefinitely."

She hated that nickname. "I know, I know." She frowned. "Hopefully, she'll come out by week's end and I'll get my *Nat Geo* shot of her."

"Kate, sweetheart, be realistic. Do you *really* think you're that kind of a photographer?"

Silence. "What kind is that?" The kind that makes it into *Nat Geo*?

"You know what I meant. Even if you did get that perfect shot and even if it did get into *Nat Geo* . . . what then? You're only as good as your last photograph. You'll be spending your life chasing the end of the rainbow."

Kate sighed. Sadly, there was some truth to what he said.

"So I've been giving your career some serious thought," Oliver said. "How about combining your interest in animals and picture taking with something more profitable? Baby pictures with puppies and kittens. People eat that stuff up. There's good money to be made."

"That's not what I want to do with my photography. I want to capture the raw beauty of wildlife." How many times had she told him that very thing?

"Raw beauty doesn't pay the bills, Katie-Kat."

She squeezed her eyes shut. It was always about the money. Kate sighed, frustration bubbling within her. "Look, I need to get back to work." That lanky photographer was coming up the bank and heading right toward her. "I gotta go," she told Oliver and hung up before he could object.

"Hey, Zoo Girl," the lanky man said. "Here's something else you can't learn in a zoo. When you're out in the field, you reduce disturbance. And you increase situational awareness."

"What do you mean?"

"Put away that blasted phone."

Oh.

Wade Schmidt leaned over his workbench, meticulously arranging his prized possession—his bow and arrow—in a sturdy case. It was a fine piece of craftsmanship; each curve and notch served a purpose to ensure a successful kill. He handled it with care, almost reverently, as if it were a delicate piece of art.

He never, ever traveled with his weapons; too risky, too much of a liability. Instead, he relied on his tried-and-true method: sending them ahead via express mail to a nameless PO box.

Feldmann had been instructed to set up the PO box specifically for this purpose. The anonymity provided an extra layer of security, ensuring his weapons stayed under the radar of law enforcement. Hidden in plain sight. It was a winning formula that had always served him well . . . unlike another bowhunter. This guy had made the foolish mistake of trying to conceal a gun with his bow in carry-on luggage. Needless to say, he made the news.

Wade smirked as he sealed up the package and affixed the typed address label on top. He didn't have much sympathy for that bowhunter. The guy had landed himself in a mess of his own creation. As for Wade, avoiding detection was everything. One close call, a hair's breadth from disaster, haunted him. Ever since, his attention to detail became obsessively meticulous, each movement calculated, every step a precise act of survival. With practiced ease, he peeled off his rubber gloves.

Tracking the prey was half the thrill of these hunts, but the other half came from outsmarting the law. And Wade Schmidt was a master at playing this game.

FOUR

In nature we never see anything isolated,
but everything in connection with something else
which is before it, beside it, under it and over it.
—*Johann Wolfgang von Goethe, German writer*

It was already past seven o'clock. Ranger Tim Rivers knew he was late closing up the Jenny Lake Visitor Center for the evening, but he'd been chatting with folks who arrived with all sorts of questions about the park. He enjoyed these initial chats with excited visitors—knowing how much effort it took to get here. Grand Teton National Park was remote, far from most everywhere. It made him happy to think that these same people would leave feeling like they stumbled upon a beautiful piece of God's creation that was even better than they expected.

The door swung open with an energetic jingle and Tim did a double take. In walked his stepdaughter Thea and her whirlwind of exuberance—Maisie. A beaming smile stretched across Maisie's face as she darted toward him, her enthusiasm contagious.

"Pops!" Maisie exclaimed, enveloping him in a tight hug.

Returning the embrace, Tim gazed at Maisie, still beaming with excitement. "To what do I owe this surprise?"

"I've missed you *so much*," Maisie said, her eyes sparkling with genuine affection. She had a way of injecting boundless energy into any space.

Thea approached more reservedly, giving her stepfather a peck on the cheek. "Hi, Tim. Um, can we talk in private for a bit?"

Oh boy. Tim raised an eyebrow, noting the seriousness in Thea's tone. "Sure, sure. Of course." Through the window, he spotted Coop out on the patio in front of the visitor center. "Maisie, you remember Coop, don't you? Why don't you go out and surprise him? I know he'd like to see you."

Maisie turned to look out the window, then did a double take. "Pops! Who's *that*?" Her eyes sparkled with curiosity.

Tim squinted to see who she meant. "That's Frankie. He's interning with Coop for the summer." It occurred to him that he had yet to share that news with Coop. Soon.

"He's a hottie," Maisie said.

Tim's head jerked around. "He's a *what*?" But Maisie had darted outside. "Since when did she start to notice boys?"

"This year," Thea said. "She turned thirteen on her last birthday."

"No. Thirteen? Really? I thought she was eleven."

Thea laughed. "Last year, you thought she was eight. I think you just don't want her to grow up."

Tim sighed inwardly, his thoughts swirling with a mix of concern and curiosity about this Frankie character. How old was he, anyway? Fifteen or sixteen? Watching him through the window, Tim's eyes narrowed. He was going to keep a close eye on that boy.

"So, Tim, there's a retreat in Park City that sounds like it's made for me."

A retreat. "What about your job?"

"Well, you see, I'm between jobs right now. And then this came up. It all worked out, timing-wise."

Tim was starting to put the pieces together. "So you thought you'd drop Maisie off with me and head off to this retreat."

She stiffened. "Just for a little while."

Tim's eyebrows practically jumped off his face. "So, uh, how long exactly is this 'little while'?" Last summer, what began as a "little while" turned into a three-week stay for Maisie. Thea just kept calling to extend her visit. Now, he adored his granddaughter and cherished every moment with her. But sometimes he wished Thea would check in with him first before making plans. Actually, come to think of it, there were quite a few things he wished Thea would do differently.

"Not long. Really. No matter what Maisie tries to talk you into."

"How long is not long?" Tim said.

"Maybe a week, tops. A week-ish. I might stay on a few days and see what the art scene is like. I've heard good things about Park City."

Tim quickly translated: Thea was leaving Denver behind to move to another city. Uprooting Maisie yet again. But that would have to be a conversation for another day. In as calm a voice as he could manage, Tim said, "You should've called and let me know. This isn't a good time, Thea. The park is just opening."

"Right! I know. That's why I said yes to this retreat, because it was in May. You've always said that July and August are the busiest months."

"True, but this is an especially difficult time."

Thea's brow furrowed with concern. "Why? What's wrong?"

He hesitated, unsure where to start. The real reason for not wanting Maisie to stay with him right now had more to do with his off-kilter relationship with Sally than with park concerns, but there was no way he was going to bring that up with Thea. "Well, for one thing, the long winter's been rough. All the melting snow is causing heavy runoffs, and the bears, who should have come out of hibernation by now, are late and hungry, just as the tourists are arriving. I've also heard rumors about potential poachers in the park."

"Well, then," she said, relieved. "Maisie won't be in any danger."

"No, of course not. I'd never let her be in any danger. But I am preoccupied. If you'd only called first . . ."

"Maisie can take care of herself. Just give her jobs to do. Or find someone who needs help. She's a great helper." Before Tim could respond, Thea put her hand on his arm, a somewhat apologetic expression on her face. "Maisie's growing up so fast, and I thought she could use some time with you. You know how much she loves being with you."

Tim sighed, a blend of frustration and understanding. "Thea, I love spending time with Maisie. You know I do. But you can't drop her off without any advance warning." He tipped his head. "School isn't even out yet. What about that?"

Thea swept that worry away with a flick of her hand. "I've been homeschooling her. Didn't I tell you that? I thought I did."

"No. When did that start?"

"A month or so ago."

"Why?"

"Well, when we moved, it just seemed easier to finish out the school year homeschooling, instead of Maisie having to make new friends."

"You *moved*?"

Thea looked down at her feet. "Yeah. I was sure I told you."

He let out a deep sigh. "Where did you move to?"

"In with a friend. Just . . . a temporary spot."

He shook his head. "Everything's temporary with you, Thea."

"Don't start. I'm figuring things out." Thea's gaze wandered toward the mountains outside.

Tim studied his stepdaughter, caught between paternal concern and exasperation. "You've been figuring things out for a long time, Thea. Maisie deserves some consistency." He scratched his forehead. "I thought the art instructor gig was working out."

"It was. It did. And then . . . it didn't." She looked away. "The person who hired me, well, let's just say we had conflicting views on art."

"Ah. Got it." Right. In other words, something had happened and she'd been fired, or not rehired. Thea's art could be a little . . . out there. Emotive, mostly dark themes. But it was clear she didn't want to talk about it. "So what do you think you'll get out of this retreat?"

"My friend Rebecca said that it would help me look deep within."

Oh boy.

Thea narrowed her eyes. "What's that look for?"

"I know what your mother would say about that. She'd say that what you're looking for can't be found within. Only outside ourselves. Only in God."

She dropped her chin and started to dig through her purse, as if hunting for something.

Tim could sense that he'd said too much. Thea was shutting down. This was her general pattern. Whenever he brought God into the conversation, she checked out. Well, too bad. Who was going to talk straight to Thea if he didn't? He'd gone this far. He might as well go all the way. "Do you know why your mother chose your name?"

"Calathea? She said it was her favorite plant."

"Yes. It's a plant that symbolizes a new beginning."

Thea lifted her head and locked eyes with him. "And that's exactly what I'm hoping this retreat will bring me. Rebecca said it is *life-changing*."

"That's a tall order for a retreat. In my book, only God can give a person a new beginning."

Thea turned her attention back to digging through her purse, but Tim was pretty sure he caught an eye roll.

"So then," she said, lifting her car keys out of her purse, "if it's okay with you, I'll go out to the car to get Maisie's bag, then I'm heading to Park City."

"Now? You're not staying even one night?"

"Retreat starts early in the morning." She gave him a thumbs-up and headed to the door.

Tim watched her go with a heavy heart. Her mother's untimely death during Thea's freshman year of college had left a wound that never quite healed. After dropping out of college, she navigated through short stints at various jobs, got pregnant with Maisie at the age of twenty-one (Tim was thankful she didn't make a different decision regarding the pregnancy), and continued to drift between jobs and towns.

It seemed Thea's path of self-discovery had become a long and winding road to nowhere.

Thank goodness Coop had seen Maisie come running out of the visitor center before she launched herself at him with a Maisie-style hug—full-force, all-encompassing—forcing him to bend at the knees to pick her up. Coop wasn't exactly the hugging type, but Maisie's exuberance was infectious, and he didn't mind so much. He was fond of her.

Setting her down, Coop scrutinized her. She had shot up since the previous summer, her flaming red hair now cascading longer, and her cute round face adorned with even more freckles. Being around Maisie, Coop mused, was like someone cranked up the world's dimmer switch. Colors glowed brighter, sounds reverberated louder, and even the sun seemed to shine warmer. She had that undeniable effect on her surroundings, on people.

Maisie's attention had shifted to Frankie. "You're Frankie, right?" she asked with an ear-to-ear grin that made Coop slightly uneasy. She was growing up too fast. "I'm Maisie. My grandfather is Ranger Tim Rivers." She jabbed a thumb behind her to the visitor center.

Frankie responded with a smirk. "The drill sergeant? Lucky you."

"Thanks!" Maisie said, not aware that Frankie was being sarcastic. "Pops is my favorite person in the entire world. I absolutely *adore* him. You will too, when you get to know him."

"Doubt it." Frankie smirked again. "I know that type."

Coop jabbed Frankie with his elbow. That was no way to talk about a ranger, especially a man like Tim Rivers. There was no better ranger in the entire NPS than Tim. Selfless, caring, committed. Coop wasn't sure how he could've weathered the Emma Dilemma without Tim's help. He was like a good boss and a good dad, all rolled up in one person. If it weren't for Maisie being here, Coop might've flicked Frankie on the back of his head.

She couldn't take her eyes off this kid. "Pops said you're Coop's intern for the summer."

Coop's eyebrows shot up. "He said *what?*"

He turned his gaze to Frankie, a mixture of disbelief and mild irritation. This was news to Coop, and he wasn't sure how he felt about having an intern. Yes, he did. He didn't like it. The last thing he wanted, besides getting pulled out of the backcountry, besides being stuck with a roommate, was having someone shadow him. Especially a teenager, especially Frankie, who seemed to carry a brooding air with him.

Frowning, Coop reconsidered every positive thought he'd just had about Tim Rivers. The man was a ruthless dictator. This summer, which had started as the highlight of his year, had plummeted to the lowlight. The lowest of lights.

The next morning, the predawn chill hung in the air at Pilgrim Creek, where a congregation of wildlife enthusiasts eagerly gathered, awaiting the emergence of Grizzly Bear 399 from her winter's hibernation. Amidst the sea of lenses, Kate set up her tripod, anticipating a glimpse of the famous sow. This was the very spot where the bear had emerged in previous years, and Pilgrim Creek, nestled in the heart of Grand Teton National Park, offered a picturesque and serene landscape. The creek wound its way through a pristine wilderness surrounded by towering peaks, dense pine forests, and lush meadows. The air was crisp, carrying the scent of pine and earth.

With her zoom lens attached, Kate adjusted the focus, surveying the silent photographers, all focused on the line of trees. A grim realization struck her—each one of them would capture the exact same image. Every single one. She straightened, distracted. Disheartened.

Then she recognized that ranger's voice, the one from Oxbow Bend. Coop. He was cautioning a photographer nearby to maintain a safe distance if the bear appeared. "We're here to observe, not disturb. Keep your dist—" His eyes met Kate's and he paused mid-sentence. Clearing his throat, he greeted her. "Oh, hello there. I see you found the right place."

Behind him, Frankie, the ranger's shadow, popped up with a grin. Yesterday morning, at Oxbow Bend, he had hung around Kate until Coop scolded him to stay on task. Frankie joined Kate just as a rustling sound emanated from the trees. Everyone froze, their eyes fixed on the rim of trees behind the creek.

Suddenly, a loud ringing pierced the quiet. Kate gasped. Her phone! She fumbled to find it, the ring echoing in the silence. When she saw Oliver's name on caller ID, she stepped away to turn it off. Why in the world would he call at this hour? Had he forgotten the time difference? Unbelievable.

As she returned her phone to the bag, she heard murmuring. "Thanks a lot."

"What did I do?" She looked up to see the photographers glaring at her.

"You scared off the bear."

Kate felt her cheeks grow warm. "I thought for sure I'd put it on silent."

Coop took a few steps closer, until he stood between Kate and the other photographers, almost protective. "Bears have keen senses, including acute hearing. Unexpected noises can startle or unsettle them."

That, Kate should've known. But in the zoo, bears were so conditioned to most sounds that they seemed oblivious to the presence of human activity.

Frankie had slipped away into the darkness and then reappeared. "It wasn't a bear. It was a moose."

"Are you absolutely certain?" a photographer said. "Did you actually see it?"

Frankie scoffed at the doubt. "I can definitely tell a moose from a bear." He illustrated his point by placing his hands on his head and wiggling them to mimic moose antlers.

"Ranger," another photographer said, "399 is overdue."

"Don't look at me." Coop lifted his hands in a helpless gesture. "She's on her own schedule."

"Maybe you should go looking for her," another said. "Maybe you should see if there's any evidence that she died."

"And why would I do that?"

That photographer scowled at him. "Because we're all standing out here in the cold, morning after morning."

Even in the dim light, Kate saw irritation in Coop's eyes. "I think you are all well aware that Mother Nature bats last." He moved along the line of photographers, yanking Frankie's arm to keep him moving.

The same photographer who irritated Coop turned to scowl at Kate. "Wildlife doesn't wait for phone calls."

"It *was* a moose," Kate said, eyes on the ground.

"This time. With any luck, next time it'll be 399. And if your phone goes off, I'm smashing it to bits."

This would be Wade's final hunt. No more chasing, no more games. He had a collection of trophies, enough money to last a lifetime. Hunts were starting to lose their spark for him; when you're the best of the best, what's left to prove? And after bagging this last prized possession—the ultimate catch—what more did he really need?

Halting his activities now was crucial if Wade wanted to remain under the radar of law enforcement. He had been a marked man on the NPS's watchlist for years. It all started in Denali, when he was covertly tracking an endangered wood bison that had strayed into the park. He thought he was being covert, anyway. While setting up camp one night, he caught a glimpse of a light, off in the distance, moving in his direction. Someone was following him. In his haste to pack and flee, his wallet must have slipped from his pants pocket. Such a careless mistake. The tracker, an overly diligent ranger, Donald Franklin, found it, including Wade's driver's license. Though the address was his mother's, the NPS now had his name and his face. It felt like a ticking time bomb; sooner or later, they'd try to make a move on him.

Maybe it was time to settle down. Time to live the kind of life his mother always nagged him to get. A charming house in the suburbs with that classic white picket fence, a pretty wife, and a couple of kids to keep his mother happy with grandchildren.

His mother would heartily approve of the woman he was currently dating. Maybe this one would work for him. Maybe not.

She was attractive, easy to manipulate, and slightly more interesting than most of the women he pursued. Pursued . . . until he caught them. He grew bored easily.

What would life be like without these games he'd been playing? Could he really walk away from the thrill of the chase? There was something addictive about being the predator, always a step ahead of his prey. Outpacing, outplaying, outguessing.

Outfoxing.

FIVE

*Nature is slow but sure, she works no faster than need be; she
is the tortoise that wins the race by her perseverance.*
—Henry David Thoreau, American philosopher

The afternoon sun felt good. Maisie ambled down the trail
alongside String Lake while her grandfather chatted with some
rangers. This morning, they'd gone into Jackson for church.
Pops had afternoon duty, so she'd tagged along, happy to be
with him, happy to be at the park.

Being in the Grand Tetons felt like a slice of heaven, surrounded by the towering trees, the fresh scent of lake water,
and the clean, sweet air. It was a far cry from bustling, noisy,
trafficky city life.

Her thoughts drifted to her mom and this supposedly life-
changing retreat. Mom definitely needed some changes in her
life. Rebecca Woodbine had provided the money to go to this
retreat, and even gave Mom extra gas money to deliver Maisie
to Pops. On the drive from Denver, Mom had seemed so excited. She said that this time, everything was going to get better.
Mom *promised*.

A wave of uncertainty washed over Maisie. Mom made a lot

of promises that didn't come true. Band-Aid-better promises. Things might get better for a little bit, but not for long.

As she strolled, the towering pines created a canopy, casting dappled sunlight on the path. The farther she walked, the more her worries over Mom slipped away. She took in a deep breath of crisp mountain air. She *adored* being out in nature. Even more so, she loved being with Pops. The future seemed brighter when Pops was in the story.

And then, to her delight and astonishment, she thought she spotted Frankie, trimming branches from a bush encroaching on the trail. She bolted over to him. "Hi!"

Frankie looked up, confused.

"You're Frankie, right?"

"Yeah, that's me." He finished the bush and gathered up the branches, tossing them into a black plastic garbage bag.

"I'm Maisie. My grandfather is Tim Rivers. The ranger. Remember? We met at the visitor center just yesterday."

Frankie grunted.

"Looks like you're doing trail maintenance. Can I help?"

"No." Frankie slung the bag over his shoulder and headed down the trail.

Undeterred, Maisie followed along.

"Hey." He stopped and narrowed his eyes. "Did your grandfather send you to spy on me?"

"Of course not! He's telling the rangers what they need to do today. I just thought you could use some help. Or maybe someone to talk to? I'm a good listener. Well, it's not my *best* quality. Talking is my *best*. But I'm working on my listening skills."

"I don't talk and I don't listen." He stopped at another spot and started cutting a root that was lifting up on the trail.

"You're Coop's roommate, right? How's that going? Don't you just love Coop? I *adore* him. I think he's wonderful. Next to Pops, he's my favorite person in the world. I suppose I should put my mom on that list. Usually she is, but right now, I'm a little frustrated with her, you know?"

"Man, do I *ever* know. Parents are useless."

"Well, not exactly useless. But definitely exasperating. Anyway, don't you just love Coop?"

"He's the one who's put me on trail maintenance today. So no, I don't love him."

"Why'd he give you trail maintenance?"

He let out a huff. "For a very minor deed."

Maisie grinned. "How minor?"

"Something ridiculously small." He whirled his finger around his ear, as if to say that Coop might be nuts. "I left my wet towel on his bed and it made his precious pillow damp to sleep on."

"Whoa." She laughed. "That's not a minor deed. You messed up. You're lucky you're on trail maintenance and not emptying latrines."

Frankie gave her a look, then a hint of amusement filled his eyes. He handed her a plastic bag to carry. "Here, kid. Make yourself useful."

"I'm not a kid." But Frankie wasn't listening. He walked along the trail, Maisie trotting beside him with the bag of branches. She wasn't looking where she was going and walked right into a spiderweb. "Yuck!" She swiped at her face and hair, pulling silky strands off.

Frankie turned to watch her. "Here's a tip, kid. Always walk behind someone taller than you. That way, your face doesn't have to be the first to make contact with a cobweb."

"Fun fact. It only takes a spider thirty to sixty minutes to spin or repair a web."

He tapped his head. "Something to remember on your return trip." He stopped now and then to pick up litter and stuff it in his plastic bag. "Why do people come to the wilderness and toss their litter?"

"Maybe it falls out of their backpack."

"Right." He picked up a couple of empty cans of beer. "Just fell right out of their backpack." He stuffed the cans in the bag. "Idiots. They should be banned from the park."

"Maybe it was someone who'd been injured, bitten by a wolf, maybe. Or face-planted on one of those roots you're cutting away. And they desperately needed an anesthetic, and that was all they had. And they drank the beer, crawled back to their car, and drove off."

Frankie looked at her like she was nuts. "Then, hopefully they'd get pulled over for DUI on the way and be locked up in jail."

"Well, I suppose that would be a fitting conclusion for idiots."

Bending over to pick up another beer can, he paused at her comment. When he straightened up again, she thought he had a look on his face like he was trying to not laugh.

"Fun fact," Maisie said, changing the subject from litterbugs. "String Lake used to be called Beaver Dick Lake. Beaver Dick was the trapper who married Jenny, the Shoshone woman. You know . . . Jenny Lake was named for her. Really sad love story." She opened her mouth to explain more, but he was walking down the trail. She hurried to catch up. "Don't you want to hear it?"

"No. I don't do love stories."

"Sad ones? Or happy ones?"

"Neither. Too sappy."

"Look!" Maisie said. "Are those Clark nutcrackers?" She pointed to a couple of birds flitting about on the ground near them.

"Wrong. Gray jays. Also known as Canada jays. In the family of blue jays and crows and ravens."

"But they're so small."

"Smaller, less noisy than their cousins. Tame too. They'll eat out of your hands."

Maisie drew closer to see their markings, and the birds seemed unfazed.

Eyes fixed on the bird, Frankie said, "Some think a gray jay's whistle or chatter means a predator is nearby."

She glanced up at Frankie. She had a hunch he liked being here more than he let on. She wanted to find out.

As they walked, they reached a scenic viewpoint overlooking String Lake. Her keen eyes caught sight of a large white bird gracefully gliding on the lake. "Is that a snowy egret?"

"Not even close." Frankie raised an eyebrow. "Trumpeter swan. See the black bill? Black legs, too. Largest bird in the park."

Her eyes widened. "It's a beautiful bird."

"Yeah. It's one of the rare government success stories. Trumpeter swans used to be hunted so much they were endangered, but they've actually recovered their numbers."

She could hear a hint of pride in his voice. Even though Frankie tried to act chill, Maisie could tell he loved sharing what he knew. And wow! Just wow! He knew a ton.

In fact, once Frankie finally started to talk, he didn't stop. "You'll see a lot of trumpeter swans around here. They like to breed and nest in the park. Anywhere there's water, you'll find them. Usually two together. They mate for life."

"Oooh," Maisie breathed as she clasped her hands over her heart. "Don't you just love romantic moments in nature?"

A peculiar expression washed over Frankie's face. "Don't your cheeks hurt?"

"My cheeks?" Her hands clasped her cheeks.

"Yeah. From all that happiness."

She pondered the question for a moment before responding solemnly, "Yes. Yes, sometimes they do."

His eyes softened. And then a laugh burst out of him, first one and then another. His laughter was contagious, and soon, they were both laughing. It felt as though the sun had emerged from behind a cloud, casting a warm glow over them.

That was the moment when Maisie fell head over heels in love with Frankie. She didn't even know his last name.

Zoo Girl.

The nickname had spread fast among the other photographers. Kate had heard their whispered snickers in the quiet of the chilly, predawn morning when she'd been at Pilgrim Creek to watch for the emergence of Grizzly Bear 399 from hibernation.

No sign of the bear.

Plenty of jabs at Kate's inexperience.

She refused to let the other photographers get under her skin. It was like seventh grade all over again, when her parents sent her to a private school because she was falling behind in the public school. That first month was horrible—she ate lunch alone each day, she was the victim of all kinds of mean-girl pranks. The only way she survived was to act like she didn't care a whit. And in a strange way, that worked. By month's end, she started to get included at lunch, then invited to girls' houses after school. Before long, she was one of them.

So, maybe it was time to pull out her old seventh-grade trick: acting like she didn't care what people thought of her. Truth is, she did care—like, a lot. But what was the harm in pretending? She had nothing to lose, right? Cool and detached, that was going to be her new vibe.

Later that day, she stood on the banks of the Snake River at Oxbow Bend, adjusting her camera with precision. She focused on the task at hand—capturing untold stories through her camera lens. She'd noticed a spot on the river with so many otters that she was sure there was a den. Wearing waders, Kate started slowly walking into the river, with a plan to photograph the river otters close to home. They used dens, often abandoned burrows from other animals, to retreat and rest, to sleep, to give birth, to wait out inclement weather or avoid predators. Using her awesome zoom lens, she hoped to get some close-ups of the den, of otters coming in and out, from the river's view.

As she stood in the middle of the river, she paused. About fifty feet away, two otters caught her eye, leisurely floating on their backs and gracefully passing each other. They seemed utterly at ease, like two friends lounging in a pool on inflatable mats. She quickly adjusted her lens and snapped a few shots, capturing the serene moment. In her mind, she playfully captioned the scene: "I'm fine. You?"

From the bank, a voice called out, "I wouldn't do that if I were you, Zoo Girl."

"He's right," another one said. "You're asking for trouble. Your camera shouldn't be that close to water."

She glanced back, seeing the looks exchanged between photographers. Until now, she hadn't noticed how many photographers were situated along the riverbank, and even more up on the road. All eyes were on her, watching with mixed expressions. Trying to appear unfazed, Kate pressed forward, intent on proving that she belonged to this wilderness as much as any seasoned photographer. Her confidence was intact.

However, nature had its own plans. A submerged branch caught her foot, and with a sudden jolt, Kate found herself tumbling into the water. She caught herself before going completely under, one arm instinctively holding her brand-new camera high in the air, but the splash echoed, punctuating the stillness. The wildlife sensed her presence. Birds took flight, otters vanished. A flock of geese darted far away, leaving ripples of discontent in their wake.

Laughter erupted from the spectators on the shore. "Great job scaring off the river otters, Zoo Girl," one of them sneered. "Scaring off everything."

"Yeah. We didn't come here for your theatrics," another added.

The gray-haired pigtailed woman had come out of nowhere. She stood on the road with her hands on her hips, glaring down at Kate. "I have spent the last hour up at the crook, trying to get photos of clouds reflected on the river, and in less than thirty seconds, you have created endless ripples of wake and disturbed every wild creature at Oxbow Bend."

The worst thing of all was that pigtailed woman was right. Instead of settling down, the birds grew noisier. They circled overhead, their irritated squawks a chorus of disapproval, a symphony of disgruntled fowl.

Humiliation washed over Kate. Her confident demeanor had slipped away, replaced by an awkward vulnerability. Discomfort, too, as icy water drenched her clothes and dripped into her waders.

As Kate made her way toward the riverbank, fighting to keep her composure, she did her utmost to block out the accusatory glances and murmurs of disapproval from the seasoned photographers. "You don't belong here," she heard one of them say, with another loudly agreeing. A flush of embarrassment spread across her cheeks as she stammered out an apology.

"Cut her some slack."

Kate looked up to see a ranger—*that* ranger, the handsome one, Coop—heading down the steep bank toward her.

"Ranger," the gray-haired pigtailed woman said, pointing an accusatory finger in Kate's direction, "that Zoo Girl disrupts everything! Birds, otters, geese, the whole show."

Halfway down, Coop stopped. "She's learning the ropes. Give her a break."

"Learning the ropes? We're here for serious shots, not a comedy act," another photographer said. "Maybe you should go back to the zoo."

Kate shot that photographer a *look*.

Coop noticed. He turned to that particular photographer. "Hey, everybody starts somewhere."

As the photographers dispersed, still grumbling under their breaths, Coop turned his attention back to Kate. He took a few more steps down the bank to reach out a hand and help her onto the bank. "You okay?" he asked, his tone softened.

"Yeah, I'm fine. Just embarrassed." She frowned. "I do wish you hadn't told them I was a zoo photographer. My nickname is now Zoo Girl."

"Me?" A puzzled look came over him. "But I didn't tell them."

She eyed him. Was he telling her the truth? "You were the only one who knew. Who else could've told them?"

Coop's eyes narrowed. "Must've been Frankie. My summer intern." He rubbed his forehead. "I'm sorry."

"I'll survive." She was shivering, and she could feel her heels starting to rub raw from the waders. "I'd better go change." She started up the bank, then stopped and turned to Coop. "Thanks for not throwing me to the wolves back there."

Coop grinned. "Wolves might have been less forgiving. Listen, don't let them get to you. Wildlife photography is no walk in the park. You've just added a splash of unpredictability to it."

"Very punny." She strode up the bank, acutely aware of the sound of water sloshing inside her waders, her clothes dripping water as she walked. Aware that Coop was watching her.

A little smile tugged at her lips.

Wade peered out the window of the plane, his eyes fixed on the rugged landscape below as the aircraft descended toward the lone runway at Jackson Hole Airport. The sight of the granite peaks in the distance and the vast valley of sagebrush meadows stirred a sense of anticipation in him. "Where are you, bear?" he whispered under his breath. "I'm coming for you."

As the plane taxied to the gate, Wade wasted no time in unbuckling his seat belt and reaching for his phone. With a quick flick, he powered it on and tapped out a message to Feldmann, letting him know he had safely arrived. The hunt was officially on, and Wade was anxious to get started.

He hadn't met Tony Feldmann face-to-face yet, a fact that niggled at the back of his mind. He hoped it wasn't a mistake. He trusted the man who had given a strong recommendation of Feldmann. He'd said that this guy knew how to scout and prepare a hunt. So far, everything checked out. The information they had exchanged, the plans they had laid out over countless calls and messages. Still, there was a small flicker of doubt—what if this was a misstep? What if he had underestimated the importance of meeting Feldmann in person before contracting him as the frontman for such a significant hunt?

This hunt was going to be the ultimate test of Wade's skills and cunning. A fitting end to his career as an expert marksman. His masterpiece.

If this was the last one, then it was going to be the best hunt of his life.

SIX

The wildlife and its habitat cannot speak,
so we must and we will.
—*Theodore Roosevelt*

Later that evening, lying in bed with a book on her chest, too exhausted to hold the book aloft, Kate couldn't shake the scorn she'd received from the other photographers. She had tried to defend herself, to not take it to heart, but these last two days had given her a rude awakening to reality. While she had observed all kinds of animal behavior at the zoo, and she'd had the opportunity to photograph rare species, the truth was that she had no idea what it took to be a wildlife photographer. She'd planned for everything—the right equipment, the right clothing, the right venues. But she couldn't plan for unpredictability. She couldn't fake experience.

That was the difference between being a photographer of animals in the zoo or in the wild. Predictability.

Kate had grown up immersed in a family that upheld the tradition of predictability. Both parents were history professors at American University in Washington DC, and her older brother was diligently following their lead by pursuing an academic career. Their house in Alexandria, Virginia, a six-generation relic on the historical registry, bore witness to the family's aversion to change. Even the wallpaper remained untouched, a nod to their steadfast commitment to the Cunningham Way of Life—safe, risk-free, and firmly grounded in the past.

Kate tried to fit in, but she was definitely a square peg in a round hole. It might not have been obvious to outsiders, but to anyone in the family, it was clear as day. She wanted to carve out her own path, find her own way. The family's way just wasn't going to cut it for her.

Unlike Kate's brilliant brother and parents, school posed a lot of challenges for her. Rather than attending a traditional four-year college, her only option was a community college, much to her mother's mortification. With an uncertainty about her vocation, Kate explored various classes until she stumbled upon photography. It was recognition from her instructor, who saw promise in her work, that marked a pivotal moment in her life.

With encouragement from the instructor and with his help, she embarked on a career of photography. Freelance, of course. Birthday parties, bar mitzvahs, a super casual wedding. One job led to another and another. She'd finally found something she excelled at.

The turning point came with a gig at the zoo, and just like that—*boom*—everything came into focus. She was hooked. Capturing animals became a thrilling pursuit. She felt she had grown to understand the creatures in the zoo, and she loved them dearly. She recognized their patterns, their habits. But there were no untold stories in a zoo. She had learned all she could from the zoo about wild animals. It was time to start applying her learning to the actual wilderness.

And then, six months ago, she'd learned about Grizzly Bear 399 for the first time. Consumed by curiosity, she delved into every available piece of information about her. For the first time, stirred by the tale of this grizzly, Kate yearned to confront the unknown. She'd done a deep dive into grizzly bears—their behavior, habitat, patterns, and everything she could learn about 399 (hours and hours of watching bear videos). She'd worked out to build her endurance and learned some survival skills (maybe not as many as she should have). She'd bought the Sony Alpha (maybe hadn't quite mastered it, but she was getting there). But she hadn't thought to study the fieldcraft—how different it would be with animals in the wild.

For that, she was getting a crash course.

Thoughts of photographing 399 in Grand Teton National Park, finding a shot that no one else had yet taken of her, occupied Kate's mind incessantly. She planned to quit the zoo and head to the park, supporting herself as a freelance photographer . . . until her parents, horrified, strongly objected. Kate compromised (caved in?) and agreed to use her vacation time at the park. For now.

Her phone rang, and she glanced at caller ID. Oliver. She let out a deep sigh. She couldn't talk to him now, not when she was exhausted, needed a shower, and even more importantly, was feeling insecure. He'd sniff out her self-doubt and make it worse.

She remembered when she had first told Oliver about her plans to go to the Grand Tetons. They were sitting on her couch (Always at her place. Never at his. She'd never even seen where he lived. He traveled so often that he said his apartment was bare-bones. Modest and messy. She doubted it, though. Oliver was the kind of guy who never had a hair out of place, who even had his jeans dry cleaned.) and she was showing him her portfolio of animals taken at the zoo. When she came to the photos of the brown bears, she told him about her idea to photograph Grizzly 399 in the wild.

Amusement decorated his face, but there was something else behind his eyes, lingering just for a moment. He actually seemed intrigued. "Tell me more."

So she did.

"The most famous bear in the world, you say? And you think there haven't been enough photographs of it?"

"Well . . . I guess it's about finding a photograph that tells a new story about her."

"Perhaps you should try a less challenging subject."

"Why?" she'd asked.

"You've never gone camping. You've never gone hiking, for that matter. You live in a city."

"Urban skills can translate to the wilderness."

He gave her a look as if to say, *Are you joking?*

But she wasn't joking. She really believed that city life had given her survival skills. Flexibility, heightened awareness, adaptability.

"What are you going to do when the weather gets bad?"

"What do you mean?"

"You spend rainy weekends at the Smithsonian. Hot ones too."

Well, sure. She lived in Virginia where summers were beastly hot. Where rain could come down like bullets. "I can manage a little rain. Besides, I'm not expecting this to take very long. I just need to get the right photograph."

He sighed. "Then I'll come with you."

No.

No, no, and no.

"Thank you, but I need to do this on my own." Kate appreciated Oliver's offer, but she needed to tackle this project solo. If he tagged along, it would become his show entirely. He'd be convinced he had all the answers—lighting, location, everything. In his mind, he could probably even control the bear if given the chance . . . and knowing him, he might just pull it off.

She needed space from Oliver. Time to think. She'd felt this way for a while now, and those feelings were only growing stronger. A couple of times, she'd suggested that they take a break, but he always cajoled her into staying in the relationship, staying committed. He was big on that—hanging in there, remaining faithful. Good times or bad. That's what God wanted from them, he would remind her.

His own father had abandoned their family and Oliver was determined to be a different kind of man. He was big on men being men. On not abandoning others. He would get tears in his eyes when he talked about his dad's departure from the family, and Kate would cave in.

Kate had known Oliver for about six months, having met at the zoo one quiet afternoon when she was photographing a black bear for the zoo's annual calendar. They chatted for a long while, especially about their mutual interest in bears. Then he pointed to the logo on her T-shirt and said he happened to attend the same church. It was a large church, with a lot of young people, but she was surprised she hadn't noticed him, or that her friends hadn't. He was *that* good looking. He asked for her phone number, a bit brash for having just met, and she politely turned him down. That Sunday at church, he was seated a few rows away from her. After the service, he came over to say hello. He asked her out for coffee, but again, she said no. He just came on so strong. The following Sunday, he asked again. This time, she agreed to go out with him.

Over coffee, he told her that when he had first seen her at the zoo, he sensed God telling him that she was the one meant for him. It was a pretty heady thing to hear from someone like Oliver, the kind of guy women drooled over. Strikingly handsome in a preppy way, confident, charismatic, successful. He was everything most any girl would ever want in a guy. Kate's friends reminded her of that very thing over and over.

But here's the thing: God had never told Kate that Oliver was the one for her. She felt as if she didn't have a choice in the matter. He was calling her his girlfriend long before she was ready. That's the way it had always been with them—he was way ahead of her.

"Look," she had told him. "I want to do this on my own, Oliver. Besides, you're allergic to the outdoors."

"Just to trees. And anything that blooms."

"It's spring. Everything is blooming right now or just about to. You'd be miserable."

"Katie-Kat. Think."

She cringed. She *really* didn't like that nickname. She'd told him that it sounded childish, but he brushed off her objection, insisting it was a term of endearment.

"How are you going to know where to go to find this bear? You've never been to Wyoming."

"I have a guidebook."

He burst out laughing.

She blew out a puff of air. "I can do this. I want to do this. It'll make me brave."

"Kate, you're the least brave person I know. You scream when you see spiders."

Well, spiders were creepy. But saying she wasn't brave was hard to hear.

"How can you think that you're going to get a photograph of a wild grizzly bear?"

Imagine what he'd have to say tonight if she told him that she had fallen into the river while photographing otters, forgotten to silence her phone while trying to catch sight of 399, and was now tagged as Zoo Girl by the truly professional wildlife photographers.

Pathetic. She was pathetic.

She rolled over and set the book she'd been trying to read

on the nightstand. It was well past dinnertime, but she was too frustrated to feel hungry. The weight of the reason she'd come to Grand Teton filled her gut with a *thunk*. Who was she fooling? She should go home and photograph puppies and kittens for the rest of her life.

Her phone buzzed, and she glanced at the incoming text. Oliver. *Again*. Impatient, as always.

Why am I thinking like this?

She let out a deep sigh and read his text. So many of her friends would give anything for a boyfriend who communicated constantly. To Kate, Oliver's persistence made her feel caged. Scrolling through his long text message, she couldn't shake the sense of being cornered.

Tim Rivers left a hastily scribbled note on the worn kitchen table, ensuring his granddaughter Maisie knew he'd be away for a few hours and to help herself to breakfast. The early morning sun was just starting to paint the sky with hues of pink and gold as he stepped outside, the cold mountain air awakening his senses. Another tip about a possible poacher had disrupted the tranquility of the morning. Sally woke him out of a sound sleep to insist that he head over to Willow Flats to investigate. Normally, protocol dictated that rangers went out in teams for safety and efficiency, so Tim suggested bringing Coop along, a reliable partner in the field.

Sally's response had been sharp, cutting through the air like a sudden gust of wind. "No," she said. "He's needed at Pilgrim Creek this morning. Then I told him to head over to the Gros Ventre River to check on the wolf rendezvous site. I'd go with you myself, but I have an important early morning meeting. You'd better save some time and get up there now. Oh, and before you leave Willow Flats, I want you to put signage up to restrict the area from public access."

"That seems a little rash." Unless there was a specific reason to do so, Sally had always been reluctant to restrict the public from what she considered America's land.

"Tim, hon, I wish you wouldn't question my decisions."

"How about if you hold off on that decision until I find out what's going on at Willow Flats?"

"How about if *you*," she said, her high voice curt and uncharacteristically tense, "do what I say and stop second-guessing me?" On that note, she hung up.

Not a good start to the day.

The coordinates provided by the informant led Tim deep into the wilderness, the trail meandering through thick foliage. As he navigated the terrain, his mind couldn't help but circle back to his conversation with Sally. There was an edge in her voice that unsettled him.

The ringing alarm in Tim's head grew louder. Going alone to confront a potential poacher was a deviation from established safety protocols. Sally knew this well; she had emphasized the importance of teamwork in a recent talk to the seasonal rangers. Her decision left Tim with a nagging sense of unease. What early morning meeting could have been so important?

Added to that was Sally's urgent insistence that she be the first to know when Grizzly 399 was spotted. She wanted a direct call on her cell, avoiding radio communication to prevent eavesdropping.

If something was bothering Sally, why hadn't she confided in him? He thought they were friends. More than friends.

After his wife had died, Tim never thought he'd feel the stirrings of romance for another woman. He'd had a great love, and memories of Mary were enough to live on for the rest of his life.

But then he met Sally Janus. She was nothing like his wife, not in looks or personality or demeanor, yet he found himself rather . . . smitten. Perhaps it was their mutual love of the great outdoors, something Mary had never fully embraced. Or maybe it was just sharing this mid-century time of life that ignited the spark. Something clicked between them last summer, and the spark caught fire.

All winter, things had been progressing rather nicely. They ate dinner together nearly every night. They spent their days off together, snowmobiling, skiing at all three nearby ski resorts—Snow King, Jackson Hole, and Grand Targhee—or just relaxing in front of the fireplace. They talked about everything—their love of the national parks, their plans to visit every single one of them in their retirement years. A month or so ago, he had noticed a shift in their discussions of the future. They spoke as a couple, in plural. *"We've never been to Banff in Canada. That should top the list."* Or *"First summer after retirement, we're heading to Alaska to see all eight national parks."*

Then, two weeks ago, Sally returned from an annual meeting of NPS chief rangers, directors, and superintendents in Yellowstone and now seemed distant, a little cool toward him. He'd asked her if anything was wrong, but she insisted she was just preoccupied with the opening of the park. He wondered if he'd done something or said something. Had he pushed too far when he brought up combining a Christmas trip to Florida to see the Everglades with a visit to his eighty-five-year-old mother? Had that freaked her out? He wondered. He planned to bring it up at dinner one evening this week, until Maisie, his all-consuming darling of a granddaughter, had entered the picture. Quiet, romantic dinners with Sally were off the calendar for the duration.

He shook off his frustration. Approaching the given coordinates, Tim took a moment, taking in the breathtaking scenery around him before shifting into ranger mode. Personal musings were pushed aside as he focused on the task at hand. Duty, in the form of investigating potential poaching, demanded his attention now.

As the sun rose in the sky, he searched the area for telltale signs that someone had been there. He saw no footprints or tire tracks in remote areas, no illegal camping, no sign of traps or snares or firearms. No evidence of recent kills or carcasses. No blood stains. Poachers were in a hurry and usually left behind valuable clues. Traces of bait or attractants used to lure animals, disturbances in wildlife habitats, or even litter. A few years ago, he had tracked down the identity of a poacher from fingerprints left on a candy wrapper.

Two hours later, after thoroughly combing Willow Flats, Tim found no signs of the reported poacher. Nothing. Frustration weighed on him as he retraced his steps. Before heading to his car, he radioed Sally.

"Ranger Janus here," her voice crackled through the radio.

"Hey, Sally. It's Tim. I've been out searching the area, but no sign of any poacher."

"You were supposed to call me on my cell."

"That would require cell reception," he said, sounding a little testy himself. He was cold and hungry, and had spent hours chasing a bad lead. "And where I am, I'm lucky that the radio is working."

She sighed. "No sign of her?"

"Who? The poacher?" A female? That would be unusual.

"399."

"No." His brow furrowed. "Sally, is that why you sent me out here? To look for 399?" The frustration was evident in his voice.

"You were sent to investigate a poacher tip," she said, her words clipped and businesslike. "That's why I need direct communication, off the radio. We can't risk information leaks."

"There's no leak because there's no poacher in this vicinity, Ranger Janus."

A heavy pause lingered before Sally spoke again. "Thank you for checking, Tim," she said, a little softer. Then back came her no-nonsense voice. "Head over to Gros Ventre River and inform Coop that he will be giving the ranger talk tonight."

"Coop? He'll balk at that."

"It's your job to make him want to do it. Tell him he can pick any topic he wants. Over and out." She ended the call abruptly.

Tim sighed, stowing his radio away. As he started toward the valley, he wondered if there was more to Sally's prickliness than met the eye. He wondered if she might be giving him the elbow.

Maisie slept late that morning. When she read Pops's note, she ate breakfast and thought about her day. She had hours and hours with nothing to do, so she put on her yellow puffy down jacket and decided to go for a bicycle ride, borrowing Pops's bike again. She didn't think he'd mind, though the bike was too big for her. The seat was awkward. The handlebars were too wide apart. It took her a while to get the hang of it. Once she could get moving along, she was okay. Starting and stopping were the tricky parts. Worth it, though. She loved exploring the park on two wheels, feeling the rush of wind against her face as she passed by towering trees and stunning vistas. The faster she went, the easier the bike was to manage.

As Maisie rounded a sharp bend in the path, her attention drifted for just a second. Those towering trees lining the trail were seriously mesmerizing. Lost in their beauty, she totally missed the two figures standing right in the middle of the bike path.

At the last second, the unsuspecting pair saw Maisie coming straight for them and stumbled backward to get out of the way. Maisie lost control of the bicycle and crashed, landing in a heap on the ground with a startled cry. She rolled over and checked her bleeding knees and elbows. "Ouch, ouch, ouch."

"Kid, are you okay?"

Maisie looked up to see two people, both rangers in official uniform, staring down at her. The man was crazy tall, his stiff ranger hat making him even taller. And the other one was a tiny woman whose head was almost entirely swallowed up by her ranger hat.

And she looked *mad*. "Honey," the tiny ranger said, in a tone of voice that didn't match the soft word, "you need to watch where you're going."

The crazy tall ranger nodded in agreement, a wry smile tugging at the corners of his lips. "Yeah, my sister always said I didn't make a very good speed bump. Too skinny."

Maisie scrambled to her feet. "Oops, my bad. This bike's new to me. It's not a new bike, obviously." In fact, it was pretty ancient. "It belongs to Pops. He's my grandfather. Well, not really. Not officially. He was married to my grandmother, but I never knew her and I've always known Pops." Maisie cringed inwardly at her own chatter, knowing she should zip it. In the best of times, she knew she was . . . how did Pops word it? "Blessed with the gift of conversation." But when nerves kicked in, Maisie's mouth turned into a runaway train, and there was no stopping the word avalanche. Like now, with the tiny ranger eyeballing her like she'd committed a felony. Just as Maisie started to explain more, the tiny ranger held up her tiny hand like a stop sign.

"Hon, just be more careful next time," she said, before turning to walk away with the tall ranger in tow.

As Maisie watched them go, she couldn't shake the feeling that she had seen the tiny woman somewhere before. Then it hit her like a bolt of lightning. She hopped on her bike, which took a little time to properly maneuver, and pedaled fast to catch up with them.

"You're Sally Janus!" Maisie called out, hoping to stop them. "I met you last year when I was visiting Pops."

The tiny ranger stopped in her tracks, turning to look at Maisie with surprise. "Who is Pops?"

"Ranger Tim Rivers."

"Tim Rivers is your grandfather?"

Maisie nodded eagerly, a grin spreading across her face. "Yep, that's him!"

Recognition lit Sally Janus's face. "Why, you're Maisie!"

"That's me!"

"You've sure changed a lot since last summer." Sally's expression softened considerably, and she gave Maisie a warm smile. "Well, it's sure nice to see you again, hon. Your grandfather talks about you all the time. He's a fine ranger. One of the best."

"Thanks!" Maisie beamed, feeling a surge of pride at the praise for Pops. She slid her backpack off to unzip it and look for her favorite picture of her and her grandfather. She wanted to show it to Sally Janus. While she hunted through her backpack, she chattered away about how she spent a portion of every summer with Pops. "Ever since I was little," she said. "Pops always wants me to spend a couple of weeks with him each summer, in whatever national park he's been assigned to." She dug through the backpack until she found the picture. "Here it is!" She looked up.

But Sally Janus and the tall ranger were gone.

Wade Schmidt's standards were sky-high, he was well aware of that. But the moment he met Feldmann, he felt a hitch in his gut. The thing that bothered Wade the most was how tall Feldmann was. Memorably tall.

Memorability was the last thing Wade wanted to be associated with. He used different disguises when traveling, both internationally and domestically, and had quite the collection of driver's licenses and passports. Thanks to his impressive acting skills and knack for accents, he could easily slip into various roles. It was all part of the game.

He tapped his fingers rhythmically on the small desk in his dimly lit hotel room. All around him were topographical maps of the park, satellite images, weather reports, and various other pieces of critical information. His eyes narrowed as he studied the detailed maps of Grand Teton National Park, etching into his mind every contour, every creek, every trail.

He checked the latest weather report again, noting the forecasted conditions for the coming days. Afternoon storms were common in the mountains. Rain could be an advantage, masking his scent. He knew not to underestimate a bear's keen sense of smell. But rain had its drawback—it made tracking paw prints and scat more difficult.

Calculated planning before the execution was half the fun for Wade. Hunters often said that the toughest part was the waiting game, especially when it came to glassing—sitting still at a prime spot for hours on end, staying alert for that perfect moment when your target makes an appearance. Glassing separated the men from the boys.

For Wade, the waiting game wasn't a challenge at all. In fact, he relished it. He understood the value of patience in hunting—it was what set him apart. Unlike many of his peers who relied on technology like animal calls from their phones, Wade preferred the old-school approach, even to the point of spreading musk all over to cover his scent. To him, there was no thrill in using gadgets to shortcut the chase. Waiting patiently for the right moment was where the real excitement lay.

Anticipation built as he visualized the hunt in his mind, preparing for every scenario. He imagined the thrill of tracking 399, the world's most famous grizzly bear. It was all about strategy, patience, and precision. A game of cat and mouse. The cat always won.

And Wade was the cat.

SEVEN

For one that comes into the wilderness with a pencil to sketch or sing, a thousand come with an axe or rifle.
—*Henry David Thoreau, American philosopher*

The midday sun beat down on Coop as he rambled through a meadow that led up to the Gros Ventre River, tracking a set of gray wolf prints. Helped by circling vultures, Coop spotted the remains of an elk calf that had been taken down during the night. He was pretty sure the wolf to whom these prints belonged was responsible for the carnage.

Coop had to admire the survival skills of wolves. They used to roam the area freely, but ranchers put an end to that. When they were reintroduced to nearby Yellowstone Park in 1995, a pack wandered down to Grand Teton and denned there, producing a litter of pups, the first in the park in over seventy years. Now, they were permanent residents in the neighborhood. At last count, over six packs were in the park. Over forty-three wolves and counting.

Coop was tracking this wolf to find its rendezvous site, which was closer to the river than he originally thought. He considered recommending an enclosure around the site to minimize human disturbance to the wolves. After abandoning their dens, wolves tended to stay in one area for pup-raising activities. In the fall, mothers and pups would start to travel through the territories, moving as a pack.

The steady rush of the Gros Ventre River provided a serene backdrop, and Coop reveled in the solitude, relishing the sounds of nature. Such moments had gone missing for him this summer. When awake, Frankie was a perpetual noise machine—tapping his hands like drums to the blaring music in his earbuds or ranting about the world's troubles. When asleep, his snoring rivaled that of a buzz saw.

As Coop neared the river, he spotted a couple of human footprints on the bank, as if they walked in the river and stepped onto the bank, then back into the river. He turned in a circle, wondering if these individuals might have been following the wolf's tracks, like he was. And if so, why.

His thoughts went immediately to the poacher threat that Tim had told him about. There was a thriving black market for wolf pups. He studied the footprints again. One was large. He guessed it must be at least a male's size 13 or 14. Bigger than his size 12, that was for sure. The other footprint was small. A female? Maybe a child? Both boots had thick tread. He took pictures of the footprints and thought he'd check at HQ to see if there'd been any chatter about wolf poaching. He heard someone call out and looked up. Two fly fishermen stood in the river, casting their lines. Wearing waders. Thick treads on the soles. He peered through his binoculars. A man and a woman. Coop sighed and deleted the footprints from his phone.

Tim's poacher talk was getting to him. Turning him into the park's meter maid. Suspicious about everybody.

Seeing the fishermen's waders reminded Coop of yesterday's encounter with that cute photographer. Kate Cunningham. He chuckled to himself, thinking of how she tried to hold on to her dignity after a dunk in the river. His smile faded as he remembered the mocking she'd received from the other shutterbugs. When he got back to his room last evening, he chewed Frankie out for telling the others that Kate worked as a zoo photographer.

He wondered if, after that humiliating moment, Kate might've packed up and gone home. She wasn't at Pilgrim Creek this morning. He knew because he had looked for her amongst the other photographers. She wasn't there, but neither was 399. The bear still hadn't been sighted. Even Coop was starting to worry that the old sow didn't make it through the long winter.

Suddenly, his thoughts were interrupted by a familiar voice. He turned to see Tim Rivers strolling toward him, a wide grin plastered on his face. He liked Tim, liked him a lot, but he knew that grin meant trouble.

"Coop! Just the man I wanted to see," Tim said, clapping Coop on the back with a force that nearly sent him stumbling. "Got a minute?"

"Do I have a choice?"

"Nope. I've got some fantastic news for you," Tim said, rubbing his hands together as if about to unveil a grand surprise.

"Why do I doubt that?" He cast a longing glance back at the wolf tracks.

"You, my friend, are going to be our star attraction at tonight's evening ranger talk."

Coop's eyes narrowed. "I hope you're kidding."

"I'm not," Tim said, a touch too cheerfully. "The ranger who was supposed to give the talk is down and out with a nasty stomach virus. Sally wants you to step in."

He felt sympathy for the poor ranger, but much more for himself. "Tim, I'm here to manage the bears and protect the park. Not to entertain tourists."

"Part of a ranger's job is to educate visitors. That's why Stephen Mather relieved the army from the task of protecting the parks when he became the first director for the national parks. Second task was to implement rangers. Greet and educate, that was his mantra."

Coop sighed. Stephen Mather, Tim's hero. John Muir, a close second. He quoted them endlessly. "You're talking to the wrong ranger."

"Coop, you're a teacher. You talk to people all the time."

Tim seemed oblivious to Coop's dismay. "And that's exactly why I'm here—to escape that." He let out a sigh. "You know how much I prefer the company of grizzlies to people."

"Well, here's your chance to enlighten the public about your favorite topic. Sally said you can choose to talk about anything you want. Tell the visitors everything you know about bears. That's all you have to do. Give a bear talk."

Tim wasn't backing down.

A voice piped up from behind them. "Did I hear there's going to be a talk about bears?"

Coop whirled around to see *that* photographer, Kate, standing about two feet away from him, an intrigued expression on her face. Man, she really *was* pretty. So far, he'd only seen her at dawn or at dusk. This was the first time in broad daylight. He felt his heart rate quicken a bit.

"Perfect timing," Tim said, gesturing toward Coop. "Ranger Cooper is going to give the first evening ranger talk for the season about bears. Tonight."

Kate's eyes lit up. "That sounds interesting."

"It will be. I'd be hard pressed to find anyone at the park who is more knowledgeable about bears than this man." Tim looked at Coop. "So I'll tell Sally that you're on board and the topic is bears, right?"

Coop hesitated, glancing at Kate, before giving Tim a nod. "Yeah, yeah. Sure."

Tim's eyes went from Coop's to Kate's and back to Coop's,

before landing on Kate. "I'm Ranger Tim Rivers. I see from the camera around your neck that you're a photographer. This is a great time to be at the park, before crowds come. Lots of wildlife in the area."

Kate smiled. "Ranger Cooper has been helping me find the right places to be at the right time."

"Has he, now?" Tim's voice was full of delight. "So, then, you two have already met."

Coop cringed. He avoided Tim's eyes.

"Well, that sounds typical of our highly esteemed Ranger Cooper. Always willing to help out." Tim slapped Coop on the back, a little too hard. He grinned at Kate, a little too happy. "So I'll save you a seat right up front tonight." He started to walk away but stopped and turned. "Sally wants a title for the talk. What do you want to call it?"

"A title?" Coop hated this kind of thing. "How about . . . something like . . . 'information on bears so you don't get mauled to death in your sleep.'"

Tim grimaced. "We're not trying to scare visitors right out of the park."

"Here's one," Kate said. "'Be Bear Aware.' Oh, wait . . . here's another idea. 'Bear Necessities.'"

Tim wagged a finger at her. "Young lady, I like the way you think." He lifted a hand in the air. "Almost forgot. It's to be held at the Jenny Lake Visitor Center. Seven o'clock." He paused and looked around the river. "Where's Frankie?"

"Probably still sleeping," Coop said. "He said it's his day off."

Tim grinned. "Specially assigned interns don't get a day off. I'll go wake him up."

"That's another thing, Tim. Since when is there such a role as a specially assigned intern? And why is he assigned to me?"

But Tim was already walking away and lifted his hand in a parting wave.

Coop frowned at his retreating back.

"I can't wait to hear your talk tonight."

Coop turned to Kate, ready to say something clever, and got caught up in the blue whirlpool of her eyes. Seriously, what color were those eyes? Blue like a calm tropical sea. Blue like the sky on a perfect summer day. His brain, usually on point, just went *poof* in the face of those eyes. All he could muster was a nod, playing it off like a total bobblehead. An awkward silence followed.

"Well," Kate said, "I'll be off, then."

She started off, and suddenly Coop's mind erupted with words. "You weren't there."

She stopped and turned, a question on her face. "Where?"

"Pilgrim Creek. You weren't there this morning."

"I overslept. I didn't get to bed until after midnight. I was photographing some elk in a meadow with a full moon behind them . . . and it was just . . . magical." She gazed up at the sky. "This place. I can't explain how I feel here. I am so overwhelmed with . . . well, with gratitude to God for creating such a place. For giving me the gift of experiencing it." Suddenly embarrassed, she dropped her head.

"I agree. Completely. I feel that same way when I drive through those gates in May."

She took a few steps toward him. "You're not a year-round ranger?"

He shook his head. "I'm a high school biology teacher from September to May."

She smiled. "No kidding? Do you like being a ranger?"

"I do. I love it. Being out in nature is my passion. And being a ranger lets me protect nature. People give rangers a lot of respect." He tipped his hat. "My theory is that it's the uniform. There's something about wearing the uniform that makes people stand up straighter. Sometimes I think teachers should wear one."

She laughed. Pleased, he grinned. She was easy to talk to.

"But you like being a teacher too?"

"I do. I like being both. But if I had my druthers, I'd be a full-time Jenny Lake Ranger."

"Is it much different from what you're doing now?"

"Yeah, it really is. They're a highly trained search and rescue team. Very James Bond."

Kate laughed. He liked making her laugh.

"Have you ever applied to be a full-time ranger?"

His smile faded. "No."

"Because . . ."

"For a lot of reasons. It's really hard to get hired full-time, especially if there's a specific park you want to work in." He felt a little sting, as if he could hear Emma asking him the same question. *"Why are you so afraid of change?"* she would ask him. *"Why can't you just try something? What's the big deal?"*

He didn't know why he was so resistant to risk. Kind of ironic, considering he was in the bear management business. But the truth was, if he applied to be a full-time Jenny Lake Ranger and was rejected, it would crush him. Sour him on being a seasonal ranger, which he loved.

It was easier not to try.

He glanced at Kate. Now, she was one willing to take risks. He admired that quality in her. She had come to the park as a novice and took plenty of jabs from the other shutterbugs. Yet she was still here. She didn't quit.

As if she sensed he was thinking about her, a curious look came over her face. "Just what are 'druthers,' anyway? I've heard that expression my entire life and I've never known what it means."

Surprised, he chuckled. That remark was unexpected. "I think it's slang for 'I'd rather.'"

"Makes sense." Kate nodded. "I heard 399 wasn't spotted

this morning, and I was so relieved I hadn't missed her. I'm determined to not leave the park without that one-in-a-million shot of her."

Coop took a step closer. "What makes you so sure you'll be able to get something unique?"

She stiffened, as if she'd heard that question one too many times. "Because my experience is from a zoo, you mean."

"Not at all. I think it's cool you got your start in a zoo. I only meant to say that a lot of photographers have gotten incredible shots of 399. Thomas Mangelsen, for one."

"True. His work is remarkable."

"Seems like you're banking a lot on something that's already been done."

"Because . . . she's such a familiar subject."

"Right."

"I think the challenge of photography is creating new and different images of a very familiar subject."

Okay. That was a new thought to him. "So . . . you're trying to find a new angle?" What new angle could there be of the world's most famous bear?

Listening to him, she tipped her head, as if trying to decide how to answer him. "Let's just say," she said, "I have something up my sleeve." She patted her camera and left him with a parting smile.

Left him wondering what in the world she meant by that.

Tim Rivers made the drive from Gros Ventre River to Jackson Lake Lodge, where he had tasked himself with the mission of rousing Frankie the intern out of bed. Not the most thrilling task, but it was part of his duty as a district ranger. Sally had been insistent that Frankie receive special attention this summer due to his father's position in the NPS, which had made her act a bit jittery about the boy potentially being overlooked in the YCP. More than a bit jittery. She was adamant that he should be carefully supervised. Tim knew that Coop had more experience with teens than other rangers had, so he brought up the internship concept and Sally jumped on it.

So that was the reason behind reassigning Coop from back-country duties, though the official explanation was his out-spoken behavior toward hikers. It wasn't a deception, though. Tim had been in full agreement with Sally to pull Coop after those complaints. It wasn't like Coop to treat people that way and it didn't bode well for the start of the tourist season. Tim sensed that something had been eating at Coop from the day he'd arrived at the park. There was a tension simmering beneath the surface, and it seemed to affect his interactions with others.

So, other than having to keep an eye on a pampered teenager, Tim thought being down in the valley might be a good change for Coop. And after seeing the exchange of looks between him and that good-looking lady photographer this morning, he didn't feel too badly about how the summer was rolling out for his young friend.

Tim's mind rewound to when he first met Coop at that school talk about careers in the NPS. Coop had come up afterward and told him how he'd spent every summer of his life back-packing in one national park or another. There was a certain look in Coop's eyes that resonated with Tim—a familiarity. A passion for the great outdoors. It was clear to Tim that this biology teacher had the potential to do more than just explore nature during his summers; he could contribute significantly to preserving and protecting it.

On the spot, Tim offered him a seasonal position as a Jenny Lake Park ranger. It was a decision Tim never regretted, as Coop's dedication and impact in the park were evident from the start. He had an uncanny intuition about wildlife. Bears, especially.

Not so much with people, though.

But he changed his mind on that after he knocked on the door of the shared room where Coop and Frankie were stationed for the summer, knocked and knocked and knocked, and after Frankie finally stumbled out of bed to open the door. Coop should be nominated for sainthood.

Frankie blinked several times and mumbled, "Dude. Where's the fire?"

Tim couldn't help but ratchet up the intensity. "You have five minutes to take a shower, get dressed, and meet me back here. Move it."

Frankie's grogginess quickly turned into confusion, then belligerence. "I'm taking the day off!"

Tim raised an eyebrow. "Who gave you permission to have the day off?"

"I did," he said, as if he'd been crowned king of the interns. And there were no interns but Frankie. "I need a break."

"Are you sick?"

"I sure am. Sick of getting bossed around. Sick of being treated like a servant."

Tim checked his watch with exaggerated interest. "Four minutes left."

"Dude! It's not like I'm getting paid or anything."

"Volunteerism is a duty that should be taken seriously." Tim stared him down until the boy buckled.

"Fine, fine, drill sergeant. Keep your cool on." Frankie grabbed his jeans before shuffling down the hall to the bathroom, a scowl etched on his face.

Tim shook his head as he surveyed the chaotic room. *Oh boy.* It was a complete mess. Frankie's clothes were strewn everywhere. So was his garbage. Poor Coop. Tim had no idea that sharing a room with the boy meant . . . *this.*

He picked up empty chip bags and fast-food wrappers and

candy and tossed them in the wastebasket. Even Coop's desk was covered with Frankie's sweatshirt and underpants.

Too bad Maisie wasn't with him right now. Maybe seeing this disgusting living condition would keep her from thinking this kid was such a . . . what did she call him? A hottie.

While cleaning off Coop's desktop of Frankie's dirty laundry, Tim noticed a thick envelope addressed to Grant Cooper in elegant calligraphy. He had a gut feeling what it was, confirmed when he saw the return address. The seal had been opened, so he pulled out the contents. He wasn't proud of snooping, but he cared about his friend. *Oh boy.* Just what he had thought. A very formal invitation to what looked like Emma's fancy wedding. He slipped it back into the envelope and noticed the postmark. No wonder Coop had been testy to the hikers. He must've received this right after he'd arrived at the park to start the summer.

Hearing Frankie approach, Tim swiftly put the envelope back where he found it, hiding it under the boy's dirty laundry.

One thing was clear, at least to Tim. It was high time for Coop to move on from the Emma Dilemma. She wasn't coming back to him.

Maisie pedaled furiously along the winding trail, the wind whipping through her hair as she made her way toward the Craig Thomas Discovery and Visitor Center. She was eager to see if Pops was there, maybe grab a snack from the café, and possibly persuade him to take her out horseback riding later. She *adored* horses. She'd never actually ridden one, but she knew she'd be good at it.

As she rounded a bend, her eyes caught sight of that super tall ranger standing near a bench, facing a different direction. She slowed her bike to a stop, pulling off to the side of the trail. She'd like to show him that picture of her and Pops, so she took off her backpack and unzipped it.

She realized that he was talking on the phone. Not really talking but listening. Maisie could hear someone on the other end. She couldn't make out the words, but she could tell the caller was angry.

Now and then, in a strained voice, the ranger would say, "Yes . . . Understood . . . Entirely my fault . . . I'll go right now."

Maisie wondered if he was getting chewed out by Sally Janus, the tiny lady ranger, but the voice sounded deeper, more like a man's. She zipped up her backpack. Now probably wasn't a good time to show off that photograph of her and Pops. She put both feet on the pedals to head off, but she couldn't reach one pedal and the bike toppled over. "Oooff," Maisie said, landing on the ground. These falls hurt, and she'd been falling a lot.

The ranger spun around. "I'll call you back," he said and hung up. "Were you eavesdropping?"

"No!" She had tried, but she couldn't hear anything. Nothing specific.

The ranger's expression softened slightly as he looked at Maisie sprawled on the ground. "Kid, you need to learn how to ride a bike." And off he went.

Maisie got herself up and brushed off her knees. As she picked up her bike, she looked at the tall ranger's receding back. "I'm not a kid!"

But he was too far away to hear her.

Wade couldn't believe it. Feldmann had given him the wrong PO box for the address. The package that was due in today had been returned to sender.

"I'm sorry, sir. I must have been distracted when I gave you the number for the PO box."

Incredibly frustrated, Wade's hands tightened into fists.

"That package was critical to the hunt, Feldmann." It held Wade's favorite bow, a custom-made compound bow that he had affectionately named "Whisper." The bow had a sleek black design with intricate engravings along the limbs, a testament to its craftsmanship. Its draw weight was precisely calibrated to Wade's strength, allowing him to handle it with ease even during long hunts.

Accompanying Whisper were arrows, each meticulously crafted and fletched to perfection. Wade favored broadheads with their razor-sharp blades. Each arrow had a marking near the fletching, a small detail that revealed the unique property of the arrow—its weight or balance. Wade's prowess with a bow was his greatest pride. He spent hours fine-tuning his bow and arrows, ensuring they were in prime condition for the next hunt.

"Don't you worry, sir. I'll find a replacement."

Wade scoffed. "Impossible. My bow is not just a weapon, Feldmann. It's my partner. You need to get it here."

"Right. Of course."

Just like a rider and their trusted saddle, Wade's bond with Whisper went beyond functionality. It was a symbol of his skill, dedication, and connection to the ancient art of archery. And when he drew Whisper's string and released an arrow, it was a dance of precision and deadly intent, a connection between hunter and tool.

"Uh, Mr. Schmidt," Feldmann said, "archery is for small game. You can't shoot a bear with a bow and arrow."

"You're right," Wade said. "Most people can't. But I'm not like most people."

EIGHT

Any glimpse into the life of an animal quickens our own and
makes it so much the larger and better in every way.
—*John Muir*

The sun began its descent behind the rugged peaks of the Grand
Tetons, casting a warm amber glow across the landscape as
Kate hurried toward the Jenny Lake Visitor Center. Twenty
minutes ago, she had been knee-deep in the Gros Ventre River,
clad in waders, attempting to capture the perfect shot of a
beaver dam bathed in the golden hues of a long summer night.
She loved these long twilights! Perfect lighting for so many
shots of wildlife. And there was so much wildlife to be seen at
dawn and at dusk.

She'd only been here for a few days, and she'd already learned
so much. How to walk in a river wearing waders without trip-
ping, for one. Stay away from where other photographers were
camped out, for another. She was proud of herself. Oliver said
she'd be running home after the first howl she heard. Well,
she'd already heard plenty of howls, bugles, and eagle screeches.

But Kate had yet to photograph 399. It was a small comfort

that no one else had, either. But only a small comfort, because that could mean the bear hadn't survived the winter.

With no time for a shower or change of clothes, she drove to Jenny Lake and found one last open spot in the parking lot. Jenny Lake was an area she wanted to explore, so she planned to hike out here tomorrow. The visitor center was much smaller than she'd expected, cabin-like, and when she opened the door, she found it packed with people sitting on metal folding chairs.

Coop was at the front, near a large rock fireplace. Kate stood by the door, looking for a seat. The older ranger, the one she'd met this morning at the river, saw her and waved her to him. He pointed to an empty seat right up front. "Next to my granddaughter, Maisie."

With a resigned shrug, Kate made her way to the front row, and Coop momentarily faltered. The fabric of her still-wet waders made a *swish-swash* sound as she walked. The room fell into an uncomfortable silence, and Kate could feel the weight of everyone's eyes on her. The gray-haired pigtailed woman made a snippy remark as Kate swish-swashed past her. "Take another dip with the otters before coming here?"

On the other side of the pigtailed woman was a friendly young face next to an empty chair. "I'm Maisie," she said, patting the chair. "Pops told me to save a seat for a beautiful woman who loves bears." She smiled at Kate, a big smile, full of metal braces.

Kate guessed the girl was around twelve or thirteen. She had an almost old-fashioned look about her: copper-colored hair tumbling down her back in a tangle of curls, sparkling blue eyes, and a round, freckled face with a slightly upturned nose. "Sorry to be late," she whispered. "I lost track of time." She settled into the chair and looked at Coop, whose eyes were still on her.

Coop gave his head a slight shake, then lifted his notes, as if trying to remember where he'd left off. Standing along the side of the room, Tim Rivers said, "You were telling us about the cozy world of bear hibernation, Ranger Coop."

"Right," Coop said. "Right." He searched his notes, a streak of red rising along his cheeks.

Kate reached into her bag and took out a notepad and a pen. She hoped she hadn't missed much. This topic of hibernation fascinated her. Such a mystery.

Coop kept looking through his notes as an awkward silence filled the room.

"Bears and me," the older ranger said, "have something in common. When we find that perfect spot, we take our napping seriously."

The audience chuckled, and Coop seemed to loosen up with the ranger's light touch. "As I was saying," he said, glancing briefly at Kate as he started again, "you might think hibernation is all about a long nap, but there's much more to it. So let's break down what happens during a bear's winter hibernation. When it comes to choosing a den, bears go for remote, high-country locations, maybe a cave or a hollowed-out tree. It's all about peace and quiet. And they usually return to the same den each year, like coming back to your favorite vacation spot."

"Like Disney World," Maisie said. "Even though I've never gone. I hear it's *awesome* though."

"Save your money," Frankie said. He stood at the far end of the front row, leaning against the wall, arms crossed, looking like he'd rather be anywhere but here. "It's a complete rip-off. Long lines, overpriced churros. American capitalism at its worst."

"You're exactly right, Maisie." Coop's face softened as he addressed Maisie's question, clearly fond of her.

That look was a little heart melting, Kate thought. Like a tough guy with a tender heart.

"*Most* people"—now Coop cast a frowning side glance at

Frankie—"love going to Disney World or Disneyland repeatedly. It's familiar and enjoyable. That's exactly how a bear considers its lair.

"Bears are the DIY kings of the animal kingdom," Coop continued. "Each bear's winter retreat can be as unique as their personality. Some might go all out on the den upgrades, while others keep it simple."

Maisie clapped her hands together. "They give it their own personal touch!"

Down the row, Kate noticed how Frankie kept rolling his eyes at Maisie's exuberance. When his eyes met Kate's, he straightened up, a sheepish look on his face.

"Does anybody know what happens to a bear's body during hibernation?" Coop's gaze swept the room.

Maisie's hand shot up. "Fun fact: A grizzly bear can gain up to four hundred pounds in preparation for hibernation!"

"You're right, Maisie," Coop said. "Anybody have something to add?"

No one did. Kate knew nothing about it. Bears in a zoo didn't hibernate. No need to.

"When a bear finally settles in for the winter," Coop said, "its heart rate drops to a mere five beats per minute."

Maisie burst out with a laugh. "Whoa! That's slower than my mom's chilled-out yoga instructor!"

As chuckles rippled through the room, Coop shot Frankie a "don't do it" look of warning before he could roll his eyes again.

"Exactly, Maisie," Coop said. "It's like they go into full chill-out mode. The real magic happens, at least for a pregnant sow, in January or February. Bears give birth in their dens. Mother Nature's maternity ward right there."

Kate raised her hand. "How does a bear know when spring has come?"

Coop's eyes met hers, a subtle pause hanging in the air

before he replied, "Excellent question. Bears have sensors in their eyes that detect the increased light, signaling their bodies to wake up."

"Like," Maisie said, "someone turns on a light and they wake up, ready for breakfast?"

Frankie's eyes rolled around and around. Now Kate shot him a frown.

"Kind of," Coop said. "Maybe, more slowly than a light switched on. They wake up hungry. Famished. And that's the condition the bears are in right now, after this long winter. Male grizzlies emerge from their lair earlier than females. They're looking for food. So if you encounter a bear while you're in the park, and chances are that you will, remember a few bear safety tips. Rule number one—never surprise a bear."

"Surprise a bear?" Maisie furrowed her brow. "But I thought bears were more scared of humans than we are of them."

"Generally, bears will avoid people. But surprising them might trigger a fight-or-flight response. Hopefully, flight. So make your presence known. Talk or sing as you walk. Some hikers use bells on their packs."

Kate took this all in.

"If you do see a bear, do not approach it. Stay at least one hundred yards away from it. That's the length of a football field. Remain calm. Don't run. A bear can outrun a horse, so you'd better believe that it can outrun you. Don't make eye contact with it. Walk slowly backward, maybe start talking in a gentle way, so that it realizes you're not threatening it. Most likely, the bear is only interested in protecting its cubs or guarding its food source. It might try bluffing."

"Aww, cool!" Frankie said. "Bears play poker."

Coop released a long-suffering sigh. "Bluffing means a bear will charge and stop. It might huff loudly at you. If so, it's trying to warn you away." He cleared his throat. "Finally, whatever you do, never feed a bear. Bears grow easily accustomed to human food and will become dangerous and unpredictable. Feeding bears causes them to lose their natural instinctive fear of humans and that's when trouble happens. Remember the mantra—let wildlife be wild."

"In other words," Frankie said, "a fed bear is a dead bear."

Maisie leaned forward to look down the row at him. "What do you mean?"

"Exactly what it sounds like." Dramatically, Frankie drew a line across his neck.

"No!" Maisie gasped. "You don't mean . . ."

"What he means," Coop said in a tight voice, "is if a bear interacts too much with humans, it could end up having to be euthanized."

"But that's TERRIBLE," Maisie said. "It's not the bear's fault! It's the humans' fault!"

"Ya got that right, kid," Frankie said.

Still leaning forward in her chair, Maisie squinted at him. "I am *not* a kid." She sat back and raised her hand high. "Coop, how often do bears attack people?"

"Statistically, it's extremely rare."

Frankie scoffed a laugh. "Not if it's happening to you."

Coop grimaced. "Again, bear attacks are extremely rare. They're not out to get you."

Maisie's hand hit the sky again. "But if a bear does attack . . ."

"Attacks have usually happened because a bear was surprised. So remember the basics and you shouldn't have any problems. Don't hike alone. Talk or sing as you hike. Wear a loud whistle around your neck. Carry bear spray on your hip and know how to use it. Stay aware of your surroundings." He cast a meaningful glance at Frankie. "For example, it would be foolish to wear earbuds and listen to loud music when you're hiking."

"How 'bout . . ." Frankie said, "eschewing the earbuds and

just listening to loud music? That's like a win-win. Perfect way to warn the bears that you're coming through." He grinned. "Unless bears like rock 'n' roll."

Maisie leaned over to Kate. "What does 'eschew' mean?"

"Forgo," Kate said. "Skip 'em."

"Why doesn't he just say that?" Maisie's hand shot up again, but Coop, clearly ready to wrap it up, ignored her.

He clapped his hands together. "There's one last point I want to drill home tonight. It's the most important one too. If you happen upon a sow with cubs, give them plenty of space. Never, ever get between a mother bear and her cubs. If you ever find yourself in that situation, say a prayer. You are in trouble."

"He's right. Lots of babies in our park right now. The phrase 'mama bear' ain't for nothing." A female ranger, small and petite with a squeaky little voice, walked up to Coop. "Let's all thank Ranger Cooper for his fascinating talk about bears."

Maisie clapped enthusiastically. "It was wonderful, Coop! You should give it every night!"

Coop's face conveyed how terrible an idea he thought *that* was.

The little ranger took over, standing right in front of Coop. "I'm Sally Janus, acting chief ranger for the park. Don't forget that you're always welcome to ask a ranger anything. That's what we're here for. Thank you all for coming tonight. Ranger Cooper will be giving lots more ranger talks this summer, so check the schedule at the visitor center."

Clearly, that was news to Coop. Kate had to swallow a smile at the shocked look on his face.

The small ranger lifted her hands in the air. "Enjoy your time here in the park, but always respect the wildlife."

Kate reached down to pick up her camera bag, and by the time she sat back up, Frankie stood in front of her.

"Hello, Kate." He wiggled his eyebrows. "We have to stop meeting like this."

"Frankie!" Maisie jumped up. "I was hoping to see you tonight. Where were you all day? I rode Pops's bike everywhere, but I couldn't find you. How's the internship going? Do you think I can shadow you and Coop sometime?"

As Maisie continued to fire questions at Frankie, Kate quietly slipped away into the crowd and out the door. Frankie the intern was the last person she wanted to see. She was still peeved at him for blabbing about her zoo background to the other photographers. The nickname "Zoo Girl" stung like nettles—leaving tiny barbs that pricked at her skin.

Tim Rivers made his way through the dispersing crowd after Coop's ranger talk on bear safety. He spotted Sally near the edge of the group and approached her with a friendly smile. "Coop did a great job, didn't he?" Tim said, gesturing toward where Coop was still answering questions for a few park visitors.

"He did just fine," Sally said. "Tell him I appreciate his willingness to give a ranger talk at the last minute."

"And you're expecting more talks from him this summer?"

"Sure am. He's good at them. He has a knack for engaging the audience and getting the message across." Her gaze shifted to Frankie. "How's that one doing as an intern for Coop?"

Frankie stood up front, hands in his pockets, looking bored. Maisie was chatting away to him, obviously enamored. Her schoolgirl crush on him was a worry to Tim. "Actually, I'm glad you asked. Frankie seems like a troubled kid."

Sally scoffed. "I'll say. Kicked out of three boarding schools."

"You know, I'm not sure how fair this is to Coop. He's stuck with him as both an intern and a roommate."

Sally turned to him. "Coop can handle it. He understands teenagers better than most any other ranger. Goodness, he deals with kids all through the school year."

Exactly why it didn't seem fair to dump Coop with the burden of Frankie.

She leaned in a little. "You and I both know that Coop's role really is to be a mentor to Frankie."

"How do you mentor a kid who's determined to be unmentorable?"

Sally waved that off. "Like I said, Coop can handle him."

"Sally," Tim said, pressing further, "why is this kid so important?"

Sally hesitated, her demeanor clouded with reservation. "Frankie's father asked me personally to give the boy special treatment and attention."

Tim raised an eyebrow. "Ah, I see. It's about connections."

Sally gave a rueful smile. "You know what it's like, climbing the ladder, Tim. It gets harder and harder to reach that next rung."

Then why do it? Tim wanted to ask. *Why not be content with where you are in life? It's a pretty good life we have here.*

But he knew not to ask those questions out loud. This was the first relaxed conversation they'd had since she'd come back from the Yellowstone conference, and he wanted to get things back on track between them. "After I lock up, would you like to grab some coffee?"

"That sounds nice, Tim, hon."

Calling him hon was just the encouragement he'd been needing. "We haven't had a good talk in a while, Sally. I've missed our talks." He noticed a softening in her expression, a hint of something unspoken in her eyes. He took a step closer. "I've missed you." He took another step, but suddenly Maisie stood between them.

"Hi!" Maisie said, in her enthusiastic way. "Ranger Janus! I met you on the bike path today! Remember? Early this morning. Really early. I nearly ran Pops's bike right into you and that super tall ranger."

Why hadn't Sally mentioned that? Tim talked about Maisie all the time. "What super tall ranger?" he asked.

Sally's attention was on Maisie. "Of course I remember. You were riding your bike pretty fast, there."

Maisie grinned. "Yeah, sorry about that. I'm still learning how to manage Pops's bike."

Sally waved to a ranger across the room. "I see someone I need to go speak to." She put one hand on Maisie's arm and another on Tim's. Two birds, one stone. "Nice to meet you, sugar. Slow down on that bike. I'll have to take a rain check on that coffee, Tim."

That sudden departure left Tim slightly puzzled. It was starting to become a familiar feeling after an encounter with Sally.

As soon as Coop finished answering questions for a group of women who planned to hike in the backcountry but were terrified of bears, he looked around the room for Kate. Disappointed, he realized she must have already left. He went outside the visitor center and peered around, then saw her standing by the open trunk of her car, fiddling with some camera equipment. He bolted over to the parking lot but slowed about fifteen feet away from her. To borrow a phrase from his irritating roommate, he should keep his cool on. "Oh, hey there, Kate."

She turned at the sound of his voice, a surprised, then pleased look on her face. When he drew close, she said, "Great talk! But you didn't mention her."

"Who?"

"Grizzly Bear 399. Did I miss that part? I know I was late. Sorry about that."

"No, you weren't that late." Just late enough for Coop to think she had blown it off, leaving him disappointed. When she did arrive, he completely lost his train of thought. He could feel his face warm up as she'd made her way to the front row.

She had a kind of delightful yet annoying effect on him. Like he couldn't quite trust himself around her.

"So why didn't you talk about her?"

"Sally, the head ranger, said she didn't want me to draw attention to 399. We don't know yet if the bear made it through the winter. Sally thought I should focus on bear behavior and safety. So I did." He cleared his throat. "I, uh, hope it was helpful."

"It was. In fact, you did a great job." Kate grinned. "I can see why she wants you to do more talks. You're a natural at imparting information in an interesting way."

Coop felt himself flush. It sounded like he'd been fishing for a compliment . . . and the truth was that he had been. That self-awareness made him feel embarrassed. And when he got embarrassed, he acted gruff and tough. It was a teacher trick. "What exactly did you mean when you said you had something up your sleeve?"

Kate seemed genuinely puzzled. "Sorry?"

"You told me you have a trick up your sleeve, then you patted your camera bag." His tone held a mix of curiosity and suspicion. Why was he trying to sound so rangerish? What was wrong with him? He was such an idiot.

She instinctively put a protective hand on her camera bag. "I'm not sure why you're asking."

"It's just . . . there's been some talk of poachers in the park." Coop mentally cringed. Did that really just come out of his mouth?

Kate stared at him, astounded. The air practically vibrated around them. "And you think I might be trying to kill Grizzly Bear 399? That wonderful, incredible, wild creature? You think"—she slapped a palm against her chest—"that I'd want to hurt her?"

Oh man. He'd hit a nerve. "No! No . . . it's just that . . ." What was wrong with him? "I'm just doing my job."

Kate unzipped her camera bag and pulled out her camera. "It's a Sony Alpha, with all kinds of amazing features."

"Like what?"

"Like . . . real-time Eye AF."

Coop took the camera from her and examined it. "AF?"

"Autofocus. It's incredibly fast. Even if an animal is moving, this camera locks on the subject's eye with precision in real time."

He tried to look like he knew what she was talking about. He had no idea.

"It's also got High Resolution EVF."

"Uh, remind me what EVF means?"

"Electronic viewfinder. Makes it easier to compose shots."

This was all Greek to him. "In other words, this is the Cadillac of cameras." *Oof.* That sounded stupid.

"More like a Tesla than a Cadillac." She took it back from him and placed it carefully in her camera bag. "Technology moves at a swift pace, Ranger Cooper."

"But you can't approach the bear." There he went again, sounding like a new sheriff in town.

Kate shot him a look that said, *Do you really think I would do that?* "I don't plan to."

The tension between them hung in the air, like a storm waiting to break.

"Then," Coop said, "maybe I can help."

How could this have happened? Wade felt a surge of frustration when Feldmann returned from Jackson without any clear idea about when the package that held Whisper could be rerouted. Even more exasperating was the equipment he did bring back. All he could think of was his beloved bow, somewhere on a truck or plane heading east.

Wade picked up the knife Feldmann had purchased and examined the edge. "This isn't going to work."

"Why not?"

"Not sharp enough."

"For . . ."

"For the pelt, of course," Wade replied, trying to keep his irritation in check.

"I thought we'd be hauling the carcass to a taxidermist. I even found a few names of ones in Jackson. Ones that were known for being discreet."

Discreet. Wade couldn't help but roll his eyes. "And how exactly did you plan to sneak a four-hundred-pound bear out of the park without raising any alarms with the rangers?"

"I was going to ask the turncoat to grease some palms. That's worked before."

"Absolutely not," Wade said. The more people involved, the greater the chance for a slipup. "I don't want the whole bear, just the pelt. Get a better knife. Get a couple of them."

"Okay. I'll get coolers for the organs too."

"No, no coolers."

Feldmann looked puzzled. "But isn't that kind of wasteful? I have plenty of connections who'd be eager for harvests."

"I just want the pelt."

"Mr. Schmidt, you're leaving money on the table."

Wade couldn't help but chuckle at the absurdity of that remark. "This is one hunt, Feldmann, that has nothing to do with money."

NINE

*Study nature, love nature, stay close to nature.
It will never fail you.*
—Frank Lloyd Wright, architect*

Kate drove at a leisurely pace along Moose-Wilson Road, savoring the scenery, her heart full with the day's wonders in the park. As she rounded a bend, her eyes caught sight of a small bear crossing the path up ahead. She eased her foot off the gas, slowing the car to a crawl, then to a stop. The bear seemed oblivious to the car's presence, continuing its leisurely stroll across the road. Kate flashed her lights off and on, hoping to warn her off the road. Surprisingly, instead of darting away, the bear paused and glanced in her direction, standing up on its hind legs and sniffing the air. Kate remained still in her seat, feeling a mix of awe and caution. She was safe inside the car with the engine running, doors securely locked, but the proximity of the bear still sent a thrill through her.

As Kate watched the young bear, she wondered about its chances in the wild. She guessed it to be a juvenile black bear cub, probably just one to two years old. Most likely, it had recently been nudged away by its mother to fend for itself. She knew the first year on its own was a real test for an inexperienced young bear. Over half didn't survive. Kate learned that fun fact from Maisie just tonight.

With a steady hand, Kate retrieved her camera from its case and slowly raised it, while cautiously, carefully leaning out of the open car window. Her amazing camera's silent shooting feature made it possible to capture the bear's calm yet curious expression without any clicking sound to alarm it. The bear's nose stretched forward inquisitively. Then it dropped down on all fours to approach the car. Every few steps, it paused to sniff the air, as if to assess whether it should continue forward, and each time it did, it came closer and closer until it was only ten feet away from the hood of the car.

"Easy," Kate said, wondering what to do next.

Too close, too close. It occurred to Kate that the bear, even if adorable, could eat her.

Slowly, she pressed on the gas pedal and steered the car away from the bear. The bear turned to watch Kate pass by, a surprised look on its face, as if to say, "Hey! Where ya going?"

I wish you well, little bear, she thought as she drove off. *But I don't want to be your supper.*

Later that night, as a long summer evening settled over the valley, Tim and Coop sat in Adirondack chairs on the velvety lawn in front of the Jenny Lake Lodge. They turned their chairs to face the steep granite mountains. The fading light painted the Grand Tetons in warm hues, creating a breathtaking panorama. Without any foothills, the mountains soared in front of him. It was what Tim loved most about Grand Teton. "Another beautiful day in paradise," he said, taking a sip from his mug of hot tea.

Coop nodded, his gaze fixed on the view. "Can't argue with that."

"How's it going with Frankie?"

"Terrible. I don't want him for an intern. I don't want any intern, but I especially don't want him."

"Give him time."

"For what? For his attitude to improve? His work ethic? That kid is in a world of his own. Can't you assign him to someone else? Or put him in the Wildlife Brigade? He says that's where he wants to be."

"Nope. Not old enough."

"I thought a parent could sign off and give a minor permission to be on it."

"Not this boy's parent. Apparently, he needs supervision."

"I'll say," Coop scoffed. "Then send him back to the YCP."

"Can't."

"Why not? What is the deal with that kid?"

"His father is an NPS bigwig. Sally wants to give the boy special treatment."

Coop grunted. "And that means sticking him with me?"

"It does." Tim leaned back in his chair. "Sally thinks highly of you. Says you understand teens better than the other rangers."

"But I come here each summer wanting to get away from teenagers."

"You did a fine job at the ranger talk. I bet you're a popular teacher."

"So-so." Coop rocked his hand back and forth. "My last review suggested that there's room for improvement."

"Was that from Emma?"

"Yeah. She thinks I have a bad attitude toward administration."

Tim had to swallow a laugh. Emma, Coop's former fiancée, was the school's vice principal. Two summers past, she had broken off their engagement after she was plucked out of the classroom and promoted to vice principal by the principal. Soon after, according to a heartbroken Coop, it was clear that those two were much more than colleagues. "Have you ever thought of leaving the school? There's got to be plenty of teaching jobs for someone with your experience."

"Not that simple. For the most part, I like teaching there. I like the parents and kids. And I especially love that the school calendar ends the year in early May."

Coop was a loyal guy. It was one of the qualities Tim admired most in him. "And maybe you're hoping Emma will change her mind about the jerk principal and come back to you?"

Coop shot him a sidelong glance. "He *is* a jerk."

Tim chuckled. "Maybe so. But maybe it's also time you let go of the past and move on."

Coop didn't say anything for a long time. Then he leaned forward in the chair. "Tim, Emma and I, we had our whole life planned out. We were going to be teachers so we could have summers free for camping and hiking. We wanted to see all the national parks by the time we were thirty. Emma had it all mapped out. Every single park. We even thought we'd do a blog together about it, or Instagram the whole thing. Maybe a podcast. But then, out of the blue, she suddenly decided she wanted a different kind of life."

Tim raised his hand. "I get it, Coop. I really do. But holding on to anger isn't doing you any favors."

Coop looked away.

"It's like a poison." Tim knew he was pushing it, the way he knew he'd pushed it with Thea, but he'd gone this far. What was there to lose? "Forgiveness is the antidote."

Coop looked skyward in annoyance, but there was a glimmer of amusement in his eyes. "You missed your calling. You should've been a preacher."

Tim laughed. "Nah. I'm just saying that letting go of the anger you feel toward Emma might do you good, that's all."

He finished off the last of his tea. "Even better, come to church with me this summer."

"I've gone with you."

"I mean regularly. You can't be here in this part of the world and not feel drawn to the Creator, to getting to know the mind behind it all."

"You know, maybe you should think about applying to the NPS chaplain program. Then you wouldn't have to retire at fifty-seven, right?"

Tim glanced at him, not sure if Coop was serious or just fending off further inquiry into his somewhat dormant spiritual life. He'd actually given some thought to that chaplain program. But for now, he'd said enough. On that topic, anyway. "Seems like there might be a little something stirring between you and that pretty photographer. The one in the waders."

Coop raised an eyebrow. "Kate?"

"Is that her name? I heard a few people call her Zoo Girl."

"She's worked in a zoo, photographing the wild animals. Thanks to Frankie, the other photographers call her by that nickname. It's not meant to be friendly."

Tim chuckled. "I don't doubt it. She's fresh meat to a competitive bunch. They're all after the next best shot. But maybe you should consider asking her out. You're not getting any younger, in case you hadn't noticed."

Coop scoffed in defense. "You know, John Muir didn't get married until he was nearly forty-two. He enjoyed his solitude."

Tim leaned forward, a more serious expression on his face. He knew how badly Emma had hurt Coop. The real issue was that Coop was reluctant to risk caring for someone else. "Well, just remember, solitude might be comfortable, but it's not where you find the most growth." He put his hands on his knees. "Finding a companion is a true gift. But it doesn't happen without a little effort."

"It did for John Muir. He was set up by well-meaning friends."

"Then, consider me to be your well-meaning friend. I recommend that you try and get to know that Zoo Girl. I like her. She seems very genuine."

Coop grumbled, not entirely convinced. "Once she gets her shot, she'll be gone."

"Maybe so." Tim nodded, understanding. "Sometimes you need to embrace what's right in front of you, even if it's just for a season."

"Speaking of embracing what's right in front of you, what's been going on with you and Sally?"

Tim nearly choked on his tea. How did Coop know about him and Sally? He felt a blush creep up his neck. "I'd better go find Maisie. I left her talking to the woman at the front desk inside the lodge. I have a feeling the woman might need rescuing." He stood, took a few steps, then turned. "Coop, I've always wondered. Was it really so sudden?"

"What?"

"Emma. Her . . . change of heart. Was it really so sudden?"

Before Coop could answer, or maybe before he knew how to answer, the lodge door opened and the woman from the front desk was gently pushing Maisie out the door.

⌇

On the drive over to his room near Jackson Lake Lodge, Coop pondered Tim's parting question. Was Emma's change of heart so sudden?

His thoughts drifted into memories, of Emma and the dreams they once shared. They had met in college, spent summers working in the parks, and planned their life together—a life "paid in sunsets." In experiences. Not in a fat 401(k). Not in material wealth.

He knew he sounded bitter. He *was* still bitter. Coop had thought he found his life partner, but instead, he found himself alone.

So . . . was Emma's change of heart sudden?

Maybe there *were* a few things he had overlooked.

Some slight disagreements that might have been more significant than he had thought. His mind wandered back to painful memories with Emma, picking apart moments that now seemed like subtle shifts hinting at the unraveling of their relationship. There'd been some big arguments, like the one about accepting money from her parents for a down payment on a house. He'd resisted, fearing it would tie them down, needlessly complicate their life, while she accused him of avoiding adulthood. Ridiculous! They'd patched things up, only for more cracks to appear later.

Then there was the summer she opted out of their annual park adventure to plan their wedding, or so she'd said. When he returned in August, she dropped the bombshell—there was not going to be a wedding. Emma didn't want to marry him. Adding salt to the wound, she told him she had been promoted to vice principal, climbing the career ladder without so much as a warning sign. She was now his boss.

It all cast a different light on his recent performance review. She had recommended that he consider shaking things up, maybe teach different classes or think about further education. He had dismissed the idea. Why would he want to change anything when he was content with how things were? It was that long sigh she let out afterward, the one he didn't think much of at the time, that nagged at him now.

Why hadn't he connected the dots? Any of them? Because he was a big fat idiot, that's why.

Tim's advice echoed in his mind as he parked at the lodge. *Forgive Emma. Let go of the past.* It was easier said than done, but Coop knew there was truth in it. Maybe it was time to stop dwelling on what could have been and focus on what was.

As Coop gazed out over the darkening land, Emma's failure to love him the way she had promised, the way he had loved her, weighed heavily on his heart. But in that moment, a realization dawned upon him: he didn't have to hang on to that hurt anymore. Tim was right. Anger was toxic.

As he stepped out of the car, he caught sight of Kate Cunningham walking up from the overview area behind the lodge, heading to the lodge entrance, camera slung around her neck. The sight of her brought a faint smile to his lips and he felt a flicker of something stir to life within him.

Tim thought he should ask her out. Should he?

His smile faded. What if she had a boyfriend? Or what if she said no?

He could almost hear Tim's voice saying, *What if she said yes?*

A slight smile began to return.

Kate's day ended with a deep exhale as she capped her camera lens, the last slivers of sunlight kissing the Grand Teton peaks. A long day but a satisfying one, filled with moments captured through her lens that she hoped would convey the raw beauty and untamed spirit of the wilderness she had immersed herself in. Her boots crunched on the path back to the lodge. She couldn't wait to get these waders off and sink into a hot bathtub.

Her room in the lodge felt stuffy after being out in the fresh air all day. Kate set her camera bag down, sat down on the edge of the bed, and slipped out of the waders. She set them in the bathroom, started the water in the tub, then turned it off as she suddenly remembered her phone. She searched for it and found it in the bottom of her camera bag. The device felt almost foreign in her hands after hours of disconnection, a tether she was reluctant to reattach.

Cringing slightly, Kate unlocked her phone, her screen lit up with a barrage of notifications. The thing was on silent, but boy, did it have a lot to say. Her eyes immediately caught a flurry of texts from Maisie, each message adorned with an array of colorful emojis. Kate winced. Why did she think it was a good idea to share her contact information with a thirteen-year-old? After the ranger's talk, before Kate left the visitor center, Maisie had peppered her with questions about her wildlife photography and Kate offered to show her a few tips sometime this week. But she hadn't expected Maisie to bombard her with texts.

Ones like *Just had a FABULOUS idea!!!* (All caps, lots of exclamation points.) *I can be your assistant!!!*

Seriously? Kate was here on an assignment, not to run a summer camp.

Scrolling past Maisie's digital enthusiasm, Kate's gaze landed on the messages from Oliver. His texts were a mix of concern and mild frustration, wondering about her whereabouts, her safety, if she'd seen the bear and, if so, when was she coming home. The tone of his messages, though laced with care, felt like . . . too much. Just too much. Kate sighed, her frustration mounting. Before she could even digest Oliver's texts, Maisie hit her with another message, this time a meme that made Kate's head roll back in exasperation.

She flopped backward onto the bed, her phone clutched loosely in her hand. She gazed at the ceiling. Why didn't anyone think she had serious work to do? No one did! Not the oh-so-charming fellow photographers, who crowned her as "Zoo Girl." Certainly not Oliver, who thought she should be home, available to him. And now a thirteen-year-old girl had Velcroed herself to her. She could just imagine how the other photographers would feel about having a chatterbox in their midst.

An image of Coop popped into her mind. She'd only known him for a few days, but he seemed to understand why she'd come to the Grand Tetons. And he didn't patronize her, the way those photographers did. Tonight, when he told her that he might be able to help her . . . well, that was very unexpected. Very touching. It gave her some hope that she might get what she came for. In fact, it might be just the right note to end the day on.

She clicked the switch on her phone back to silent and went in to take a bath.

About an hour before the sun dipped below the horizon, Wade made his way into the national park. Sure, he had topographical maps, but there was something about being right there, feeling the land beneath your feet, taking in the grandeur of the place, breathing the air, that no map could replicate.

Tonight's drive was a bit of a wildlife parade. Moose sauntered, elk grazed, but alas, no bears made an appearance. He hardly saw any cars. No rangers at all.

The lack of visitors and rangers was a bonus in his book. Early in the season meant fewer crowds, and Wade was never one for crowds.

Just as he rounded a bend, a large creature caught his eye in a meadow. Wade pulled over and parked the car, reaching for his trusty binoculars, wondering if it could be a bear. His bear.

He adjusted the focus on his bins. A bison stood grazing in peace.

Wade entertained the thought of a bison head adorning his wall, a prized trophy. Where would the arrow need to hit for a fast, clean kill? Straight into the femoral artery? He watched the bison graze for an inordinately long time, pondering his options. But in the end, he shook off the temptation. He hadn't come all this way for a cow.

TEN

Everybody needs beauty as well as bread.
—*John Muir*

Lo and behold, there was Maisie at Pilgrim Creek at four in the morning, searching through the long line of photographers for Kate. She'd talked her grandfather into bringing her. As soon as she spotted Kate at the far end, she bounded over to her with a big hug. "I came to help!"

Kate cringed. "Okay, but you have to be quiet."

"Gotcha." Maisie put her fingers to her lips. "Fun fact. Grizzly Bear 399 has her own Instagram. She says it's hard to type with claws." Her face lit up. "Oh, I almost forgot! She has over 50,000 followers." Her face fell. "I only have three."

The other photographers made a hushing sound, so Kate moved her equipment even farther away from them, feeling a little half-hearted in the process. She knew full well that even if 399 appeared this morning, it wouldn't be the shot that would get into *National Geographic* magazine. She needed something different, something unique. And she really needed Maisie to focus on something else. Maisie made her nervous as she eagerly watched every move Kate made. She was already nervous enough around these judgy photographers.

"Kate, look! It's Coop." Maisie sucked in a breath. "And *Frankie*."

"Morning," Coop said as he approached them.

"Frankie!" Maisie said. "I didn't expect you to be here so early."

Frankie scoffed. "Neither did I. I don't want to be here. I want to be back in bed."

"Part of the internship program," Coop said.

Maisie drifted away from Kate, cozying up to Frankie, bombarding him with questions, inadvertently providing a welcome distraction.

Coop took a step closer to Kate and lowered his voice to ask, "I get the distinct impression that Maisie is more of a nuisance than a help."

Was Kate acting that obvious? "What makes you say that?"

"You're about as far away from the others as you can be."

Kate, still attaching her zoom lens, looked up, surprised at Coop's perceptiveness. "I know she means well. She's very . . . enthusiastic. About everything." She let out a puff of air. "It's not just Maisie that has me bothered. I know there's a better story to tell of this bear than"—she swept her arm in the direction of the long line of photographers—"this." She looked at Coop. "Did you mean it when you said you could help me?"

Coop glanced at the other photographers, then leaned in. "Now's not the time. I'll find you later." He maneuvered back down the line, pulling Frankie along.

But how? How did he think he would find Kate? She planned to hike up to Hidden Falls near Jenny Lake this afternoon. Hopefully, Maisie wouldn't ask to go with her.

"Isn't he cute?" Maisie said.

"Actually, yeah, he is," Kate said, watching Coop engaged with another photographer.

"Do you think he noticed me?"

Kate turned to her. "Isn't he a little old for you?"

"Not hardly! I'm almost fourteen."

"When's your birthday?"

"Next April."

It was only *May*! Kate had to bite on her lip to not laugh out loud. She didn't want to embarrass Maisie. She remembered how it felt to be a young teen and long to be older, to be taken seriously. Sadly, that didn't resolve with age. She was twenty-five and still struggled to be taken seriously.

"Think of the story we could tell our children." Maisie covered her heart with her hands. "We met and fell in love at a national park."

Again, Kate had to bite her lower lip until she knew she could respond without laughing. "Still, I think your grandfather might have something to say about you setting your cap for a man who's a decade or two older than you."

Maisie looked at her, a puzzled look on her face. "Frankie's only a few years older than me."

"Right," Kate said, cheeks growing warm. "Right. He, um, just seems older for his age."

"I think so too!" Maisie's eyes were on Frankie.

Kate turned back to her camera to finish attaching her zoom lens. She took several photographs to get different shots of how the morning light spread over the area, then reviewed the shots to see what needed to be improved.

Watching her, Maisie said, "Why are you taking photographs if the bear isn't here?"

"All about lighting. There's a time of day, shortly after sunrise and before sunset, that's considered a golden hour. Some photographers call it the magic hour. Sunlight is soft, warm, and diffused."

"Why would it matter in a photograph?"

"Softer sunlight provides more favorable lighting conditions," Kate said. "It creates long shadows and a golden glow that can enhance the photograph." She didn't mind answering serious questions about photography for Maisie. Many people had been patient and helpful when she first showed interest. It felt good to pass along that kindness.

Much too soon, the sun rose in the sky, and photographers started to pack up and leave, one by one.

"Why's everybody leaving?" Maisie said.

The woman with the gray pigtails, busy packing her gear, caught Maisie's question. "If that bear hasn't graced us with her presence by now, chances are she's taken a rain check for today."

Maisie's eyes widened, and she persisted, "But why? How do you know that for sure?"

Kate shared Maisie's curiosity. It was nice to have a thirteen-year-old ask the questions that she wanted to ask.

"Bears prefer dawn, dusk, and night to do their hunting. Conditions are more ideal for them." The pigtailed woman cast an eyeroll look in Kate's direction. "Quite unlike the luxurious lifestyle they lead in a zoo, where they get their meals served on a silver platter . . . with a side of predictable routine." On that snarky note, the woman left.

Maisie turned to Kate. "Why'd she compare *this* to a zoo?"

"Because," Kate replied, beginning to dismantle her camera from the tripod, "she knows most of my experience in photographing wild animals comes from my time at a zoo."

"SHUT UP," Maisie said. "That is so cool."

Kate saw Maisie's face light with wonder and pride. "It is cool." Very cool. And she was grateful that someone acknowledged it, even if it came from an overly enthusiastic thirteen-year-old girl who thought everything was cool.

Later that day, Maisie was practically flying on her bike, the wind tangling her curly hair into what her mom would call a bird's nest. She was on a mission, eyes peeled for Kate somewhere around Jenny Lake Visitor Center. Kate had been vague when Maisie asked her what their afternoon plans were going to be. Oddly vague. But she happened to overhear Kate ask another photographer about a trail that wound around Jenny Lake and led to a fabulous waterfall. Maisie had a hunch that's where Kate was headed this afternoon. If so, she would need an assistant.

As Maisie swerved into the parking lot at the Jenny Lake Visitor Center, she spotted Kate's car. Better still, she spotted Kate's yellow slicker! She was bent over, rummaging through the trunk of her car. "Kate! Hey, Kate!" Maisie skidded to a halt, gravel crunching under her tires like popcorn.

"Whoa!" Kate had to squeeze against her car to avoid getting hit. "Watch out, there!"

"Yeah. My starts and stops on this bike need work."

Kate adjusted the camera strap on her shoulder. "I thought you'd be with your grandfather this afternoon."

"No! He's super busy today. So I thought I'd go looking for you."

"Oh." Kate didn't sound as excited as Maisie thought she'd be.

"I'll be your assistant," Maisie blurted out, her words tumbling over each other. "Like, I can hold your equipment. I can even carry it for you."

Kate's smile wavered, then fizzled. "That's a really sweet offer, Maisie, but today I've got a specific plan. I'm hiking on the Jenny Lake Loop Trail to head up to Hidden Falls. It's a bit of a trek, and I'm chasing the light, you know?"

Maisie's excitement dimmed but only slightly. "But I can keep up! And I won't get in the way, I promise!"

Kate looked Maisie right in the eye, her expression soft but firm. "I believe you, Maisie. But photography . . . a task like today is kind of a solo thing for me. You get that, right?"

"Yeah, I guess." She didn't, though. "I just thought it would be cool to hang out with you."

"And it would be," Kate said. "It will be. But today's not the best day for that. How about we plan another time? I'll teach you how to use my camera. Sound good?"

No, it didn't sound good to Maisie, but she could tell Kate wasn't budging. "Okay, deal. But you better not forget!"

"I won't." Kate gave Maisie a playful salute.

With a heavy sigh, Maisie turned her bike around. "Alright, I'll be off, then. Don't do anything too awesome without me!"

Kate laughed, a genuine sound this time. "Don't worry about that. Ride safely, okay?"

"Always!" Maisie called over her shoulder, already pedaling away. Disappointed but not discouraged, she made a note to herself to hold Kate to that promise of teaching her how to use the camera.

For now . . . she thought she'd go find Coop and see what he was up to. Hopefully, Frankie was with him. She pedaled faster, smiling.

～

The sun disappeared behind a curtain of clouds, casting a sudden shadow over the main road where Coop stood alongside fellow rangers, managing the situation with a bear and her cubs. Keeping traffic moving, keeping visitors away from the sow, keeping photographers at a distance. It was the task he dreaded most after being pulled from the backcountry. A traffic cop for bears.

This was not what he had signed up for as a seasonal ranger. He thought about complaining again to Tim but dismissed the idea. Each time he griped about getting stuck with Frankie or about getting pulled from the backcountry, Tim gave him something else he didn't want to do. Like a ranger talk. Tim insisted it was Sally's idea, but Coop wondered.

He noticed a bicycle out of the corner of his eye, swerving along the road as if its rider were intoxicated. Suddenly, it veered sharply in his direction, coming to an abrupt stop just before colliding with him. "Coop!" The rider pulled off her helmet. "What's everyone looking at?"

"Maisie! Watch where you're going," Coop chided, his irritation softened by her familiar face.

"Sorry. I'm not very good on this bicycle." She looked around her. "Is Frankie here?"

"Yeah, he's around here somewhere."

Maisie scanned the area. "Where? I don't see him anywhere."

"He's probably off doing his own thing." That happened a lot with Frankie. Easily bored, easily distracted. A tendency to wander off.

Returning her attention to Coop, Maisie asked, "So what's going on here?"

Coop gestured toward the trees. "We've got a grizzly and her cubs back there. They've been peeking out now and then."

She gasped. "Grizzly 399? I have to go tell Kate!"

"Hold up. Not 399. This one is called Blondie." Coop eyed the gathering storm clouds. "You should head back to your grandfather. There's a storm rolling in."

"Fun fact. Wyoming has more deaths by lightning strikes per capita than any other state. Did you already know that? I read about it in Kate's guidebook this morning while we were waiting for 399 to show up, which she never did."

Coop glanced around. "Where is Kate?"

"She's photographing a big waterfall."

Concern spiked in Coop's chest. "What do you mean? Where did she go?"

"Some waterfall on Jenny Lake. Or maybe near Jenny Lake."

"Hidden Falls?"

"Yes! That's what she called it."

"She took the shuttle boat to cross the lake, right?" If so, the pilot would hold the boat at the dock until the storm passed.

"Hmm, not sure. I don't think so." Maisie squinted. "She said she was going to hike around Jenny Lake."

"How long ago?"

"I left her just a little while ago," Maisie said.

Coop wasted no time. "Go find your grandfather and let him know where I'm headed. Tell him I'm going to find . . . um, the Zoo Girl." Tim was bad with names, but he'd remember Zoo Girl.

"Can I come with you?"

Coop shook his head. "No."

"But, Coop!" Maisie looked crestfallen. "I can help!"

"No. Too risky." Out of nowhere Frankie appeared, and Maisie brightened. "Frankie, get Maisie to her grandfather."

A smile spread across Maisie's face.

Coop instructed two rangers to remain vigilant about the bear jam before rushing to his truck. As he raced to the trailhead of the Jenny Lake Loop Trail, the once tranquil sky loomed with foreboding clouds, signaling the imminent storm. Why had Kate put herself at such risk? How could she not know any better?

More importantly, why was he so concerned about her? Why was Coop all twisted up over her? Normally, he was pretty clear-cut about park visitors: they had to look out for themselves. He and Tim would go round and round on this after hours. Typical of Tim, he argued that the ranger role extended beyond mere oversight. To Tim, it was about education, about going the extra mile to ensure the safety of even the most uninformed visitor.

126

Coop was all for the education part, but if visitors ignored all the signs, warnings, and up-to-date information that rangers provided, then whatever happened was on them.

But Kate? Something about her threw a wrench in his works. She just didn't fit his usual "you're on your own" policy. She was all wide-eyed wonder, and yeah, maybe a bit naive. But not in a bad way. It was kind of endearing, actually. He found himself wanting to make sure she wasn't getting bullied by the other photographers, wanting to help her get the shots she came for, wanting to be sure she stayed safe while she did it.

It was like she hit some soft spot he didn't even know he had.

Kate felt a few raindrops and pulled the hood of her yellow raincoat up over her head. She tightened the straps of her backpack and adjusted her camera bag as she set off on the trail around Jenny Lake. Now and then, the sun peeked through the clouds, casting a golden glow on the quaking aspens that lined the path. Almost fluorescent.

Beneath the towering dark trees, Kate found herself in a world of contrasts. The canopy above cast deep shadows that enveloped the smaller plants below, creating a serene yet mysterious atmosphere. Now and then she spotted a delicate yellow glacier lily or a cluster of pink spring beauty, early wildflowers that appeared as the snow melted.

As she hiked around the southern end of Jenny Lake, Kate's excitement to see Hidden Falls only grew. This morning, she had overheard a photographer tell another that he'd never seen so much water pouring over the waterfall, fueled by the melting snow from the mountains. A hundred-foot cascading waterfall. She couldn't wait to get a look at it.

She thought about the kinds of shots she hoped to get this afternoon—light dancing through the water, creating a mesmerizing play of colors and textures. It was moments like these that fueled her passion for photography, trying to capture nature's shocking beauty in a single frame. She felt a tender intimacy as she hiked, as if the tall trees she passed and the shallow streams she crossed were familiar, despite never having set foot on this particular trail before. The familiarity was comforting yet intriguing, adding a layer of connection to her wilderness experience. It reminded her . . . well, of how it felt to sit in church on Sunday. She felt closest to God in such moments. Sensed his presence, his pleasure.

Dark clouds overhead snuffed out the sun, and sprinkles turned to droplets. She had to stop now and then along the trail to step aside and let descending hikers pass by.

"Are you sure you want to keep going?" a woman asked. "The rain's picking up and it's getting pretty slick up there."

"Thanks, but I'll be fine." Kate loved the challenge of shooting in changing weather conditions. The rain made the rocks glisten and added a dramatic touch to the scene. She had to slow down, though, as the rain was coming down steadily and the uphill dirt trail was getting slick. Runoff began to wash out parts of the trail, causing her to scramble to step over or around them without slipping.

When she reached the Hidden Falls junction, another clutch of hikers passed her on their way downhill. "There's a storm coming," one said. "Better turn around."

Kate looked up at the clouds. Growing up in the East, she was no stranger to thunderstorms; they often passed as quickly as they arrived. She heard thunder, but it was far off. Now and then, lightning scattered through the sky. Nothing directly overhead. For a moment, she considered turning back but then decided to press on. It would be such a bonus if the waterfall had no visitors. She wanted to photograph the falls without anyone around, to capture the pure essence of nature. She just needed to do it fast.

The sound of rushing water grew louder as Kate neared Hidden Falls. The rain intensified, but she wasn't concerned yet. She walked up and down around the waterfall, peering over the different overlooks, until she found the perfect spot to set up her camera. She adjusted the settings to capture the fast-moving water and the interplay of light and shadows.

Just as she was about to take the shot, a tiny sliver of a break in the clouds allowed a beam of sunlight to pierce through, illuminating the waterfall in a breathtaking display of natural beauty. Kate clicked the shutter, capturing the moment in all its glory. Perfect. Absolutely perfect.

She smiled, her heart hammering in her chest. Her hands felt tingly.

This had been her dream! And she was actually living it.

Wade Schmidt stood by the hotel room window, scowling, watching the thick black clouds roll in. Thunder rumbled in the distance, announcing the impending storm. He had expected to have completed the hunt by now. Expected to be home by now. If he'd had any idea that this hunt would've taken so long, he would've driven and saved himself the distress of not having his weapons.

It was all Feldmann's fault. Not that the weather had turned sour; Wade knew how unpredictable the mountain could be. But he had picked a turncoat who didn't know the coordinates of the bear's lair. Unbelievable! And it was entirely Feldmann's fault that Wade's equipment had gone missing.

As the raindrops splattered against the windowpane, he turned away and paced the room. He needed to figure out a solution, and fast. Maybe he should go ahead and replace the missing gear. He would need hours of practice to get the feel of the new bow, but missing the chance to go after this bear was not an option. He'd come too far to call it off.

With a sigh, Wade grabbed his phone and dialed Feldmann's number. The call went straight to voicemail. Typical. He left a terse message, ordering him to return the call immediately.

Outside, the storm intensified, lightning flashing across the sky. Wade cursed under his breath, feeling the pressure mounting. He could feel himself tighten up, and he rocked his head from side to side, shook his hands out. Something about how this hunt was unfolding made him jittery. His nerves felt all twisted up, like he was fearful. He had never before been fearful.

If only he had Whisper. Everything would be alright if he could just get his trusty bow back in his possession.

Then he reminded himself who he was—Wade Schmidt, master hunter. He wasn't one to let anything get in the way of a hunt, especially this hunt. Not even his missing bow.

ELEVEN

*In nature there are neither rewards nor punishments—
there are consequences.*
—*Robert G. Ingersoll, philosopher*

Coop was lucky enough to get the last trip across Jenny Lake on the shuttle boat. An eerie stillness hung over the lake. There was a long line of people who wanted a return trip, and he was pretty sure the boat wasn't coming back for him, at least not until the storm passed. He bolted up the narrow trail that led to Hidden Falls. No other hikers crossed his path, no birdsong filled the air. Every living creature seemed to realize a storm was heading in . . . except for Kate.

Minutes felt like hours before he thought he spotted a dot of bright yellow up ahead and he quickened his pace. There she was! Blissfully unaware, standing near a cluster of rocks, framed by towering trees and a raging waterfall. He cringed. The worst place someone could be in a thunderstorm. He knew the dangers that awaited ignorant hikers—trees, rocks, and water would become conduits for deadly lightning strikes.

"Kate!" Coop's voice was nearly drowned out by the waterfalls.

"Kate!" She finally heard him as he reached her side. "We need to get out of here. Now."

"What's wrong?"

A burst of lightning lit the sky. Coop pointed to the ominous clouds. "That. That is on its way." As if on cue, a thunderclap roared.

Without a word, she packed up her camera, zipped up the bag, and folded her tripod. "Let's go."

He grabbed her bag and took her hand to start back down the trail to the boat dock, where at least they'd have some cover with the awning.

They were drenched by the time they reached the dock. Amazingly, a towel had been left on a bench by someone. He grabbed it and handed it to Kate.

Kate dried off her face. "How did you know where I was?"

"Who else? The Grand Teton Crier."

"Maisie."

He nodded. "You put yourself in real danger up here."

She looked away, as if embarrassed. "I'm sorry."

"Why did you head up there if you knew a storm was heading in?"

"There were just a few clouds overhead when I set out. I honestly thought I had enough time to get the pictures and get back down. More than enough." She wiped off her camera bag. "I didn't mean to cause you concern. I was planning to head down soon."

"Kate, you can't be so . . ."

"So what?" She looked up, waiting for him to finish his thought.

"You really need to be more careful. These mountains don't forgive mistakes."

"I promise I'll pay better attention to my weather app."

"Not just that. You were hiking alone up there."

132

"Not at first. Lots of hikers were heading down the hill."

"Exactly. Heading down. Not up. You have to be more aware of your surroundings, Kate. The bears are starting to show up and they're hungry. They're aggressive. Especially the males. You shouldn't hike alone. No one should. Even rangers rely on teamwork."

"Noted." She had a sheepish look on her face. "I really am sorry. I feel so . . . dazzled by this park. Just when I think I couldn't get a better photograph, I turn a corner and there's an even more breathtaking view."

"I get that." He let out a sigh. "Do you know that bears are drawn to the color yellow?"

She looked down at her slicker. "Yellow? I wonder why?" She lifted her head. "Oh, I bet I know. It reminds them of honey."

A laugh burst out of him. She was just so . . . sweet.

She smiled. "You'll have to try to stump Maisie with that fun fact."

"Can't." He grinned. "She's the one who told me."

⁓

Coop's concern for Kate during the thunderstorm was touching. And embarrassing. To think he came to find her! They sat under the dock awning, huddling close together to keep warm, the patter of rain on the roof creating a soothing backdrop to their steady conversation. They never seemed to run out of things to talk about.

She felt her phone vibrate in her pocket and pulled it out to glance at caller ID. *Oliver.* She turned her phone completely off. "So, after the ranger talk," she said, glancing at Coop beside her. "You mentioned you might be able to help me get a unique shot of 399. What exactly did you mean by that?"

"You tell me." Coop turned to her, his expression guarded.

"You said you wanted to know more about her. So what do you know?"

"Well, I know the facts about her. She's a legend and the face of bear conservation around the world. I know she's called the Queen of the Tetons. I know about her track record, that she's the oldest known grizzly to have cubs. Eighteen at last count."

"Twenty-two, that we know of," Coop said. "She's an excellent mother. She provides for them, teaches them to hunt, to stay out of trouble."

"See? That's just the kind of information that I'm looking for. How does she keep her cubs out of trouble?"

"She's learned to spend time near areas with people. Male grizzlies can be a threat to cubs. They'll kill cubs to mate with a female. But they tend to avoid people. By staying close to human activity, 399 has figured out a way to keep her cubs safe from predators. She's even taught her cubs to look left and right before crossing the road."

Kate couldn't help but smile at the image of bear cubs cautiously checking for traffic. "So is that what makes her stand out among grizzlies?"

"Frankly, most female grizzlies are good mothers. But 399 is special to people. I think it's probably because of a few stories that hit a human chord."

Kate tilted her head. "What stories?"

"Well . . . like a few years back, one of her cubs, Snowy, was killed by a hit-and-run driver. She wailed, foamed at the mouth, mourned like a . . . well, like a mother would. It gave everyone a glimpse into the emotional depth of these creatures."

Kate's eyes widened with surprise. "Do you think a bear feels sorrow on that level?"

Coop hesitated, his gaze distant. "Hard to know for sure," he said slowly. "But 399 definitely exhibited sorrow over Snowy's death. And people, well, they resonated with her sorrow. She's not just a wildlife subject. She's got a personality, a history. People root for her, celebrate her triumphs, and mourn her losses."

"A living, breathing legend."

"Exactly. She's a symbol of the wild, a reminder that even in the heart of nature, there are stories, personalities, and connections waiting to be discovered. And every spring when she emerges from hibernation, it's a grand spectacle. People come from far and wide just to catch a glimpse of her."

"People like me."

He smiled. "Like you."

Kate's mind swirled with questions. "I read a lot about her, but I never found out how she got her name."

"She was tagged as the three hundred ninety-ninth bear in the Yellowstone ecosystem. First one found in Grand Teton after a long absence. The bear population had been wiped out in this park by hunting. But then grizzlies were put on the endangered species list back in . . . hmm . . . I think it was 1975."

"Still on it?"

"No, but they do have threatened status. Lots of conflict over that issue."

"So tell me more about the end of hibernation."

"Sows emerge slowly. Sows with COYs are generally the last bears to leave their dens."

"Hold it. What's a COY?"

"Cub of the year. Brown bears and grizzlies—and, of course you know that grizzlies are a subspecies of brown bears, though only grizzlies have that hump on their back—their yearlings generally stay with their mothers for three to four years."

"So when you say they emerge slowly, what does that mean?"

"They start out cautiously. After emerging from the den,

mothers and cubs tend to spend their first few weeks around the site. That helps the COY to slowly explore their world and start to learn some skills. Only half of COYs make it to their second year."

Sad. Nature could be so cruel. Kate remembered going to an exercise class where the instructor wore a T-shirt that proclaimed "Say yes to the universe!" At the time, she had thought it silly. Now, she thought it foolish. The universe was heartless. It didn't care what you thought.

Listening to the rain on the awning above them, Kate mulled over whether she could ask the question that had been on her mind since their earlier conversation. Finally, she turned to Coop. "Do you know where her den is?"

Coop shifted in his seat, his gaze flickered away, a hint of reluctance in his expression. "Somewhere near Pilgrim Creek. In the high country."

Maybe Kate shouldn't have asked. Or maybe . . . he seemed uncomfortable because he did know.

"You do know, don't you?" she pressed, her tone gentle but insistent.

Coop sighed, his shoulders sagging slightly. "This time last year, I found her den." He rubbed his forehead. "With each passing day, I've thought about heading up there to check on her, to see if she made it through the winter."

A surge of excitement washed over Kate. "Would you take me there?" she asked eagerly, her eyes shining with anticipation.

He shook his head. "First of all, it's a difficult trip. Straight up."

"I won't slow you down."

"Well, the area is restricted to the public for now."

"We're not the public. We're a ranger and a photographer."

"True, but interfering with wildlife can have serious consequences."

"But I wouldn't be interfering. I know the mantra—observe, don't disturb. I have no intention of disturbing anything. But I do have an idea for a unique photograph."

Coop narrowed his eyes. "What kind of idea?"

"I want to set up my camera and capture her as she emerges."

"Do you realize how long that could take?"

"Not for me. My camera has a motion detection feature. If she's coming in and out of the den, like you said, it would just be a twenty-four-hour thing."

He glanced at her camera. "So you'd leave it and we'd come back for it?"

She nodded.

"Let's say, just for the sake of discussion, that she ventures out of her den. Bears are insatiably curious and they have an incredible sense of smell. If she sniffs your scent on that camera, she'd tear it apart."

"I'll take unscented wipes and make sure I've eliminated every trace of me."

"Still sounds risky."

"It is. But I'm willing to take that risk."

Coop hesitated, his brow furrowing with concern. "I don't know, Kate."

Kate nodded, understanding she was asking a lot of him.

Coop studied her for a moment, his expression softening. "Let me think about it," he said, a hint of reluctance in his voice.

Kate nodded slowly, her heart pounding with excitement. She hoped he couldn't hear its thump.

The radio on Coop's belt crackled to life, interrupting their conversation. "Coop, where are you? Frankie said you were going after the Zoo Girl."

Kate cringed. How many people were worried about her? Embarrassing.

"I found her, Tim."

Tim's voice conveyed a stern warning. "Make sure the Zoo Girl knows she shouldn't be taking chances. Thunderstorms are no joke."

As lightning lit the sky, following by thunder, Kate nearly jumped. She cast a glance at Coop.

"I think she realizes that," Coop said with a grin. "Over and out."

"Did you actually tell Maisie you were going after the *Zoo Girl*?"

"I . . . might have. Tim's bad on names. I knew he'd remember that."

Kate tried to frown, but she couldn't keep it up. A smile tugged at her lips. That terrible nickname was stoking her inner fire to prove people wrong. There was still a story to be told about a grizzly named 399, and she was going to go after it.

And the handsome ranger with the seawater eyes was going to help her get it. Fingers crossed.

The Jenny Lake Visitor Center was packed while everyone waited out the thunderstorm. Tim was answering a day hiker's questions when he saw Sally approach him, a concerned expression on her face.

"Tim, I need you to check on a nearby campsite. Campers have overstayed their permit, and I wonder if the rain has caused them some trouble." Sally's eyes scanned the storm outside. "Can you handle it?"

"Sure thing," Tim said, reaching behind the counter for his rain jacket. "I'll take Frankie with me."

"Aww, *man*," Frankie said, disappointed. "Haven't I done enough hard labor for one day?"

Tim wished Sally had heard Frankie, but she'd already moved on to another task. He thought it would be good for her to get a sense of the responsibility she'd dumped on Coop for the summer. "Maisie, stay here at the visitor center until we get back."

To his surprise, Maisie didn't ask to come along. He couldn't blame her. The rain was coming down in sheets.

Twenty minutes later, Frankie followed Tim through the rain-soaked campground to the specific campsite Sally had mentioned. No vehicle, no tent, but piles of discarded items littered the campsite, food wrappers scattered everywhere, and a campfire pit filled with half-burned logs. The campers had gone but left their trash.

Frankie made a face of disgust. "If I were part of the Wildlife Brigade, I wouldn't let this happen. What happened to the 'leave no trace' principle?"

"If you were part of the Wildlife Brigade, you'd be dealing with animals, not campsites."

Frankie kicked at a pile of empty beer cans. "So much for that old saying."

"What old saying?"

"The closer you are to nature, the further you are from idiots."

Tim chuckled.

"You'd think so, anyway." Frankie turned in a circle. "Man, people are so messed up."

"Not all people." *But some sure were.* Tim surveyed the campsite. "I'll get the trash bags out of the jeep."

Frankie groaned. "You mean, we've got to clean it up? In this rain?"

"More campers are due in. We don't want them to have to face this, now do we?"

"Yeah, actually. We do. Maybe it'll stop 'em from messing up the park."

Tim chuckled. "Better still if they leave it the way they find it."

They spent the next half hour cleaning up the campsite. Tim tied up the last bag of trash and tossed it in the back of the jeep.

As they made their way back to the visitor center, the rain began to ease up, and a faint rainbow appeared in the sky. Frankie didn't say anything, but his eyes were on it. Tim hoped he felt some satisfaction in being a steward of the park. He sure did.

Inside, he spotted Sally at the far end of the room, bent over a table with Maisie, their heads close together as they pored over a stack of topographical maps. "Hey, you two," he said, hanging up his raincoat on a coat tree.

"Hi, Pops!" Maisie said, a smile lighting up her face.

Sally looked up. "What'd you find at the campsite?"

"Nothing. Abandoned. Empty of everything except trash. So we cleaned it up. Four trash bags full."

Sally grimaced. "Sorry about that."

"Par for the course," Tim said. "So what's with the huddle?"

"I've been showing Maisie how to read these maps. Figured it might come in handy for her Junior Ranger badge." Sally sounded her cool, calm, collected self, which made Tim relax a bit.

"Actually," Maisie said, "I got my Junior Ranger badge a couple of summers ago. Pops made sure of that."

"Right," Sally said, looking a little embarrassed. "Well, hon, I guess you've been around national parks for a long time."

"Every summer for as long as I can remember," Maisie said proudly.

Tim felt a swell of pride at Maisie's words, but beneath it lingered a sense of unease. He knew he was the only father figure in his granddaughter's life. And he couldn't help but wonder if he was doing enough to prepare her for life. Her mother certainly wasn't. He even had to push for Maisie to get braces for her very crooked teeth, offering to cover the cost himself.

"So how's Coop doing with Frankie?"

Tim looked behind him, thinking Frankie was nearby, but saw no sign of him. "Pretty much what you'd expect."

Maisie's eyes lit up. "Where is Frankie?"

"He's around here somewhere," Tim said.

As Maisie slipped away to go find Frankie, without her as a buffer, Tim and Sally were left in an awkward silence. What had caused the change between them? He still couldn't figure it out.

"Hope I didn't offend your little gal," Sally said. "I'm not around kids much. I can barely tell a five-year-old from a ten-year-old."

"No, I don't think you offended her. Maisie doesn't offend easily. She's pretty happy-go-lucky." With a wide-eyed innocence that Tim cherished. He knew it wouldn't last much longer. Look at Frankie. Only sixteen, yet there was a perpetually bored look in his eyes. Clearing his throat, he said, "So I haven't seen much of you lately. Everything okay? You seem a little . . . distracted." Cold. Distant. Aloof.

Sally's smile faltered slightly, her eyes darting away for a moment before meeting his gaze again. "Just the usual start of the season madness." She rolled up the maps she'd shown to Maisie.

Really? Tim wondered. He couldn't shake the feeling that Sally was holding something back, creating a distance between them that hadn't been there before. "Well, if I can help in any way, just let me know."

Sally nodded, her smile strained. "Just keep doing your job, darlin'. Let's keep this park running smoothly." She picked up the maps and left him.

And with that, Tim realized where he now stood—just another employee to her.

Wade hated to be wrong.

He had made a mistake by entrusting so much to Feldmann. He couldn't afford any more mistakes.

With so much riding on this hunt, Wade thought it would be wise to put Feldmann's turncoat to the test. What better way than by a real hunt? But not just any hunt would do. Elk and moose were too predictable, too straightforward. They roamed openly, making them easy targets. A bear, on the other hand, would attract unwanted attention from the park rangers.

No, Wade needed something more challenging, something that would truly gauge Feldmann's discernment. And that's when the idea hit him like a bolt of inspiration—a wolf hunt. Wolves were cunning, elusive, and far more challenging to track down. And they weren't endangered, so there'd be less backlash from park rangers if they found any evidence of the poach. Unlikely, though.

With a grin spreading across his face, Wade made up his mind. A wolf hunt it would be.

TWELVE

The continued existence of wildlife and wilderness is important to the quality of life of humans.
—*Jim Fowler, American zoologist*

It was Coop's day off, a precious opportunity for the solitude he craved. He planned to hike to the headwaters of Pilgrim Creek and look for signs that 399 might have emerged from her den. He couldn't make up his mind about taking Kate to set up her camera near the bear's lair, and thought a visit to the vicinity might give him the answer he was looking for—especially if 399 hadn't made it through the winter. If the old girl hadn't survived, it might be better for everyone to know. As he strode toward his truck, his peace was disrupted by an unexpected companion.

"Hey, Coop! Wait up!" Frankie's voice echoed through the quiet parking lot.

Coop quickened his pace, hoping to outdistance him. He wasn't in the mood for company, especially not Frankie's. He wanted this day to think through a few things, like how to ask Kate Cunningham out on a date.

Frankie caught up with surprising ease. "Mind if I tag along?"

Coop shot him a glance, annoyed. "Yes, I do mind. This is my day off. I was hoping for some time to myself."

Frankie grinned, undeterred, and opened the passenger side of the truck. "I saw what you put in your pack. I know you're going hiking. And that probably means the backcountry. You know the park rules—use the buddy system."

Coop sighed, knowing better than to argue that point. The kid was right. "You better not expect me to share my food with you."

"Not to worry. I can handle my own sustainment."

Turning onto the main road, Coop scoffed. "Your pack looks way too light. Did you even bring a can of bear spray?"

"No worries. Bears are just as afraid of me as I am of them."

"What about a warm coat? There's a lot of snow up there."

"My body has a low thermostat setting."

Fine. Coop was well familiar with a teen's know-it-all attitude. The only way to break through it was by experience. He slowed down as he drove the truck past a line of Boy Scouts, all in uniform. "They're working on their hiking merit badge. I spoke to their leader yesterday."

"Yeah. That badge is a piece of cake."

"Yeah?" Coop glanced at Frankie. "How do you know?" This kid didn't strike Coop as the Boy Scout type.

He shrugged. "I know things."

They didn't chat much until Coop pulled into the parking area off Pilgrim Creek Road. After parking the truck, they hit the trail. The Middle Pilgrim Creek Trail started off easy, with a wide, flat stretch alongside the creek. As they delved deeper into the wilderness, he and Frankie encountered more snow, not just in the shaded areas. They also had to navigate several creek crossings, which could be quite tricky at this time of year, if not downright impossible. Coop couldn't help but wonder if the hike might be too challenging for Kate. He glanced back at Frankie to check on his progress. With a sigh of relief, Coop realized he had nothing to worry about with that kid. Frankie moved like a gazelle, effortlessly conquering the ascent.

An hour or so into the hike, Frankie slipped away to water the bushes, he said, and Coop found a sunny spot to rest for a bit. He drank a few sips from his water bottle, closed his eyes, and soaked up the sun. Frankie returned with a surprise—berries, carried in his shirt like a hammock. He held one hand out to Coop. "Try these. They're underripe, but still provide nourishment."

Coop raised an eyebrow. "Huckleberries."

"Yep. They thrive in montane forests." After polishing off the huckleberries, Frankie pulled out a pocketknife and walked over to some plants. Bending over, he dug the plant out of the ground. He walked back to where Coop sat and held out the plant. "I recommend the leaves, though the tuber can be prepared like a potato."

Coop shook his head, cringing. "Isn't that a spring beauty?"

"More correctly known as Claytonia virginica." He chewed a few leaves, then swallowed. "Vitamin rich, full of nutrition."

As they nibbled on the sour berries, Coop said, "So, I'm guessing you might have had more experience with the great outdoors than you let on."

"Maybe."

"Boy Scouts?"

"Possibly."

"How far'd you get?"

"Far enough."

Coop watched him for a while. "You're an Eagle Scout, aren't you?" He slapped his knee when he saw the embarrassment in Frankie's eyes. "You are! Man, that's impressive. I sure didn't get that far. I think only a small number ever reach Eagle."

"Four out of every one hundred."

Coop had to swallow a smile. There was more to this kid than met the eye. "How old were you when you made it?"

"Fourteen."

Coop practically choked on the berries. "No way. You have got to be kidding me! That makes you one of the youngest Eagle Scouts. Ever."

"Eh. I think there's like nine or ten of us." Frankie looked away. "It was something my dad and I did together."

Coop took another swig of water. "Tell me about this dad of yours. I hear he's a muckety-muck."

Frankie lifted a shoulder in a careless shrug. "He rose through the ranks of the forestry service."

"So you basically grew up in national parks?"

"Pretty much. We kept getting moved around."

"Like which parks, exactly?"

"Alaska, a couple of times. Acadia, Great Smokies, Yosemite."

"Not Yellowstone or Grand Teton?"

"Yeah, but I was really small. I don't remember them."

"So where are your folks now?"

"Dad sold out and went to the den of iniquity."

Coop practically choked on a mouthful of berries. "I take it you mean Washington DC." There was a saying among rangers—all roads in the NPS led to the nation's capital.

"Yep."

"How long ago?"

"Last year. I refused to go with him, so I got shipped off to boarding school."

"What about your mom?"

"She died. Car accident. Drunk driver crossed the median and crashed right into her."

Oh man. That would be tough to get over. With a jolt, Coop realized he'd completely forgotten to call his mother on Mother's Day. *Tonight*, he told himself. *Call Mom tonight.* "So it's just you and your dad."

"Yeah. Kinda. Mostly, it's just me."

Coop nodded, gaining a new perspective on Frankie. They got ready to resume their hike when the sound of a distant gunshot pierced the quiet. Coop froze, high alert, expecting another shot to ring out, ears straining to capture the location. But none came.

Frankie pointed behind them. "Came from that way."

Coop's mind jumped to Tim's warning that there was a credible threat of a poacher after 399. "Let's go," he said, grabbing his backpack.

They rushed along the trail, boldly leaping across the creek in spots where they had struggled just thirty minutes earlier. They saw nothing unusual until they weren't far from the start of the Middle Pilgrim Creek Trail. Frankie saw it first—a blood trail running into the creek from the bank, where someone had dragged an animal.

Climbing up from the rocky creek, Frankie suddenly crouched to check something out. "Hey, Coop!" he yelled, trying to be heard over the creek's roar, waving him over excitedly.

Coop hurried over to see what had caught Frankie's attention.

"Check out these tracks." Frankie pointed out their outlines pressed into the wet, matted debris. "Definitely not big enough for a full-grown bear, but they could be from a cub, you know, a COY."

Coop bent down to look more closely. "I think it's a wolf." Still crouching, he gazed around at the peaceful setting. So much wildlife frequented creeks, looking for food, water, or low spots to cross over.

He wondered why this wolf had been targeted and if the

poacher planned to return. He stood up. "Frankie, help me look around for bullet casings."

Frankie wandered along the creek bank, stopping now and then to bend down. He straightened up and turned around. "Found it!" He came back to where Coop stood and held out his open palm. In it was a shell.

"Nice work," Coop said, growing more impressed with the kid. He pulled out his cell phone and tried to call Tim Rivers. "Dead zone. I should've brought the radio." He took pictures of the scene and checked coordinates on his phone. "I think Tim said he was going to be at Mormon Row today. We'll head over there and let him know what we found." So much for his peaceful day off.

Frankie frowned, confusion written all over his face. "What is Mormon Row? Because I'm not going to any church service."

"Follow me and I'll educate you." Coop gestured for Frankie to follow as he headed back toward the narrow path that led down the hillside. Frankie trailed behind.

Once the terrain leveled so they could walk side by side on the trail, Coop launched into his impromptu history lesson. "Alright, Frankie, let me tell you about Mormon Row. Back in the late 1800s and early 1900s, a bunch of Mormon settlers came here looking to start a new life. They built these sturdy log cabins and barns and set up farms, thinking they could make it big in the Wild West. But boy, were they in for a surprise."

Frankie nodded, seeming intrigued. "What happened to 'em?"

"The winters here are brutal," Coop said, glancing at Frankie to gauge his interest. "Snow piled up like you wouldn't believe. Probably a lot like this winter had been." He gestured to snow under a tree. "It was tough for those folks to survive, let alone thrive. Some of them gave up and headed for greener pastures, but others stuck it out. They figured out ways to tough it out, growing crops, raising cattle, and making do with what they had. Nowadays, you can still see some of those old cabins standing tall, like the Moulton Barn."

"What's the Moulton Barn?"

This kid surprised Coop with his wilderness knowledge, but he still had a lot to learn about the park's history with people. "The Moulton Barn is probably one of the most photographed sites in the entire Grand Teton National Park."

"A barn?" He scoffed. "Seriously?"

"Yeah. It's kind of . . . poetic, I guess. It reminds me of the grit and determination those settlers had." Coop finished his impromptu history lesson, feeling pleased with himself. He picked up his pace, eager to get to his truck. Frankie kept up, not saying anything, and Coop assumed he'd probably grown bored.

But as they reached the truck and climbed in, Coop noticed Frankie didn't automatically reach for his earbuds to listen to music. Instead, he said, "I could've survived back then."

Coop couldn't help but grin. "Think so?"

"Know so," Frankie said with a scoff.

Yep, Coop had definitely hooked him. Finding a way to engage Frankie wasn't all that different from teaching in the classroom. He just needed to find the right angle.

⁓

Kate sat at the desk in her room at Jackson Lake Lodge, carefully examining each photograph she'd taken this morning after downloading her camera's memory card onto her computer. In one photograph, a white egret took flight off the still-as-glass Snake River. Kate frowned. It was a slightly fuzzy white egret. That moment could not have been more perfect. Her skills as a wildlife photography were so . . . imperfect.

Scrolling through, she felt her frustration grow. Amateurs wouldn't even notice the flaws, but she was painfully aware of how these pictures revealed her inexperience with wildlife photography. One glaring error was misjudging the lighting conditions, resulting in overexposed shots that washed out the vibrant colors of the birds she'd been so excited to capture. Another mistake was not adjusting her camera settings quickly enough when the birds took flight, leading to images that lacked the sharpness she had envisioned, like the egret.

To make matters worse, Kate realized she had chosen the wrong lens for some of the shots, resulting in a lack of magnification and detail in her subjects. As she clicked through the photos, each one highlighting a different mistake, she felt a sickening disappointment settle in her chest. She'd put so much pressure on herself this week to capture stunning images, like those she'd seen from the seasoned professionals at the park with whom she rubbed elbows each day. Now, faced with her own serious shortcomings, with an impending time limitation from the *National Geographic* editor, she couldn't help but question her abilities.

Should she even be here? Maybe the zoo *was* where she belonged.

With a sigh, Kate closed her eyes and leaned back, taking a moment to collect her thoughts. She reminded herself that mistakes were a natural part of the learning process. "Each one has a lesson to teach," she said to herself. She gave her head a shake. It was time for a change. She took a pad of paper and pen from the desk drawer to make notes on each picture, to identify the mistakes she'd made. Later today, she'd try out different settings on her camera and practice with different lenses.

Reinvigorated, she scrolled back to the first picture of the day, to the egret. She was focusing so intently that she jumped when her phone buzzed. Oliver's name flashed at the top of the screen. She hesitated for a moment before answering, bracing herself for the conversation she knew was coming.

"Hey, Oliver," she said, trying to keep her voice steady.

"Kate! I've been trying to reach you." His tone was tinged with relief. "What's going on? Why haven't you returned my calls?"

She felt a pang of guilt at his words, knowing that she'd been avoiding his calls and messages for the last day or so. "I'm sorry, Oliver. I've been out in the field nonstop." True.

"Out in the field?" Oliver repeated, as if she had used a foreign phrase.

"Well, that's where the wildlife is."

"I don't understand why it's taking so long to get your picture. Hasn't that bear showed up yet?"

"No, she hasn't." There was an unmistakable tinge of annoyance in her voice.

"And no one else has spotted it? No rangers? None of the other photographers? You're absolutely sure?"

"Of course I'm sure."

"Could the photographers be lying to you? I can see why they wouldn't want to share that info. I mean, you're all competing for the same picture, right?"

"I suppose. But word travels fast around here. I'm sure I would know if someone spotted her."

"It's only that . . . I can't help but worry about you, that's all."

Kate's frustration ebbed. His concern was sweet. "I'll be home soon enough." That was true too. She just wasn't sure if she'd be back with a great photo or back to the zoo.

"I'll hold you to that," he said, a hint of playfulness returning to his voice. "You know, having you away has got me thinking about what you said before you left. About how this time apart would be good for us."

"Yes," she said, her voice laced with relief. Yes! Yes, yes, yes.

"The more I think about it, the more I think you're right. A change is needed."

Oh, thank goodness! "Sounds like we're on the same page. We can talk more when I get home."

"And when exactly do you think that will be?"

Kate hesitated for a moment. She was holding out hope that Coop would take her up to 399's den. He hadn't said yes but he hadn't said no. "Honestly, I'm not quite sure," she said. "For now, I'd better get back to work. There's something I need to finish up."

"Oh. Okay." He sounded a little hurt. "You get back to your photography adventure. Let's talk again tonight, okay?"

"Absolutely!" she said with a lightness she didn't feel. She hung up before he could try to pin her down with a specific time.

Maisie pedaled her bike hard along the winding trail that led to String Lake. She was getting better on Pops's bike. In Denver, where she lived with her mom, she didn't bike much. Partly because of the heavy traffic and partly because her bikes kept getting stolen.

As Maisie made a turn into String Lake's parking lot, her heart skipped a beat at the sight of Frankie, shooting a thrill of excitement through her. Frankie had a level of coolness that no other boy in her middle school could ever hope to match. He acted like he had nothing to prove and no one to prove anything to. *Soooo cool.*

"What happened here?" Maisie asked, hopping off her bike to join Frankie. He was cleaning up a picnic table full of half-eaten leftovers, empty cans, and discarded food wrappers.

"Coop assigned me to pick up trash left by stupid people who can't seem to clean up after themselves." Frankie grimaced as he gestured toward the mess. "What is *wrong* with people? Why do they come to a national park to litter? Why not just stay home and keep their slovenly ways to themselves?"

Frankie was brilliant. Who used the word *slovenly*? "Looks like they had fun, at least." Maisie picked up some chewed cobs of corn by their stems and added them into the trash bag. "I can't eat corn with my braces."

"I don't care if they had fun. Leaving their junk behind is how bears end up preferring human food." Frankie's voice was laced with frustration. "And then the bears end up getting euthanized. What's worse, it's usually the COY or yearlings."

Maisie froze. "Cubs?" she whispered. "Cute little cubs?"

Frankie nodded grimly as he continued to gather up the trash. "Yep. Happens all the time. A fed bear is a dead bear. They should punish the stupid people, not the bears."

Once the area was picked up, Frankie took the bags over to Coop's truck and heaved them into the open bed. Maisie trotted behind. "Where's Coop?"

"He's down by the lake talking." He made a *yak yak yak* gesture with his hand. "Somebody said there was a big ol' bear sniffing around here." He chuckled. "Then again, if I were to encounter a bear the size of Bruno, I'd raise a racket."

"Bruno?"

"Yeah. Bruno the boar."

"A pig?"

"You should know better than that. You're a ranger's grandkid." He scoffed. "A boar is a male grizzly. Biggest bear in the park. Bruno's the sire of most of 399's offspring."

"I'm *not* a kid. But I do think that's sort of sweet." Frankie gave her a look like she sounded silly. "What? It's kind of romantic to think bears pair up."

He scoffed. "Bruno has sired the cubs of a ton of female grizzlies."

"Oh. So he's not a monogamist."

A laugh burst out of him. "Not even close."

Waiting for Coop, he tipped his head toward a bench. She took that as a bona fide invitation. She had to remember this moment. Someday she would tell their children about their first date. "You know what I love most about being here? The fresh air." She took in a deep breath. "I haven't had to use my inhaler once." She lifted up her leg to reveal a lump in her sock, where she kept her inhaler in case of an asthma attack.

He glanced at her sock.

"Fun fact. String Lake got its name because it looks like a string."

He shrugged, like *big deal*.

Okay. She had more. "Another fun fact. Jenny Lake is named after the Shoshone woman who married Beaver Dick."

"Who?"

"I told you about him. You know, String Lake? Beaver Dick was an Englishman named Richard Leigh. He was a guide and a settler and a trapper. That's how Leigh Lake got its name."

Frankie didn't respond, but she could tell he was interested. Sort of.

"So Beaver Dick and Jenny had this super happy marriage and a bunch of kids, and they were really popular. Everyone talked about their generosity and hospitality and kindness."

"Why do I get the feeling there's going to be a terrible end to this story?"

"Because you're *right*. They invited this sick guy into their home and he got everyone sick, including Jenny. Not Dick. They all died, one by one. Not Dick, but everyone else."

He looked at her, astounded. "That is incredibly tragic."

"I know!"

"Where do you learn this stuff?"

"I read a lot. There was a kid in my math club who gave me a book about Jenny. And Pops tells me a lot."

He grinned. "By Pops, you mean"—he made his voice deep and authoritative—"Ranger Tim Rivers?"

"Yes. He knows everything about the park. About all of the parks." She looked at him with sincerity. "I hope you realize how lucky you are to have both Coop and Pops looking out for you this summer. They're wonderful men. True heroes."

For a brief moment, Frankie's face lost his bravado. Then back it came. "Yeah, yeah, yeah. Speaking of, here comes the warden." Coop was heading toward his truck and motioned to Frankie to come join him. "I'd better go." Frankie gave her a high five. "Thanks for the janitor help."

Maisie could've hugged him. Their first date! And it was a great success.

He stood up and took a step, then turned to her. "How old are you again?"

"Almost fourteen."

"So let me get this straight. You keep an inhaler stuck in your sock. You've got a mouth full of metal. And you're in math club."

She nodded, delighted he had been listening to her.

"When you get to high school, if you want to keep your cool on, you might want to space out nerdy things." He sauntered off to Coop's truck.

And just like that, Maisie's happy feelings popped like soap bubbles.

She heard a text come in from her phone and pulled it out of her backpack to read.

Mom
How's everything going?

> All good! How 'bout you?

Not so well. This spiritual retreat isn't what I expected.

> How so?

Bible-thumping. I might cut it short. Thinking we should head back to Denver so I can start job hunting.

156

Maisie felt panic. She didn't want to leave Pops and the park! Her week had just begun.

> Give it a chance, Mom. Remember, Rebecca Woodbine treated you to this retreat. If you leave early, she'll probably want you to pay her back.

Long pause.

> Good point.

Long pause.

> I'll give it another day.

Over the radio, Sally Janus had told Coop to come to her office as soon as possible. When he asked why, she bristled. "How 'bout you find out when you get here."

That was an uncomfortable end to a public call with the acting chief ranger that every other ranger was listening in on.

Frankie gave him a look. "Aww, man. What'd you do wrong?"

"Nothing that I know of."

Thirty minutes later, after dropping Frankie off at the Jenny Lake Stables to help the shorthanded handler clean out horse stalls—a task Frankie was not happy with, but what else was new?—Coop stepped into Sally's office, immediately sensing an unusual tension in the air. She gestured for him to take a seat, and as he settled in, the door clicked shut behind him, sealing them in the uneasy atmosphere. She folded her arms against her chest.

"Tim said you came across evidence of poaching activity." Her tone was sharp, cutting straight to the point. "What information did you gather?"

"Just what I told Tim," Coop said, trying to match her seriousness. "Pretty sure it was a wolf."

"Did you see any sign of the poacher that we can go on? Snares, traps, bait? Tire tracks?" Sally fired off questions like bullets from a gun.

Each time Coop shook his head, he felt the weight of Sally's disappointment in him settle in the room.

"Broken branches, trampled vegetation? Any clue that might have indicated the path he took?"

"Pretty sure he went through the creek," Coop said, feeling a twinge of frustration at his own lack of findings. He should've done a more thorough investigation.

"Any sign of human activity? A gum wrapper. A tissue."

"No. I filled out the report. Here, I have a copy." Coop opened his notebook, but she waved it away dismissively.

"I read it," she said, her expression conveying her dissatisfaction with both the report and Coop's detective skills. "Coop, hon, you aren't giving me much to go on."

"There wasn't much to go on. Other than the shell casing which, by the way, Frankie the intern found. So at least we know the make of the rifle."

"It was a rifle that would be common for any hunter." Sally leaned forward, her eyes probing. "What were you doing up there, anyway? You're assigned to the valley."

"It was my day off."

Sally narrowed her eyes suspiciously. "I asked *what* you were doing up there. It's off-limits."

Coop hesitated, unsure how much to reveal. He settled on a half-truth. "I assumed that meant off-limit to public access. You see, it's one of my favorite day hikes."

Sally wasn't buying it. "So did you see 399? Any signs that she's emerged from hibernation?"

"No. I didn't see her. We didn't get as high up as I had hoped to. The gunshot interrupted the hike."

"Coop, do you think she didn't make it through the winter?"

"Not sure." He hated to think so, but it was starting to look that way.

Sally's gaze softened, betraying a mix of emotions. "I sure hope that big darlin' made it through."

"Me too," Coop said.

Sally shook off her sentiment. "If there's any sighting of 399, I want you to let me know immediately. Day or night. Let me know if any of those wildlife watchers catch sight of her. How many photographers have you counted so far?"

"At least forty." Forty-one, if he counted Kate.

"Do you recognize them from last year?"

"Most." Kate was new.

"Any one photographer who might be . . . seem to have questionable motives?"

Still thinking of Kate, Coop coughed a laugh. "No. They're all . . . dedicated to 399's well-being. Their livelihood depends on her."

"Well, if they see the bear first, you're to let me know," Sally said in a firm voice. "Did you happen to pass anyone on the trail?"

"Nope. No one's up there."

"I've decided to extend the area along Pilgrim Creek to be closed to public access. All the way down to the road."

"But what about the photographers waiting for 399?"

"Unaffected. They can stay along the road."

"Sally, the whole park is going to be restricted soon."

"It's just temporary, Ranger Cooper." She gave him a look, as if to say, *Don't forget that I'm the boss here.* She cleared her throat. "One more thing." Her face softened. Even her voice grew tender. "Tim might seem to feel a little . . ."

"Tim?" Coop leaned forward. "Feel a little . . . what?"

"Maybe a little . . . put on the back burner—" But a knock on the door made Sally put an abrupt end to that sentence. "Come in."

A very tall ranger entered Sally's office. Coop couldn't help but notice how Sally's demeanor shifted. Tense. Stiff.

"Ranger Feldmann, come in. Ranger Cooper was just leaving."

I was? Apparently he was. Coop rose from his seat and reached out to shake the man's hand. "Are you new to the park?"

Before Feldmann could respond, Sally answered. "He's on loan from Yellowstone."

"Really?" It was only then that Coop noticed his Yellowstone badge. "I've never known Yellowstone to have enough staff to loan out."

"The parks," Sally said, "have been working on a way to better support each other. I met him at the conference I attended recently, and he volunteered to help us out during opening season. That'll be all, Ranger Cooper. There's a bear jam over at Moose-Wilson Road that could use your expertise."

As Coop left Sally's office, he felt unsettled. The bear jam at Moose-Wilson Road had plenty of rangers to cover it. He'd driven by on his way to Sally's office and knew it to be so. Sally wanted him out of her office when that super tall ranger came in. Or maybe he just seemed tall because he stood next to Sally and she was so small.

A lingering sense of curiosity gnawed at him. There was something else behind Sally's questions, something beneath the surface. How could she think that any wildlife photographers could be potential poachers? Especially the ones dedicated to 399.

Something struck Coop as odd about that Ranger Feldmann too. He couldn't quite put his finger on it.

And then it dawned on him. When he shook Feldmann's hand, his palm was smooth. Unusually soft.

160

Wade couldn't believe it when Feldmann told him details about the turncoat. A chief ranger. A woman. He didn't know which was worse. "What were you thinking?" Wade practically spat out the words, his eyes narrowing in disbelief.

Feldmann's nonchalant demeanor faltered slightly. "I thought I told you. She's our best bet."

"Best bet?" Wade scoffed. "She's a chief ranger, Feldmann. She's not some rookie we can manipulate easily."

"That's exactly why. I went as a mole to a conference at Yellowstone. This ranger was asking a lot of questions about park employees' retirement package, and she didn't like the answers. So, after the meeting, I made a point to get to know her. Sat next to her at meals, you know, that kind of thing. It was obvious that she was angry at the NPS and that she needed money. By the end of the conference, I knew she was willing to play ball. I actually think it's genius that she's a chief ranger. In her role, she's got power to help us."

"How?"

"By limiting public access to areas where that bear might be."

Okay, Wade thought. Apart from one clean shot at the wolf, proving the turncoat could actually hunt, he still wanted proof that she could be trusted. "I want her put to the test. Have her go after a bear." He patted his chest. "Not *my* bear. Just any other bear. Let's see if she's playing ball or if she's playing you for a fool."

Feldmann nodded. "I'll get it set up."

With that, Wade turned on his heel and stalked back to his hotel room. This turn of events only fueled his determination to succeed, but it also made him wary.

Time was ticking.

THIRTEEN

One touch of nature makes the whole world kin.
—William Shakespeare

Coop leaned against the doorframe, his arms crossed tightly over his chest, as he watched Frankie stumble groggily out of bed. Frankie had been out past midnight and turned on the light when he finally came back to the room, waking Coop out of a sound sleep.

So Coop decided to return the favor at four a.m.

Dawn would be here soon, and they were due up at Pilgrim Creek to keep an eye on the bear-eager photographers. "Speed it up," Coop muttered, his patience already worn thin.

Frankie mumbled something unintelligible—perhaps unrepeatable—as he stumbled into the hallway to head toward the communal bathroom. Coop had to step over things in their cluttered room. Frankie's junk was strewn everywhere. Coop sighed, disgusted.

As he searched for the keys to his truck, Coop thought to check the pocket of Frankie's coat. Bingo. There they were. Unbelievable! He was just starting to think this kid had some redeeming qualities, and now *this*. No wonder he kept getting kicked out of boarding school.

With a frustrated huff, he held his keys in the air as Frankie returned to the room. "Seriously? You borrowed my truck without asking?"

"I didn't want to wake you up to ask." Frankie shrugged, his nonchalant attitude only fueling Coop's irritation. "What's the big deal?"

"It's a pretty big deal to me." Coop couldn't believe Frankie's lack of remorse. He was no stranger to the self-centeredness of teenagers, but this kid took it to a whole new level. "And it's a big deal that you made me late for work."

With that, Coop left the room to let Frankie fend for himself. As he reached his truck, he threw open the door and climbed in, only to find more evidence of Frankie the slob. Candy wrappers littered the floor, empty soda cans rolled around on the passenger seat, and worst of all, the gas tank was nearly empty.

"Incredible," Coop muttered to himself as he started up the truck.

The passenger door opened, and Frankie scrambled in, boots still untied, shirt unbuttoned, coat unzipped. "Hey, I'm sorry, dude."

"Sure you are."

Frankie closed the door. "Really. I am. But if I had wheels, I would loan them to you, anytime. We're compadres."

"You don't have wheels and we're not compadres. I'm your boss and you're my lowly intern."

Frankie huffed. "Fine. I won't borrow your truck again without asking."

"You won't borrow it, period."

He rolled his eyes. "Got it."

"And you're going to buy me a full tank of gas today."

"A full tank? Dude! I only drove to Jackson and back last night."

"Plus you're going to wash the exterior and vacuum the interior." Coop tossed a candy wrapper at him. "After you throw out all your trash."

Frankie let out a heavy sigh.

"And then you're going to clean up our room."

"Boot camp," Frankie muttered.

"Pardon me?"

"I said, 'Suits me.'"

Coop nodded. "That's what I thought you said."

Maisie stood in front of the old, slightly tarnished mirror on top of the bureau, studying the picture on her smartphone and comparing it to her reflection in the mirror. On her smartphone was a zoomed-in, close-up photo she'd taken of Kate, when she was staring at a bird or moose or something out in the distance. The more time Maisie spent with the photographer, the more she decided that Kate was everything she wanted to be: smart, pretty, super focused. Everything her mom was not. Well, not the pretty and smart part but the focused part. Her mom could walk into a room and forget why she was there.

Maisie admired everything about Kate, with her effortless style and the way she seemed to forge ahead, turning heads. Mostly, Frankie's. It swiveled to stare at Kate. The funny thing was that Maisie didn't blame him. Kate was *that* pretty.

So she was on a mission to transform herself into Kate, helped by a visit to a pharmacy in Jackson yesterday when she tagged along on Pops's errands. She spent an entire month's allowance on makeup and hair products.

Hair came first. Kate's brownish-red hair was thick, wavy, gathered high on the back of her head, cascading into a long swirly ponytail. Shiny, like it was spun from sunrays. Maisie's hair was wild and fuzzy red curls that refused to be tamed. She wrestled with the straightener she'd borrowed from her mom, tugging and pulling, but each curl seemed to fight back. Gobs of hair spray helped her tackle most of it into a ponytail, but it looked like a pom-pom stuck on the back of her head.

Studying Kate's eye makeup in the photo, Maisie then applied a smoky gray liner on each eyelid. Her hand was a little shaky and the liner wasn't quite straight in places. She squinted into the mirror. *Bleh.* She made a second pass over the liner, a little wider to cover her mistakes. *Not too bad.*

Next came black mascara. One coat, two coats, three coats. She smeared a thick layer of foundation over her cheeks to hide her freckles. Lots and lots of foundation.

Finally, a shiny pink lip gloss. A sigh escaped Maisie's lips, her frustration mounting as she eyed her braces in the mirror. Kate had a perfect white smile, like in those toothpaste commercials.

Last came the outfit. Maisie had carefully chosen clothes that screamed "Kate"—she thought so, anyway. A simple top, jeans, and hiking boots. *Perfect.* Casual and cool. She turned this way and that, paced the small room, trying to catch that same ease Kate wore. She practiced Kate's laugh, light and musical. Then she peered at herself again in the small mirror on top of the dresser.

She looked *awesome.*

Maybe now Frankie would notice Maisie. He sure did notice Kate. Practically drooled.

Outside, a car horn tooted. Thirty seconds later, it tooted again. This time, a bit longer.

Pops!

He had told Maisie to be out in the jeep in ten minutes so he could get to the visitor center for a ranger meeting. She grabbed her smartphone off the bureau and checked the time. *Uh-oh!* That was twenty minutes ago.

Grabbing her backpack and her big, puffy, bright yellow down jacket, Maisie hurried outside, the door closing behind her with a soft click. When she hopped in the jeep, Pops said nothing about how late she'd made him. Not a word about her dazzling new appearance. By the time they arrived at the visitor center parking lot, he turned off the jeep, opened the door, and stepped out. Before he closed the door, he looked right at her with a thoughtful expression. "Sweetheart, a tulip doesn't struggle to be different from a rose."

Maisie shot him a side glance. What did *that* mean?

Pops just didn't seem like himself this summer. Absent-minded. Distracted. There were times when he'd stare off in the distance for long stretches or fail to hear the whistle of the tea kettle. She wondered if he might be starting to have dementia. He worried Maisie. After all, Pops was in his mid-fifties, not exactly a spring chicken. Maisie knew a lot about dementia from her friend at school, whose grandmother put cereal in the refrigerator and milk in the cupboard. Odd things like that.

A little concerned, Maisie zipped up her jacket and reached for her backpack. She would have to keep a close eye on Pops for any alarming or strange behavior. She blew out a puff of air. That meant she'd have to be worrying about both her grandfather and her mother. Different worries, but all worry felt the same.

~~~

Kate sat on the stone hearth in the Jenny Lake Lodge, her camera in hand, as a midday storm rumbled outside. The lodge hadn't officially opened for the season yet, but they had opened the large living room for visitors to enjoy. She was waiting out the rain by scrolling through her most recent photographs on her camera's screen and felt pretty encouraged by the improvements she'd made today. After studying her mistakes, she'd adjusted her camera settings for lighting and speed, and the results were much better compositions. In one, she'd captured a majestic male moose grazing in a meadow, its velvet antlers glistening in the soft light filtering through the trees. The detail was so clear, it was as if you were right there with him. Three birds stood on the back of the moose. In her mind popped a caption for this photograph: "Waiting for appetizers."

The lodge's large living room was bustling with people seeking shelter from the rain, creating a cozy atmosphere, full of humming conversations, though Kate was hardly aware of them. Then she sensed someone's eyes on her and looked up to see Coop approaching.

"You look like the cat that swallowed the canary." He sat down next to her, a warm glint in his gray eyes. "Don't tell me. You've scored a reservation for dinner at Jenny Lake Lodge tonight, with a table for two right against the windows." He gave her a light jab with his elbow. "And you're thinking of inviting me to join you."

"I only wish," Kate said, pleased he was here. She hadn't seen him since Wednesday. "One meal here would swallow my entire budget for this trip."

"Good thing they haven't opened the restaurant yet. Frankie's in the kitchen, hoping to sample their practice meals."

She held up her camera. "Here's why I'm smiling." She explained how discouraged she'd been yesterday, so she studied her work, trying to identify mistakes and figure out how to correct them. She showed Coop the photographs she had taken today, then she pulled up similar photographs from a few days ago, illustrating the progress she had made.

He scooted closer to her to look at the photographs on her camera screen. His eyes widened in appreciation as he admired the wildlife shots she had captured. "I don't think I would've noticed the differences unless you pointed them out. But now I can see what you're talking about."

"And now you can't unsee them, right?"

He grinned. "When 399 finally comes down from her lair, you'll be ready."

"I like that you said 'when' and not 'if,'" Kate said. He was so close to her that she noticed how good he smelled, a combination of soap and aftershave. A hint of coffee, maybe?

"You weren't at Pilgrim Creek this morning."

He'd noticed! But he wasn't there yesterday. *She'd* noticed. Her cheeks started to grow warm.

And suddenly Tim Rivers was right in front of them. He gave a quick nod to Kate before turning to Coop. "Bear jam at Jackson Lake Dam. I was driving past the lodge and saw your parked truck. I need you and Frankie over there now." Tim looked around the room. "Where is Frankie, anyway?"

"He went to the kitchen to ask to sample the food. I'm pretty sure they'll kick him straight out." Coop rose to his feet. "I guess that means I should be on my way."

Kate stood too. "A photographer was telling me about the dam just this morning. Something about bears hanging out there."

"That's right," Coop said. "Anglers discard suckers on the rocks at the base of the dam. The bears know to come snacking there."

Kate looked up at Tim. "Do you happen to know which bear is causing the bear jam?"

"Not sure," Tim said. "Report came in that the sow has yellow ear tags but no radio collar."

"Sounds like 610," Coop said.

610? Kate made a slight gasping sound. Grizzly 610 was the daughter of 399, nearly as famous as her mother. She'd read a story in which, several years ago, 610 had adopted one of 399's triplets and successfully raised it. Really unusual, because grizzlies were solitary animals. While Kate knew not to anthropomorphize the bears, it was remarkable that the two sows had engaged in such a way as to help each other with childcare. "Maybe I'll head over there after the rain peters out."

Tim had a sheepish look on his face. "I was wondering if . . . maybe you'd be willing to let Maisie spend a little time with you this afternoon."

"You mean . . . today?" Kate hoped her voice didn't give away her alarm at that request.

"She's keen on learning more about wildlife photography." Tim cleared his throat. "And . . . she seems to be quite impressed with you."

As if on cue, Maisie appeared next to her grandfather. "Hi, Kate!"

Hold it. Kate exchanged a shocked glance with Coop, silently questioning what had happened to the girl before them.

Maisie, typically fresh-faced and youthful, now sported a heavy dose of makeup, with her curly hair pulled into a high, stubby ponytail.

Frankie strolled in and grinned when he saw Kate.

Maisie beamed. "Hi, Frankie!"

He glanced at Maisie and did a double take. "Whoa. Are you sick?"

"I feel great," Maisie said. "Better than great."

Frankie's eyes widened, and he burst out laughing. "Oh, I get it! You're going for the mini-Kate look, huh? A Kate copy!" He practically wheezed with laughter.

Kate and Coop exchanged an *oh dear* moment. Maisie sported a thick kohl eyeliner like she'd joined a Goth band. If that's really how Kate looked to others, she might need to dial back her eye makeup.

Maisie flashed a scowl at Frankie before she turned to Kate. "Can I be your assistant this afternoon?"

"Good luck getting anything done." Frankie raised one hand

to make the blah-blah gesture while mimicking the call of a squawking bird.

Kate kept a poker face, but those were her thoughts exactly. Maisie never stopped talking.

Tim put his hands on Coop's and Frankie's shoulders. "Let's get going." He looked at Kate. "Thanks for keeping an eye on my granddaughter."

What? But Kate hadn't said she would!

"I'll grab my backpack from Pops's jeep real quick and be back!" Halfway to the door, Maisie spun around with excitement. "This is going to be *so . . . much . . . fun!*" She emphasized each word with a clap of her hands.

Coop shot Kate a playful eyebrow wiggle before he turned to join Tim and Frankie at the door. At least he understood the situation Ranger Tim Rivers had just thrown at her.

Watching Coop pass by the big picture windows, it dawned on her that she would never have shown Oliver raw photos straight from her camera. Why? Oliver had a sharp eye for detail, no doubt about it. But he would've torn apart her shots, especially the ones she'd worked hard to improve. That would've left her grappling with self-doubts and insecurities, feeling like she wasn't good enough, creative enough, bold enough, smart enough.

There was just something about Coop that put her at ease, made her feel as if she could fully be herself with him. Yet she hardly knew him. Why did she trust him so easily?

It was a question that lingered in her mind as she continued to browse through her photographs, waiting for the storm to pass. Waiting for Maisie the Magpie to return.

On the drive to Jackson Lake Dam, Maisie filled Kate in on fun facts about the dam. "When Jackson Lake was made by that dam thingy, it covered up a bunch of old buildings and stuff.

Pops said that there are old homesteads, cabins, and even an old ferry landing that got hidden underwater. He told me that, once, during a really bad drought year, he could even see parts of old places peeking out. Isn't that awesome? It's like secrets are hiding beneath the lake. Wouldn't it be cool to go scuba diving around the lake?" *Is she listening?* "Kate?"

Kate startled. "Scuba diving? No, I've never been."

That wasn't exactly what Maisie was asking, but it was close enough. "Me neither. But someday I want to learn how to scuba dive. Don't you?" Before Kate could answer, she said, "I have more fun facts about the dam."

"There's more?"

"Tons more." Maisie was just about to share more of her vast knowledge when Kate said, "Look! We're here." And sure enough, they'd arrived at Jackson Lake Dam.

Kate took her equipment out of the trunk of her car and went to work. And boy did she work. Maisie too. Kate kept sending Maisie off on errands to find out valuable information, like to go ask Coop if the bear causing the bear jam was 610 (it wasn't). By the time Maisie found Coop to ask, then looked for Frankie and chatted with him for a while, and then returned to Kate, the bear had wandered off. Kate was disappointed. Maisie, not so much. She was just happy to hang around Kate.

Later that day, as Maisie helped Kate carry her equipment from the parking lot to her room at Jackson Lake Lodge, she picked right up where she had left off with fun facts. These ones were about the lodge. "Four presidents have visited here."

"Yeah? Which ones?"

Maisie ticked off her fingers. "Presidents Kennedy, Nixon, Reagan, and Clinton."

At the top of the staircase to the upper floor lobby, Maisie stopped in her tracks. She'd been here once before with Pops, and had the same overwhelmed-awesomeness-breathtaking moment when she took in the sight of the enormous windows that framed the Grand Tetons.

Kate was heading toward the elevator.

"Kate, slow down! Come and see this." Maisie hurried around the furniture, eager to reach the window and soak in the stunning vista.

"Gorgeous," Kate said as they stared through the windows, captivated by the jagged silhouettes of the Teton Range. "You know what I love most? It's unchanged. People have been looking at those mountains for centuries, and they look just the same."

"Do you ever wonder about them?"

"Who? All those presidents you said had visited here?"

"No, no. I mean way, way back. Like, before Lewis and Clark came exploring, before the mountain men came trapping here. The tribes. The Shoshone, Crow, Blackfeet, Gros Ventre. Don't you wonder what their lives were like? Like, did they fall in love and get married and have kids and worry about their kids like people do now?" Most people. Not Maisie's mom, but most.

Kate turned to her with a thoughtful look. "Maisie, you have more on your mind than I did when I was your age. All I thought about was boys."

"Oh, I think about boys a lot." Especially Frankie. She wondered if Frankie thought about her half as much as she thought about him.

Kate laughed and picked up her camera bag. "I've got to get up to the room and change out of these wet boots. Better still, grab a shower. Why don't you just wait here for me? I won't take long. And then I'll drop you back at the visitor center to meet up with your grandfather."

"Can I see your room? I've never seen a lodge room."

"Oh. Well, sure." Kate tipped her head. "Let's go."

"First, follow me for a second." Maisie crossed the room to the Mural Room, a fine dining restaurant that she'd never eaten in but someday she wanted to. When Kate joined her at the door, she whispered, "Just look at that."

Kate was looking out the window. "A panorama of mountains."

"Yeah, but I meant the mural on those two walls. They tell the story of a mountain man rendezvous."

"A what?"

The restaurant host came to greet them. "Table for two?"

"Oh, no," Kate said. "We were just looking at the mural."

"Come in," he said. "It's quiet right now. I'll give you a tour." He took them to the start of the mural. "This is known as the mural of the mountain man rendezvous. The beaver fur trade lured trappers, hunters, and traders to this area in the mid-1800s. The mountain men would gather once a year to exchange furs for supplies, tobacco, liquor, and news. Davey Jackson trapped in the hole and left his legacy. Hence the name Jackson Hole."

Kate's gaze was on a wagon in the mural. "It looks so dangerous."

"It was," he said. "And lonely. Most of the men lived a solitary life." He sighed. "The cost of greed. They were competing for the same product. Pelts."

"So why," Kate said, "did it end?"

"I bet I know," Maisie said. "They killed all the beavers."

"Actually, the Homestead Act of 1862 put an end to trapping," the host said. "It granted land to those who promised to build on it and live there for five years. In came farmers, ranchers with big herds. That only lasted four or five years."

"Why?" Kate spun around. "What happened?"

"A devastating winter. Nearly all of the ranchers' herds perished, and they just gave up. And then Yellowstone became the first national park."

"Fun fact," Maisie said. "It was the first national park in the entire world."

The host bobbed his head in a nod. "That's true. The first national park in the entire world. Attracting visitors proved to be a more profitable venture than farming and ranching." He noticed a couple at the door, waiting to be seated. "Take your time looking at the mural." He pointed to his forehead and then to Maisie. "You are one smart kid."

"Thanks," she said, frowning. "But I'm not a kid!" He was already off, hurrying back to the host desk.

Kate hoisted her camera bag over her shoulder. "Maisie, I really need to get to my room. You stay. Just stay down here. I'll change and come back down."

"No, that's okay. I'll come with you." She wasn't going to miss a chance to see a room.

Kate's room at Jackson Lake Lodge was better than Maisie had imagined. The only hotel rooms she'd ever stayed in with her mom were bare-bone types. Like, check to see if the sheets had been changed. Kate excused herself to hop in the shower and Maisie walked all around the room, touching the curtains, noticing the mirror frames. What a life Kate lived!

Instead of being a ranger like Pops, Maisie decided she was going to be a wildlife photographer, just like Kate. Maybe she'd even get her initial experience at a zoo, like Kate did. She wouldn't tell anybody about it, though. She'd heard those photographers make fun of Kate.

Kate's phone buzzed a text, then another, and another. Then a phone call. She was just about to knock on the bathroom door to get Kate when the shower turned on. So, being the assistant she was to Kate, she answered the phone. "Hello?"

"Katie-Kat? Is that you?"

"Nope."

"Who are you?"

"It depends. Who are *you*?"

"I'm Oliver. Kate's boyfriend."

"SHUT UP! I didn't know Kate had a boyfriend." How could she not have told Maisie? That was front-page news!

"And just who," Oliver said, "are you?"

"I'm Kate's assistant. Maisie."

There was a pause. Then, "I didn't know Kate had an assistant."

"See? We're even."

"She's only been in Wyoming for a week."

"Yes! I just got here too. It was meant to be. I believe in those kinds of coincidences, don't you? My grandfather calls them miracles. What do you call them?"

"Is Kate there? I'd like to talk to her."

The shower was still going strong, so Maisie decided to not bother Kate. "Sorry, she's not available at the moment." Lounging comfortably on Kate's bed, she decided to take charge. "So, you're the boyfriend, huh?"

"Yeah, that's me. I've got something important to talk to Kate about . . . so if you'll just go get her."

Maisie rolled over on her back. "Something important, you say? Do tell. I'm all ears."

Oliver scoffed. "Exactly how old are you, anyway?"

"Plenty old enough to be Kate's assistant."

"And what exactly do you do for her?"

He seemed to have a fondness for the word *exactly*. That told Maisie a lot about him. Direct. To the point. Literal. She decided to respond in a way that would help him understand her role. "I carry her equipment. I hunt out opportune viewing sites for her. I'm basically her right-hand man . . . except I'm a girl. I mean, a woman."

"Has Kate found that bear yet?"

"Grizzly bear," Maisie said.

He chuckled. "A bear is a bear."

"Oh no, it is *not*. A grizzly bear is a subspecies of the brown bear."

Oliver let out a sigh. "So did Kate get her Kodak moment with that grizzly bear?"

That sounded like the kind of rude remark that the other photographers might make to Kate. "I can't reveal my employer's private business." She sat up on the bed and crossed her legs. "So, Oliver, tell me what's so important that you need to tell Kate. I'll relay your message to her."

"It's none of your business."

True, but that didn't stop Maisie from being curious. "If you want my help, I'll need to know what this matter is all about."

"What makes you think I want your help?"

"Because I have been extremely helpful to Kate this week." Mostly, this afternoon.

"Are you any good at keeping secrets?"

"Well, I haven't let you talk to Kate yet, have I?"

"Point taken." He hesitated before saying, "Maybe you can be helpful. I'm planning to come to Grand Teton National Park to ask Kate to marry me."

Maisie's eyes widened with surprise. She sat up. "SHUT UP! No way! That's *huge*! How romantic. I *love* a love story." She gasped. "I'm just the person to help you with this. I'm really good at this kind of thing. So what kind of proposal do you have in mind? How big is the ring? Are you hiring a videographer? And when is this going to happen?"

"Hold up," Oliver said. "I haven't worked out all the details yet."

That wasn't good enough for Maisie. "Oh, come on. You want to win the hand of the most beautiful, wonderful woman in the world. This proposal should be epic."

"Epic, huh?" Oliver chuckled. "I just want it to be special, something to remember. I'm thinking it should happen sooner rather than later. Like, in the next few days."

Maisie grinned. *This was So. Much. Fun!* "Something to remember is a very good place to start. But you need a solid plan. Is it going to be a mountaintop proposal? Or in a helicopter flying over the valley? Or how about proposing at sunset by the lake? My favorite is Jenny Lake, but Jackson Lake is a lot, lot bigger. Leigh Lake is pretty. So is String Lake, but it's kind of tiny. That's probably why they named it String, don't you think? Plus, there will be people all around, getting in our video." She gasped. "Oh, I've got it! A hot-air balloon proposal. Now *that's* memorable!"

"Hot-air balloon, huh? That's quite a suggestion. But you might be onto something." Oliver sounded intrigued. "Thanks for the advice, Melissa."

"Maisie," she corrected, but kindly, because she felt a bond with this man. They both loved Kate. "Just remember, the more creative, the better. And make sure that ring is sparkly. Big and sparkly. Girls love bling."

As she heard the shower turn off, she decided it would be best to end the call now. "Gotta go. And don't worry, your secret's safe with me. I won't spill the beans to Kate. Here's my number so I can help you with plans." She quickly dictated her phone number to him and hung up, a smug grin on her face. This was turning into the best summer of her life.

The time had come to go bow shopping. Feldmann still hadn't been able to reroute Whisper, and Wade was getting anxious. That bear was overdue.

Normally, Wade didn't venture out into public when he was preparing for a hunt, but he wasn't about to let Feldmann make this purchase for him. The bow and arrows needed to be a superior quality—a high-grade armguard and handgrip as well.

Fortunately, he always brought a disguise or two along in his suitcase. For this incognito visit to the archery shop, he constructed a getup that was a mix of the mundane and the meticulous, ensuring he'd blend into the crowd. Nothing memorable, that was Wade's MO.

Out of the suitcase he lifted a thick brownish-gray wig that was tousled in just the right way to suggest age without looking disheveled. Next came the mustache, snugly adhered above his lip and blending seamlessly with the wig's color tone. The mustache subtly altered the contours of his face, adding years to his appearance. Practicing a slight Midwest accent, he elongated his vowels just enough to sound authentic. Completing his ensemble, he donned a nondescript button-up shirt, faded jeans, and worn-in sneakers.

Standing in front of the mirror before he left, he barely recognized himself. Wade had transformed himself into a thoroughly average-looking man on the late side of midlife—the kind you pass on the street without a second glance. This was the art of invisibility.

FOURTEEN

Wildlife is something which man cannot construct.
Once it is gone, it is gone forever.
—*Joy Adamson, naturalist*

After dropping Maisie back at the visitor center to her grandfather's care, Kate decided to head over to Willow Flats, an area that was supposedly teeming with wildlife. According to the guidebook, anyway.

A little absentmindedly, she parked her rental car behind another vehicle and retrieved her camera equipment from the trunk. She was mindful of Coop's warning to not hike alone, but she had her world's loudest whistle around her neck and bear spray in her coat pocket. The presence of another car meant other hikers were here, and that gave her an additional boost of confidence. Besides, she wasn't planning to stay long. After spending the last few hours with Maisie, having some quiet time to herself felt like a breath of fresh air. Kate liked Maisie, quite a bit, but the girl could talk your ear off. She never stopped.

As she walked down the trail that led to Christian Creek, Kate was glad she'd stopped at the lodge to shower and exchange wet boots for dry ones. They protected her now as she trudged through the mud and wet grass. She walked in a state of wonder at the beauty and the silence. Especially the silence. Her ears were still ringing from Maisie.

Stopping at different points along the trail, Kate took out her binoculars to survey the flats. An eagle, or perhaps an osprey, shrieked overhead, prompting her to reach for her camera. Fat chance. By the time she removed the lens cap, the bird had disappeared into the distance.

She came to a fork in the trail and stopped to pull out her guidebook, uncertain by now that she was even on the original trail. She took out her map and compass to assess her position, and looked up in the sky to see which direction the sun was setting. Happily, not a cloud in the sky, just as her weather app had forecasted. She had checked before she set out for Willow Flats. She'd learned her lesson from Hidden Falls . . . though it was kind of nice to have Coop come looking for her.

Rooted to the spot, she peered out through her binoculars, wondering about all the life that found shelter at the flats. Out here, with the wide marshes in front of her, Kate felt as if she was stepping into the unknown.

It was a far cry from the confined orderliness of the zoo. No neatly set-up exhibits or scheduled shows. In the zoo, animals lived in synchronicity. Rhythms drew the animals together—sleeping, eating, even playing.

Here, nature was the boss. It didn't follow any rules; it had its own rhythms.

Kate had learned a tremendous amount as a zoo photographer, starting with needing an inordinate amount of patience. Especially fascinating to her was how animals used their senses to help interpret and understand the world. Owls or bats could hear a prey's movements in total darkness. Sharks used electroreception to detect electric fields, helping them navigate and locate prey. Wide-eyed deer used their vision to avoid a threat. Dogs and bears relied on their highly sensitive noses. Birds, turtles, even butterflies relied on magnetoreception to orient them on migration.

All that and more she had learned at the zoo. Watching and studying. A passive observer.

No longer. Here, she felt like a caged bird set free, soaring through the open sky with exhilarating abandon. The thought of returning to Virginia—to the zoo, to Oliver—filled her with a sense of dread.

It was a startling realization. Just a week ago, Kate wouldn't have been fearless enough to go hiking like this, alone, near sunset. Yet here she was. Bold and brave.

Kate Cunningham. The new and improved Kate Cunningham.

She heard it before she saw it. An unmistakable snort that made her freeze in her tracks, followed by utter silence. Even the birdsong stopped. Looking through her binoculars, Kate spotted a massive grizzly bear. It was far away, at least a football field. Hopefully more. Her heart started to pound. *Calm, stay calm*, she told herself. Moving slowly, because she knew that bears got excited by quick movement, she lifted her camera to take photos of it, thankful she had the zoom lens attached.

Big mistake.

The bear might have heard or seen her move or maybe it smelled Kate's presence. It stood up on its hind legs, fixing her with a piercing gaze. Standing tall, this bear was enormous. Slightly terrified, yet far more mesmerized, Kate kept taking pictures of it. She remembered advice from a book she'd read about wildlife photography—don't shy away from beautiful and jarring unsettling moments. As long as he was on his hind legs, he was merely curious. If he dropped down and started to approach her, she needed to take action. But what?

Her mind was racing through options. Back up slowly? Blow the storm whistle? Sing? *Think, think, think.* What did Coop say in his ranger talk about close encounters with bears?

Bear spray! Whistle!

Before she could decide which to reach for first, a gunshot rang out and echoed through the meadow. The bear turned and ran, its thick rump rippling before it vanished into the trees, leaving Kate alone in the now eerie silence.

Shaking, Kate scanned the area with her zoom lens, searching for the source of the shot. Unable to see anything or anyone, she decided it was best to return to her car and report the incident to a ranger. To Coop. She needed Coop.

Twenty minutes later, when she arrived back at her rental car, the other vehicle was gone.

As Coop directed traffic around a bear jam at Oxbow Bend, his attention was suddenly drawn to Kate waving to him from her car. Pleasure rippled through him at the sight of her, but it was quickly replaced by concern when he noticed the urgency in her gesture.

"I need to talk to you!" she called out as he approached her car.

Coop lifted his hand in a wave back, the spiral of pleasure in his stomach intensifying. "Sure thing," he replied, motioning for her to pull over to an empty spot.

Once parked, Coop made his way over to her car, his curiosity piqued. "What's going on?"

Kate glanced past him, her eyes scanning the line of vehicles. "Is this traffic all because of a bear?"

"Two, actually." Coop nodded. "A sow and her COY are drawing quite the crowd this evening."

"Please tell me this one is 399." Her blue eyes were wide with hope.

"Nope." Coop shook his head, sorry to disappoint her. "We think this might be one of her granddaughters."

He expected her to jump out and start snapping pictures

like the rest of the crowd, but Kate stayed put in the car, her expression serious. "Coop, something strange just happened."

"What?" Coop leaned in closer.

"I was at Willow Flats and—"

"Hold it. That area is supposed to be off-limits."

"Really? I didn't see any signs. Besides, there was another parked car. When I saw it, I just assumed it would be okay." She shook her head. "Anyway, I was walking on a trail—just like you said, stick to the trail—and I encountered a bear."

"You ran into a bear?" Coop interrupted. "As in, you surprised a bear?"

"The vegetation was pretty thick and he was far, far away."

"Did the bear see you?"

Kate nodded, mimicking the shape of a hump on her neck with her hand. "Pretty sure it was a grizzly."

"Do you realize the danger you put yourself in?" His voice held a note of alarm, so he cleared his throat. After all, he was a professional. "I mean, I can see you're still in one piece." *Stupid, stupid, stupid.* "I mean, um, you lived to tell the tale. You had bear spray, right?"

"I did! And I brought my whistle." She pulled a cord on her neck to reveal a bright orange whistle. "It's supposed to be the world's loudest whistle. I can even whistle underwater."

Underwater? How would that have helped? And why was the whistle buried in her shirt? Coop could feel his stomach tighten with concern. "You shouldn't have been hiking alone, Kate, especially in remote areas. Rangers are always told to travel in threes." With the shortage of manpower, they hardly ever did, but it was a good policy.

"Trust me, I will definitely be more careful next time. But that's not why I came looking for you."

Kate came looking for him? That spiral of pleasure stirred again.

"So the bear raised up on his back legs to look at me, and I knew that he was curious and not acting aggressive—"

"You can't know that."

"I *have* studied bear behavior." She let out a sigh. "Please. Just let me get to the strange part."

"Okay. What was the strange part?"

"As I was taking pictures, a gunshot rang out."

Coop's stomach twisted. "A shot was fired? At you?"

"No. Not me. At the bear. But I don't think it was hit."

"What makes you think that?"

"The bear turned and ran off into the trees. He vanished."

"Did the bear make any noise?"

"Noise? What do you mean?"

"After the shot, did the bear make any sound? When a bear is hit, it bellows. If it's dying, it's a death moan. Almost a song."

She looked at him, clearly affected. "No. No sound. I would've remembered something like that."

Okay, Coop thought. That sounded like an unwounded bear. "Did you see who fired the shot?"

"No. I looked, but I didn't see anyone."

Coop crossed his arms over his chest, his mind racing as he considered the implications. He wondered how to proceed. There wasn't much evidence to go on. Then again . . . "Kate, did you manage to capture anything on camera?"

"Not sure. Maybe." Kate's gaze flicked to the camera hanging around her neck. "I haven't looked at the photos yet. I came straight to you."

"Give me your memory card so I can examine the photographs."

Kate hesitated, a protective glint in her eyes. "Coop, I can't just give you my memory card."

"This could be serious. You might have come across this poacher who's been causing us some grief." Him, especially.

"I know it could be serious. I realize that! That's why I came to find you and tell you about it. But I need to protect my photographs."

Coop sighed, frustration brewing. "Don't make me pull my ranger card and commandeer the memory card."

But Kate held her ground, her gaze steady. "I'm pretty sure you can't do that without a warrant."

Blast. She called his bluff. "Fine," he muttered, defeated. "Can I at least *see* the photos?"

Kate nodded, her expression softening. "Of course. My computer is in my car trunk. I can download the memory card now, and you can see them for yourself."

Kate jumped out of the car, quickly retrieved her computer from the trunk, and began the download process of her camera's memory card. Coop's heart pounded in his chest as he scrolled through the images, relief washing over him when he identified the bear as Bruno. But his relief was short-lived as he noticed something peculiar in the background.

"We need to show this to Tim Rivers right away," Coop said, his mind already racing ahead to the next steps.

"I'll go with you."

"No need."

"I'm sorry, Coop, but there's every need. You're not taking my computer from me."

Coop hesitated for a moment before nodding in agreement. "We'll take my truck. You can leave your car here and I'll drop you back later." Walking to his truck, he had to swallow down a smile at Kate's feistiness. The more he was around her, the more he liked her.

Tim had been turning out the lights when he heard a knock at the door and suddenly Coop and Zoo Girl were in his cabin. He squeezed his eyes shut. He had to stop thinking of her as

Zoo Girl. What was her name again? Something short. Coop seemed to be a little sweet on her, which was just the scenario Tim had hoped for his friend this summer.

Coop flicked on the overhead light. "We've got something to show you."

"This can't wait until morning?" Tim said.

"Nope," Coop said, heading straight to the small kitchen table.

"Keep your voice down," Tim said. "Maisie's asleep in the other room."

"I'm awake!" Maisie said, poking her head around the door. "Hi, Kate!"

Kate! That's her name. "Go back to bed, Maisie," Tim said. "Coop's here on official business." Disappointed, Maisie's face slowly disappeared, but she left the door open a smidge. Tim went over and closed it. "Okay, what's this all about?"

Kate had her computer opened as Coop looked up at Tim. "Kate was out at Willow Flats and surprised a grizzly."

"You okay?" Tim said. She looked okay.

"I'm fine," she said. "That's not why we're here."

"What were you doing out there? Sally closed it to the public."

Coop lifted a hand to stop him. "I already gave her that talk, Tim. That's not why we're here."

Tim frowned. "But you went out there alone?"

"That's the thing," Kate said, tapping on her keyboard. "I wasn't alone. A shot rang out and scared the bear off."

Tim straightened. "A shot?"

"And that's why we're here," Coop said, turning the computer screen toward Tim.

Tim pulled out a chair and sat down. On the computer screen was a wide shot of Willow Flats. To the left, a large grizzly stood on its hind legs. "Bruno?"

"I think so," Coop said.

"I was hoping it was 399." Kate sounded disappointed.

Coop looked at her. "Definitely a he."

"I have to say that I'm impressed at how well you rangers know your bears."

Coop grinned. Tim noticed. Then Coop's grin faded when he realized Tim was watching him. "Now look to the far right."

Tim squinted. There were two fuzzy figures in front of a stand of trees. "Can you enlarge it?"

"It's already enlarged," Kate said.

"Rangers?" Tim said, hoping so.

"No one was scheduled to be up there. You said so at today's staff meeting."

Yeah, yeah, Tim knew. Which meant these two had no business being there. It meant they were hunters. Poachers.

"Tim," Coop said, "if you look closely, you can see one aiming a rifle."

Kate pointed. "I took these photos before the shot rang out."

Tim focused on the two fuzzy people, one tall, one small. And the small one held a rifle. "Think that's a child? Maybe a teen."

"I think it's a woman," Coop said. He exchanged a look with Kate. "Tim, look more closely. I think that figure could be Sally Janus."

Tim stared at him. "What? Why would you say such a thing?"

"She's holding the rifle in her left hand. And her hair." Coop waved a hand around his head. "Big fluffy blond hair. Plus Kate thought she saw a ranger jeep."

"Well, I think it was a ranger jeep. I wasn't paying close enough attention. But it was gone by the time I returned to my car."

Tim rose and crossed his arms. "That's pretty flimsy evidence to slap against Sally. Your boss and mine. A ranger who's loyal to the core."

"Slow down." Coop held up his palms. "I'm not accusing Sally of anything. I came right away to you. And this guy looks as tall as the ranger from Yellowstone who was in her office yesterday."

"What Yellowstone ranger? Coop, what are you talking about?"

Coop pointed to the picture. "That guy. Super tall. I met him in Sally's office. She said that he was on loan from Yellowstone. But that guy had soft hands."

"His hands," Tim said in a flat voice.

"They weren't calloused. What ranger doesn't have calloused hands?"

Tim frowned. "Coop, now you're worrying me. Is the Emma Dilemma keeping you up at night?"

Kate piped up. "What's Emma Dilemma?"

The bedroom door opened and Maisie's head popped out. "Emma is Coop's old girlfriend."

"Maisie!" Tim swiveled to bark at her. "Quit eavesdropping and go to bed."

The door quietly closed.

Tim turned to Kate. "Emma is Coop's former girlfriend and now his boss. She caused him a great deal of heartache. Still does."

"Hey!" Coop said, frowning at Tim. "Can we get back to the more serious issue here? I think you need to follow up with Sally. Just to rule her out."

"There's nothing to rule out."

"I hope you're right. It's just . . . she seems kind of . . ."

"Kind of what?" Tim said, annoyed.

"Different. More authoritative than I remember from last year. A little dictatorial."

"She wasn't the acting chief director last summer. Just a district ranger, like me. There's a lot on her plate this year."

"Maybe. But could you at least just find out where Sally was earlier tonight?"

Tim let out a huff. "I don't need to. I know she couldn't have been involved in this."

Coop raised his palms in the air. "How do you know?"

Tim rose to stand tall, hands on his hips. "Because if Sally Janus had fired a shot, she wouldn't have missed. She's a sharpshooter. Best I've ever seen, bar none."

After Coop and Zoo Girl left, Tim sat at the kitchen table, troubled. He refused to believe that Sally could be mixed up with anything illegal. No way. Not Sally. He'd never known another ranger who took her job more seriously. She acted like she was guardian of the park.

Coop was right about one thing—Sally was acting strangely lately. And who was this Yellowstone ranger on loan? Tim vaguely recalled that Maisie had said something about a tall ranger. Something about bumping into Sally and a Yellowstone ranger on the bicycle.

But Yellowstone didn't have surplus rangers to loan out. Even if there was a ranger on loan, Sally would've looped him in. Introduced him.

But that picture was hard to ignore. Granted, the two figures were fuzzy and distant, but as soon as Coop spoke Sally's name, Tim could see the resemblance.

He rubbed his forehead. Probably just a coincidence. He was 100 percent positive that Sally Janus would never be involved in something illegal.

As Tim got ready for bed, he couldn't shake the feeling that trouble was brewing. There were two incidents now of gunshots in areas that were off-limits to the public. That was an enormous concern.

As he lay in bed, staring at the ceiling, his mind kept wandering back to Sally. To how often she spoke of money worries. Quite a lot. He remembered a time when she had asked him how he had prepared for retirement. "Little by little," he said.

"From my very first paycheck, I've set money aside. Time plus money can work wonders."

A troubled look came over her. "The problem," she had said, "is when you've run out of time."

Tim heard the hoot of an owl, then another answer back. He rolled over to his side and punched his pillow a couple of times.

He was 99 percent sure Sally would never do something illegal.

Maybe 90 percent sure.

~

As Kate and Coop drove back to Oxbow Bend, the night air held a chill that seeped through the truck's windows. Kate, feeling a mix of relief and apprehension after the evening's events, turned to Coop. "Do most poachers get caught?"

"Not often enough," Coop said.

"Why do they risk poaching in a national park?"

He shrugged. "Lots of reasons. Trophy hunters want bragging rights. A living room rug or a head mounted on the wall or just a pelt. Ranchers want to get rid of anything that might threaten their livestock. Some poachers harvest body parts to sell for Asian medicines. And then there's just stupid people, looking for a good time."

"Wait. Back up. Did I hear you say . . . a poacher will harvest body parts?"

"Yeah. Like, for a bear's gallbladder. Apparently, it's an ingredient for an aphrodisiac. There's a big consumer demand in Asia."

Kate shuddered. "Are poachers after bears, mostly?"

"Bears, yes. Especially bruins. Boys are the prettiest of all bears. It's said they make great rugs."

Again, Kate shuddered.

"Wolves are targeted too. But most poachers go after elk,

moose, mule deer, pronghorn. They're sought out for their antlers, or hides and meat."

"Sounds like poaching is more common than I had realized."

"Not rampant, but not uncommon. Even if a poacher is caught, prosecution is a challenge. They usually plead self-defense. It's not illegal to kill an animal if it's threatening your life, even an endangered species. Evidence to convict has to be airtight. The LE rangers do their best, but it's a tough job."

"What's an LE ranger?"

"Law enforcement." Coop turned onto Teton Park Road. It was such a scenic route by day, with wilderness on both sides and the breathtaking view of the Teton Range. Even in the darkness, Kate was aware of its silent beauty. "So . . . um," she said, breaking the quiet, "Emma Dilemma." She cast a sideways glance at him. "Her surname isn't really Dilemma, is it?"

Coop's grip tightened on the steering wheel, his expression briefly clouded with uncertainty. "No. That's just Tim's lame humor." Then he went quiet.

"It's not really so lame. I can see how a little perspective in the wilderness can create relationship dilemmas. I've been having some serious doubts about my boyfriend."

He gave her a sharp look, then turned his attention back to the road. "Is that who keeps texting you?"

She sighed. "Yes." Over and over until she had to turn her phone completely off. "Something about this trip has . . . opened my eyes to a few things."

"I guess time apart can be illuminating." Again, he went quiet.

She waited a while before adding, "So is that what happened between you? Time apart shed some light on things?" What she really wanted to ask was if Tim Rivers called her Emma Dilemma because there was unfinished business between them. Why else would it be an ongoing dilemma?

Coop looked out the window, and Kate fretted she'd gone too far. After all, she hardly knew this man. But somehow, he made her feel very safe. Seen. She was trying to decide if she should apologize for prying, when he suddenly turned to her.

"Emma is my former fiancée. We were college sweethearts. We had this plan to be schoolteachers during the year and spend our summers as seasonal rangers. But . . . things didn't work out that way."

Kate sensed the weight behind Coop's words, the lingering hurt and confusion. "Can I ask what happened?"

Again, Coop hesitated, but she was discovering that his hesitations were a way of gathering his thoughts.

"I thought we were on the same page, but it turns out we weren't. She wanted one kind of life, and I wanted another. We just . . . couldn't make it work. And now she's the vice principal at my school and engaged to the principal. They're getting married this summer."

"Ouch." Kate nodded in understanding.

Coop cleared his throat. "So, how does this boyfriend feel about your interest in wildlife photography?"

She snorted. "Kinda like the other photographers. Like I'm playing at being a grown-up."

He gave her a sharp look. "That's not fair. It's not easy to be a beginner, but how else do you get experience?"

"I agree," she said, liking Coop all the more. "I'm learning that it's important to do the difficult things."

He nodded, slowly, not so much in agreement but as if he was listening carefully.

"Oliver has always had a very clear idea of the future and how he wants me to fit into it." She wasn't really sure why she was spilling her innermost thoughts to him, but it felt good to get it off her chest. "At first, I can't deny it was kind of dazzling. He's rather dazzling. But that feeling wore off and . . ."

192

"And what?"

"Well, let's just say that after one week in the park, I've changed."

He glanced at her. "What do you mean?"

"This might sound funny, but it's like God brought me here this week for a specific purpose." She could feel any self-consciousness lift and evaporate, like steam from a teacup, so she continued. "I sense God is calling me to something with my photography, like he's given me this desire and I need to listen to it." She turned slightly to face him. "I don't even know if you're someone who believes in God."

"I do."

She thought so. She'd just had that kind of feeling about him. "Even when I try to tell Oliver what I want, he doesn't really hear what I'm saying. It's like my desires don't count. Like . . . I don't count." Silence settled between them for a moment before Kate spoke again, her voice tinged with uncertainty. "I'm still trying to figure it out. I'm not sure I explained that very well."

"You explained it just fine."

They both fell silent, not knowing where to go next with the conversation. Coop's gaze remained fixed on the road ahead as they continued their journey. Kate wondered what thoughts were running through his mind, what memories of Emma Dilemma lingered in his heart.

Coop lay in bed that evening, tossing and turning as Frankie's window-rattling snoring filled the small room with a chorus of rumbles. Seriously, the kid could wake up the bears with that racket.

But it wasn't just Frankie's snoring that kept Coop awake. No, his mind was a swirling mess of thoughts, like a blender on overdrive.

That gunshot at Willow Flats just wouldn't leave him alone,

echoing in his head as if he'd been there himself. He couldn't shake the gut feeling that Chief Ranger Sally Janus was somehow entangled in the chaos. Recognizing her in that photograph had sent shivers down his spine, and he was certain Tim had felt the same.

Ever since Coop had arrived in the park, Sally's behavior had been off-kilter—yanking him from backcountry detail and replacing him with the Three Stooges. Added to that was her unreasonable restrictions, limiting public access to anywhere 399 could possibly roam. Closing areas went against everything Sally had preached about park ownership belonging to the people. It was like she was playing a game of park politics that Coop couldn't quite figure out. So not like the Sally Janus he'd worked for last summer.

The grizzly. That gunshot. Kate could've been seriously hurt.

He rolled over, staring at the ceiling. So . . . Kate had a boyfriend. Hearing that was like a punch to the gut. The first woman he'd had an interest in since Emma broke their engagement . . . and she had a boyfriend. A persistent one too, from what Coop could see. The kind of guy who put a claim on a girl and marked his territory.

He wondered how serious Kate's doubts were about this guy. When she spoke of him, her voice went distant. Was their relationship about to end? Or did she mean they just needed to make some changes? How did she describe that boyfriend? Oh yeah. Dazzling. He was a dazzling guy, she'd said.

Coop was anything but dazzling.

Wade Schmidt stood alone at the range's shooting line behind the hunting gear shop, his eyes locked on the butt up ahead. The unfamiliar weight and balance of the new bow in his hands contrasted sharply with the beloved one that had gone missing. It reminded him of how a violinist or cellist might feel when handed a new instrument just before a professional performance.

The bowstring felt tight under Wade's handgrip as he fitted the arrow in the nock, the yellow fletching pointed toward him, the carbon fiber shaft cool and smooth to the touch. His body aligned with the target as he pulled the bow to full draw with a steady, measured tension, anchoring against his face. Then, with a release as natural as a sigh, he released the bowstring and let the arrow fly, sending it hurtling.

The arrow's flight was a thing of beauty to Wade, cutting through the air with a whisper—hence the name of his favored bow. It struck the target dead center, right in the ten ring, a sign of the hours he'd poured into mastering this skill.

The shop owner, who'd been observing from a distance, approached the butt and whistled softly. "Bull's-eye," he said, admiration clear in his voice. "Apparently, you're not new at this."

Not hardly, Wade thought to himself, a smirk playing on his lips. But to the shop owner he said, "I'll take it. And I want a butt, as well."

FIFTEEN

Nature's peace will flow into you as sunshine flows into trees.
The winds will blow their own freshness into you,
and the storms their energy, while cares will drop
away from you like autumn leaves.
—*John Muir*

Tim made his way toward Sally's small office in the back of the visitor center, his footsteps echoing down the dimly lit hallway. The conversation with Coop and Kate had left him on edge, suspicions gnawing at him, and there was no way he was going to be able to sleep until he spoke to Sally. To ask her, straight up, where she'd been earlier tonight. He drove by her cabin, but her jeep wasn't there and the lights were out. Sally was a night owl. He decided to drive over to her office and see if she might be there. If nothing else, he wanted to see if her rifle was in the rifle case. It was always there, unless she was at target practice or needed it for official use. She wasn't a sport hunter. And if it was in its place, he could rest easy tonight.

Reaching the visitor center parking lot, he didn't see her jeep. He parked far off in the distance and fished his flashlight out of the glove compartment. Using his key, he went into the darkened visitor center, down the hallway, and knocked on Sally's door—knowing full well she wasn't there. Nervously, palms sweating, he slipped inside to shine the light on the rifle case against the wall. That's all he wanted to see. The only reason he was here, skulking around in the dark like a cat burglar. His heart hit the floor.

Sally's rifle wasn't there.

Before he could dwell on the implications, he heard voices coming from the interior door of the visitor center, and then a shuffle of footsteps approaching. Panic gripped him, and he ducked into the closet, pulling the door closed behind him just as Sally entered the room. He felt foolish, immature, and over-reactive. He would make a very bad spy. He thought about showing himself . . .

. . . until he heard a man's voice.

Holding his breath, Tim strained to hear the conversation, his heart pounding in his ears. Ear against the door, he heard the man say something that sent a shiver down his spine.

"So as soon as my client bags it, you'll get your money."

"Oh no," Sally said. "We had an agreement, darlin'. Fifty percent now, fifty percent after he's got what he came for."

Tim's pulse quickened. Money? What money? And bagged what?

The response came in a low murmur, barely audible through the closet door. "Fine. Fifty percent now, and fifty percent after the bear pelt is in my client's trunk."

"You ever going to tell me," Sally asked, "just who this client is?"

"I'm not." Then came the sound of a thunk on top of the desk, a crisp thank-you from Sally, and the sound of a metal drawer opening and shutting.

As the pieces of the puzzle fell into place, a sickening realization washed over Tim. He couldn't believe Sally—the best, most dedicated ranger he'd ever known—could be involved in plundering the park's wildlife for profit. *His* Sally. His sweetheart.

Tim strained to listen as Sally and the man continued their conversation. He heard the door open and shut, then their voices grew faint as they moved down the hallway toward the door that led to the area open to the public.

As soon as he heard the door click shut, Tim opened the closet a smidge to peer out. Empty. He let out a breath of relief. The lights were off, and he heard the sound of cars start up outside, so he assumed they wouldn't be back. Quietly, he slipped out of the closet. He turned his flashlight on and noticed that her rifle was now back in the rifle case. He shone the light over Sally's desktop, cluttered by the familiar maps and paperwork that constituted her daily routine.

The bottom left drawer of her desk was slightly ajar and he pulled it open to find a fat envelope. He grabbed the envelope and peered inside to find a thick wad of hundred-dollar bills. Heart pounding, he tucked it into his shirt and headed down the hallway and out the back door.

No. He wasn't going to rest easy tonight.

Coop couldn't shake off the odd encounter he'd just had with Sally Janus. In the middle of the night, she'd woken him and told him to meet her in the parking lot. "Now," she said. "I'm waiting for you. And come alone."

Wide awake, he quickly threw on some clothes and ran a hand through his hair, trying to figure out what was happening. Meanwhile, Frankie was still in the land of Nod, snoring loudly. Oblivious.

Outside, it took Coop a while to find Sally's jeep. It took her flashing her headlights once or twice for him to notice where she'd parked. He climbed into the passenger seat. "What's up?"

Sally looked Coop right in the eyes. "You know where 399's den is, don't you?"

When he started to sputter that he wasn't absolutely sure, she waved him off, as if she knew that he knew. And he did.

"Tomorrow," she said, "I want you to hike up Pilgrim Creek and find out if she's alive. If there's any evidence that she's left the lair, let me know. Report back to me with coordinates. Use my cell phone, not the radio."

"Why? What's the deal with all the secrecy?"

"Extra precautions to protect her." She pointed to him. "Tell no one if and when and where you see her. Only me. That's an order."

Stunned, Coop didn't know how to respond. Something seemed shady. Sketchy. He thought about asking Sally if she'd been at Willow Flats and fired a shot . . . but he held back. Tim seemed so sure that Sally wouldn't have missed her target. From the look on her face right now, Coop thought he was probably right. She might be small, but she could be fierce.

"Have I been clear, darlin'?" Sally said, softening a bit.

"Crystal clear."

"Then, off you go. Nighty night." To underline the point that this discussion was over, she started up her jeep. He had hopped out, glad this odd midnight rendezvous was over.

Candidly, he was not at all unhappy to be given an order to go find 399. He'd been wanting to head back up there. Sally had said not to tell anyone if and where and when he saw evidence that 399 was alive . . . or dead. She didn't tell him not to bring anyone along with him. The buddy system was always the best system.

So why not invite Kate along? The den was at a high elevation, but she seemed to be in good physical condition. If he took it slow and steady, he thought she'd be up to the steep hike. And it could give Kate an opportunity to capture that one-in-a-million shot she wanted. Just so long as Sally never found out how she got it.

The morning mist hung low over Pilgrim Creek as Kate set up her camera, waiting along with dozens of other photographers for a first glimpse of 399. The other photographers leaned against their cars, talking quietly. Everyone was waiting, waiting, waiting. Growing impatient.

Kate heard someone call her name and turned to find Coop approaching.

"Morning," he said softly, his breath forming small clouds in the chilly air.

"Good morning, Coop," she said, a smile spreading across her face.

Coop glanced around before leaning in closer. "Thanks again for sharing those photos last night."

"I'm glad I could help."

He took another step closer to her, his eyes fixed on the tree line. "If you have time today, I thought I could make good on that promise to help you out."

Kate's heart skipped a beat. So he had decided to help her! She tried to keep her cool on, whatever Frankie's saying meant. "Has there been a sighting of 399?"

Coop held up a hand. "Not yet. And no promises for one, either. We still don't know if she's made it through the winter."

Kate nodded eagerly, barely able to contain her excitement. She loved that he called the bear a *her*, not an *it*. "I understand. Coop, thank you."

Down the line of photographers, he squinted. "Frankie! You're not to take food from the photographers."

Halfway through a doughnut, Frankie frowned at him with a look on his face like, *What's the big deal?*

"That kid." He let out a weary sigh. "I'd better go. Meet me at the Jenny Lake Visitor Center at noon. Be sure you've had something to eat. Wear a lot of layers and good hiking boots. We'll be going through snowy areas. And bring plenty of water.

It's a long hike." He took a few steps, then stopped and turned around. "Maybe you should take my phone number, just in case you change your mind."

Oh, trust me. Nothing could stop me from this mission. She pulled out her phone and handed it to him. "Enter your number and I'll text you back so you'll have mine."

Coop grinned. He took her phone and typed in his contact number. "See you at noon."

Noon. Seven hours from now. How was Kate going to wait so long?

She found herself torn between two equally exciting prospects: the chance to capture 399 in a photograph, and spending a whole afternoon with Coop. It was a surprise even to herself—she was ready to tackle a treacherous, snowy, uphill trek into the wilderness, if it meant Coop would be right by her side. This kind of bravery was new to her, but she was willing to embrace it for the sake of this adventure.

A few hours later, after a shower and shampoo, Kate gazed in the mirror one more time. She looked as if she was going out on a date. Not what she was after. She gathered her hair up and put it into a ponytail, wondering if this was what Maisie was trying to imitate. She eyed herself. *Yes.* Casual but serious. Relaxed but focused. Laid-back but purposeful. She checked her camera bag a second time, just to make sure all batteries were fully charged. Her phone rang and she picked it up without checking caller ID, thinking it might be Coop.

"Katie-Kat! Where have you been? I've been calling and texting. I've been worried!"

She glanced at the clock near the bed. "Oliver, I'm sorry. This isn't a good time to talk. There's someplace I need to be in a few minutes."

He let out an irritated huff, loud enough for her to hear. "What about later? What time will you be back?"

She knew he was annoyed, but she was glad he didn't pry any further. She could feel guilt creep over her. Guilt about avoiding him. Guilt about her delight in spending the afternoon with Coop. She cupped her forehead with her free hand. "I'm not exactly sure."

"Before sunset?"

"Yeah, definitely. I would think so. I'll be back before sunset. I'll try and call you later."

"Before sunset, then. For sure."

"Gotta go." She hung up and hurried out the door, now running late.

Coop was waiting out in front of the Jenny Lake Visitor Center. Even as rushed as she felt, she took a moment to notice how appealing he looked in his ranger uniform. No wonder there was a *thing* about men in uniforms. His face lit up with a smile when he saw her, and it made her feel all soft and mushy inside.

"Ready? Let's go." He took her backpack from her and started toward his truck. At one point, he stopped in the parking lot. "Is that the kind of car you saw last night at Willow Flats?" He pointed to a ranger's jeep.

"I think so. I'm pretty sure. I have to admit that I didn't pay much attention to it."

He opened up the door to the truck for Kate, and it occurred to her that Oliver rarely displayed that kind of chivalry. It wasn't his fault, of course. He hadn't grown up with a father who would've modeled how to treat a woman.

She found herself constantly comparing the two men, although she knew that was silly. After all, she'd just met Coop. Yet he always seemed to outshine Oliver.

"So," Kate said, "when you're not here as a seasonal ranger, you're a schoolteacher."

"I am."

"Do you like being a teacher?"

"Yeah, I really do. My folks are both teachers, so it's kind of a family business. Having summers off was the best part—we spent those months on adventures. Modest ones, mostly camping, but as a kid, it was heaven. Mom and Dad and my brother and me, all jammed into a tent. All summer long." He grinned. "As I recall, Mom might have preferred a tent to herself." He chuckled. "What I really like about my summers is that it gives me a chance to recharge my batteries, so when I get back to the classroom in the fall, I'm ready for another school year. I like learning. I like seeing the light go on in kids' minds."

"School was so hard for me," Kate said. "I grew up in a family that values higher education in a big, big way. My mom and dad are professors."

"Both?" He let out a short whistle. "Professors?"

"Yep. My brother's on the same track. But I could barely get through high school. Dyslexia."

"Did you get help for it?"

"Yes, but it wasn't diagnosed until I was older."

The truck hit a bump in the road, jolting them both. "Your mind works differently from other people. It's not a bad thing."

"Well, it feels pretty bad when you're failing subjects."

"Yeah, I get that. I've had a couple of students who've had dyslexia. I like to show them that the world needs different thinkers. Thomas Edison had dyslexia. ADHD too. Albert Einstein, Leonardo da Vinci. I don't consider dyslexia to be a disability. The tricky part is how to help kids make it an asset." He glanced at her. "Like you're doing."

"Me? How am I making it an asset?"

"Dyslexia might be the very reason why you have such a good eye for photographs."

"You think I have a good eye?"

He cracked the window a little, almost as if releasing a little . . . intimacy . . . that was building between them. "Oh yeah.

Not just a good eye, but I'm still amazed you had the presence of mind to stand your ground with Bruno and get those shots . . . They were incredible."

She looked at him. "Thank you. That means a lot." More than she could express. "I have a hunch you're a pretty popular teacher."

He shrugged, but he seemed pleased. "So-so. But I do like the balance of teaching and being a ranger. It's a nice life." He glanced at her. "Can I ask you something personal?"

"Shoot."

"How does this boyfriend of yours make you feel about your dyslexia?"

Kate cringed. "Actually, I haven't told him."

"Whoa. Isn't that significant?"

"That I haven't wanted to tell him? Yes. Yes, I suppose it is." There was just something about Oliver that made her feel as if she had to hide that part of her. So many parts of her. Like her deep faith that she found hard to express. They attended church together on Sundays, yet Oliver never had much to say about the sermon. Nothing positive, anyway. Mostly, he offered critiques. It occurred to her recently that she'd never heard him pray aloud. Grace before a meal was offered in a moment of silence.

They drove in comfortable quiet for a while, the hum of the engine filling the space between them. Finally, Kate spoke up again. "Can I ask *you* something personal?"

"Shoot."

"Do you think Emma is a good principal? Is she good at her job?"

Coop pondered her question for a moment. "She's dedicated, compassionate, and she knows how to connect with parents and kids. Like, she stands at the gate every morning and shakes hands with every single kid as they arrive for the day. Yeah, she's a very good principal." He went quiet for a long while after that, and she thought it best not to ask anything more about Emma for now.

Kate studied him for a moment, pondering how conversation came so easily with Coop. She'd shared more about herself in this one conversation with him than she had in six months of dating Oliver.

Maisie pedaled her bike as fast as her legs could manage, heading up the scenic path that led to Jenny Lake Lodge. As she sailed past the lodge toward the stable, her eyes lit up at the sight of the string of horses, lined up and ready for the afternoon trail ride. She *adored* horses.

Dropping her bike by the paddock, Maisie eagerly approached the horses. She reached out to pat the long neck of a horse, relishing in the softness of its coat. Another horse nudged closer, seeking attention. Maisie laughed. "Okay, okay, I can pet you both!"

"Is that the bike you're riding? A BMX?"

Maisie spun around to see Frankie pushing a wheelbarrow filled with straw and manure. "Frankie! What are you doing here?"

He raised an eyebrow at her bike. "Why are you riding a little kid's bike?"

"I know," she said, her voice heavy with disappointment. "Pops's bike has a flat tire. This was my only transportation option."

Frankie shook his head with a smirk. "A BMX. Kid, how many times do I have to tell you to keep your cool on?"

"I'm *not* a kid," Maisie said, frowning. "So what are you doing here, anyway?"

"Menial labor without pay," Frankie grumbled, setting down the wheelbarrow. "The handler's short-staffed, so Coop volunteered me."

"I was hoping there'd be space for me on today's trail ride," Maisie said wistfully, glancing at the saddled horses.

"Yeah, there's plenty of space," Frankie replied. "The ride starts in about half an hour. See that lady over by the saddled horses? She'll have you sign a lengthy release form so you can't sue anybody if you fall off the horse and break your neck." He paused, squinting at her. "Wait a minute. Have you ever ridden a horse?"

Maisie looked down at her sneakers. If she answered this truthfully, she may not be able to go on a trail ride. She lifted her head. "Fun fact. The horses used for trail rides are bred and trained specifically for being, well, trail horses. They undergo specialized training to ensure they are well-behaved, responsive to commands, and suitable for riders of various skill levels." She'd read that very thing in a brochure at the visitor center.

Frankie chuckled. "Well, these trail horses are ready for retirement at Shady Acres. Tell that lady that the trail boss said you're fit for our ride."

"Wait." Her heart started to pound. "Are you going to be on this trail ride too?"

"Yep. I'll bring up the rear. I just need to finish cleaning a few more stalls first."

Maisie stared at him. "Is there nothing you can't do?" Frankie was UH-mazing.

He rolled his eyes, but there was a hint of amusement in his expression. "I can't seem to stop myself from getting kicked out of boarding schools." He picked up the handles of the wheelbarrow and went off to the compost pile to dump it.

Maisie went over to speak to the woman and signed the papers for the trail ride. Then she went looking for Frankie and found him in a horse stall, mucking it out. "So why do you keep getting kicked out of boarding school?"

Frankie looked up from his task, a mixture of surprise and

annoyance on his face. "Because it makes my dad mad." He heaved his pitchfork's load into the wheelbarrow. "Then he gets back at me by forcing me into indentured servanthood each summer." He straightened his back to stretch. "It's a game we play."

"Where does your dad live?"

"Washington DC."

"What about your mom?"

A shadow crossed his face. "She's dead."

She felt stupid for being so nosy. "I'm sorry."

"You wouldn't know." Frankie waved off her concern and resumed work.

"Well, I've never even met my dad. He vanished when my mom told him she was pregnant."

Frankie took a break from shoveling. "Where is your mom?"

"Right now?" Maisie leaned against the stall door. "She's at some kind of spiritual retreat."

"So that's why you're staying with your grandfather?"

"Yep. Mom got fired from her art teaching job cuz she only let the students use black and gray and brown colors."

"What's wrong with that?"

"Well, it was a watercolor class for spring flowers. Supposed to be cheerful." She sighed. "Anyway, then we had to move out of the apartment cuz Mom couldn't pay the rent. This nice lady named Rebecca Woodbine let us live in her basement and then treated Mom to this retreat. Rebecca thinks Mom'll find herself there."

Frankie smirked. "Like, your mom's gone missing?"

"Not exactly, but kind of. Like, some of her has gone missing. At least, that's what Rebecca told Mom. Something about how she needed to dig deep to find herself." Maisie had to piece it all together from bits of conversation she'd overheard. "Rebecca told Mom that this retreat would be *life-changing*." From the latest texts she'd sent, it didn't sound like that was happening. "My mom doesn't like to be told what to do." Or how to think.

Frankie placed the pitchfork against the stall wall. "Your mom should meet my dad. They sound a lot alike." He pushed the barrow past her and out to the compost pile.

Maisie's heart soared at that remark. It seemed like a clear signal that Frankie had the same longing to stay close to her as she did for him.

Unless . . . he was joking. Was he?

Wade felt a growing sense of foreboding after the turncoat missed shooting the bear. Feldmann explained that the problem was a person taking pictures in the flats, and the turncoat couldn't risk shooting the person. Instead, she fired a warning shot to scare the bear off. After all, Feldmann reminded him, the turncoat was a park ranger.

Wade felt his ears prick, like a dog's. Something felt off to him.

Taking an arrow from the quiver, Wade fixed his eyes on the butt. Thanks to the many restricted areas of the park—and, on this note, he had to hand it to Feldmann because the turncoat had practically shut the park down—he had found several remote fields for target practice. He was able to concentrate in complete and total solitude. And practice he did. Hours upon hours. Waiting for word from Feldmann's insider source that the bear had emerged from its den.

The new bow felt foreign in his hands, lacking the familiar weight and balance of Whisper. Working with an economy of motion, Wade pulled back the string into a full draw. With a swift release, the arrow soared through the air, hitting the target with slightly less precision than he was accustomed to. He frowned, dissatisfied with the result.

With each arrow he loosed, he fought a growing frustration as he worked to adjust to the unfamiliar weapon. The arrows hit the target, but without the pinpoint accuracy he had come to expect with Whisper.

After a few more attempts, Wade sighed and lowered the bow. Trying to take down a four-hundred-pound bear with a bow and arrow was a bold and risky move. Practice would eventually improve his proficiency with this new bow, but it would never replace the confidence he had with Whisper.

Could he be losing his edge?

He walked across the field to retrieve his arrows from the butt. Suddenly, he stopped, turned slowly in a circle, listened for . . . for what? He wasn't sure. He just knew he felt nervous, uneasy. He didn't like the feeling. Not at all.

SIXTEEN

Nature does not hurry, yet everything is accomplished.
—*Lao Tzu, Chinese philosopher*

Coop kept stealing glances at Kate as they checked their back-packs one more time before locking up the truck at the parking area off Pilgrim Creek Road. He had to smile at the shiny new string of bells hanging off her backpack. He was pleased she'd listened to him after her Willow Flats scare.

"I haven't been this far north. Are we close to Yellowstone?"

"Very close," Coop said.

They started up the trail that led from Middle Pilgrim Creek to Wildcat Peak Trail. His heart was racing and he didn't know if it was because of the task ahead, the altitude, or because he was spending time alone, quite intentionally, with Kate. He did know that he felt stomach-twisting nervous, like he was sixteen again and asking a girl out for the first time in his life.

He really hoped this afternoon might give Kate a chance to get that special photograph she was after. She deserved it, if for no other reason than her resiliency. It impressed him. He'd overheard the daily digs from the other photographers. And it sounded like her own family and jerk-boyfriend had their own share of doubts about her abilities. Imagine growing up with undiagnosed dyslexia in a family full of PhDs. Yet she'd found her own path, despite facing obstacles along the way.

What Coop didn't anticipate was the unexpected connection he felt with Kate, one that seemed to deepen each time they interacted. It reminded him of how he had felt with Emma, long ago. And yet, it was different too. Better. He didn't think he'd ever meet someone who could make him forget his feelings for Emma.

In a good way, Kate threw him off balance, made him reassess things. When she questioned him about Emma's role as a principal, it caught him off guard. He'd never really considered it before. The truth was, Emma excelled in her role.

As they headed up the steep rise of the Middle Pilgrim Creek Trail, single file, the rushing creek didn't allow time for talking but it did for reflecting. Kate seemed lost in her own thoughts too, and he wondered what was running through her mind. He hoped she might be thinking about breaking up with the jerk-boyfriend. He considered him a jerk because—hard to admit but it was true—he reminded Coop of himself, back when he was with Emma. It struck a chord, resonating with Tim's question about Emma's sudden change of heart. Had he been blind to the signs, too consumed with planning their future to notice Emma's feelings shifting beneath the surface?

Getting to know Kate, seeing her situation with the jerk-boyfriend through her perspective, gave him a stark clarity of how he had stifled Emma. Same thing that this guy was doing to Kate. She deserved better.

And Emma had deserved better.

Which meant that he'd been just as selfish and obtuse as Kate's jerk-boyfriend. He'd been so determined to plot the future that he hadn't taken into account how Emma's feelings were changing. And she kept accommodating him until she couldn't do it anymore.

Coop saw it clearly now. He'd been so focused on his own desires that he hadn't given her the space to flourish in her own right. Emma was thriving in her role as principal, doing precisely what she was meant to do.

He took a deep breath, as if stung by a bee. Shamed. It was time to truly let go of Emma. To let her off the hook. Yes, she had hurt him deeply. But he had a role in that too. He shared responsibility in the demise of their relationship.

It was as simple and as painful as that.

"Hey, Coop?"

He stopped and turned to see that Kate had fallen far behind. Her face was red, she was puffing from exertion. Argh. He was doing it again! Moving at his own pace, not thinking about someone else.

"Can we take a water break?"

They were exiting the cover of trees, so he knew he was close to the intersection of Wildcat Peak Trail. "We're almost to a place where it'll level off a bit. We can rest there."

She nodded, but he knew she was running out of steam. Just ahead, he spotted a fallen log in full sun to lean against, to rest and rehydrate. "You doing okay? Too cold? Too hot? Want me to carry your backpack?"

She shook her head. "I'm fine. I just need to take a little break." She unscrewed the cap on her water bottle and took some swallows.

And kept gulping. Coop scolded himself at how thirsty she'd been. The trail that followed Pilgrim Creek rose rapidly, a steep ascent of thousands of feet. The narrow path was muddy in most places too, and they had to traverse several water crossings, dead falls, and go-arounds. It wasn't an easy hike for him, and he was accustomed to backcountry hikes. He should have warned her that they'd be aiming straight up for the headwaters of the creek. He watched her carefully for signs of overexertion, but she seemed to be recovering quickly. A good sign. Her face was less flushed, and her breathing was back to normal.

"It's so beautiful here," she said.

"Even prettier in the fall, when the trees are in full color. Spruce, aspen, white bark pine. Now that's a sight worth photographing."

"You've been here often?"

"A couple of times. Tim and I spent a few days up here last fall, before the park closed for the season."

She took another swallow of water, but less like she was parched, so he decided to keep talking. He pointed to the meadow in front of them. "Hard to imagine that brown field, still with patches of snow, will be full of wildflowers in a month or so. Full of bears too. Tim calls it a grizzly-strewn meadow."

Swallowing a sip of water, she practically choked. Her eyes went wide as she looked over the meadow. "How many?"

"Grizzlies in the park? Hundreds of 'em. And Yellowstone's got even more." He gestured in that direction. It dawned on him that he might be freaking her out. "But don't stress, I've got bear radar—always keeping an eye out."

"I sure hope so, Ranger."

Yeah, he was spooking her. "Here's something cool about bears that I didn't mention in my ranger spiel. They have a habit of sitting for long periods at vista points, just staring. Scientists think they might have the ability to interpret the beauty of nature."

Gazing out at the meadow, Kate quietly said, "'But ask the animals, and they will teach you, or the birds in the sky, and they will tell you; or speak to the earth, and it will teach you, or let the fish in the sea inform you. Which of all these does not know that the hand of the LORD has done this? In his hand is the life of every creature and the breath of all mankind.'"

"Bible verse?" Coop said.

She looked a little embarrassed. "Yes. From the book of Job."

"You've memorized it?"

"Well, not the whole book. But I do love that verse. And I learned at an early age to memorize. Compensation for not being much of a reader."

See? There was that resiliency again. "Tim would be pleased to hear you quote the Bible," Coop said. "He's always trying to get me to go to church with him."

"Have you gone?"

"A couple of times." But he thought he might start going regularly this summer.

"You and Tim seem to know each other well. Have you worked for him a long time?"

"A couple of years. He's the one who talked me into being a seasonal ranger. He helped me get a job here at Grand Teton. These jobs are super competitive. Everyone's after the plum assignments. He's a great guy to work for. I've learned a lot from Tim."

"Like what?"

"Like . . . trusting your gut instincts. He's big on that. Most of the problems in life can be solved by listening to intuition, he says, so pay attention to it, especially when it rears up. As much training and protocol as rangers receive, Tim has always said that gut instinct will serve you best."

She gave him a look that he had trouble reading. He pulled out his own water bottle and drank from it.

After a while, he said, "Feeling okay?" He thought she'd fully recovered, but now she seemed awfully quiet.

"Feeling great." She gave him a side glance. "You've got me thinking."

"Yeah? About bears among wildflowers?" That made her smile. *Man*, she had a nice smile.

"About trusting your gut." She took a swig of water, swallowed, then turned to him. "About making some changes in my life."

He tapped his water bottle against hers. "Cheers to that." He wondered what changes she might be considering and hoped it might include rethinking this jerk-boyfriend. It's not that Coop was the type of guy who would ever come between a couple, but it sounded to him like this guy wasn't ready for the give-and-take of a real relationship. Not yet. Just like Coop hadn't been ready for one with Emma. He thought he was, but he wasn't. Not really.

However, watching Kate's profile as she gazed at the meadow in front of them, he thought he might have found a reason to be ready now.

Maisie sat on a park bench at the Jenny Lake Visitor Center, her legs kicking excitedly against her BMX bicycle tire as she chatted on the phone with Kate's boyfriend, Oliver. He had texted her early this morning to set up a time to talk about surprising Kate. Since then, she'd been nearly bursting with enthusiasm, her mind running wild with ideas for the perfect marriage proposal.

"Okay, okay, hear me out," Maisie said, barely pausing for breath. "You could rent a skywriter to fly overhead and write the words 'Marry me.'"

"Um, no," he said.

"How about hiring a flash mob to dance and sing while you pop the question?"

"No."

"Too much? Okay. I've got more ideas. What do you think about taking her on a treasure hunt around the park, and at the end, there's a hidden ring waiting for her?"

"Well, that's an improvement on the first two ideas." Oliver sounded unimpressed. "All I need from you is to know when and where Kate will be later tonight, before sunset. I need your help to make sure she's in the right place when I arrive."

Maisie's enthusiasm dimmed. "Oh, right, of course. Sorry, I just got a little excited there. Where do you want Kate to be?"

"Is there some general location to meet up? A place where people go to hang out?"

Maisie looked around. "Well, the Jenny Lake Visitor Center is easy to find. There's a big patio in front of it. It can get crowded, though."

"Sounds ideal."

"And then I thought you'd both drive over to Oxbow Bend for the big event."

"Why there?"

"Because . . . it's so memorable. So impressive. But there might be a crowd there too."

He chuckled. "I'm not worried about crowds. The whole world is welcome to watch me propose to Kate."

Maisie practically swooned.

"I'll be at the Jenny Lake Visitor Center thirty minutes before sunset."

"Gotcha. I'll be wearing a yellow down jacket. You can't miss me."

"Just be sure that Kate is there. Thanks, Mary. I appreciate your help."

"Maisie," she corrected. Before he could hang up, she said, "Wait a minute. Have you given plenty of thought about what you'll say? You need a romantic speech that'll make her cry happy tears."

"I'll worry about the speech. You worry about getting Kate to the right place at the right time."

"Got it, got it," Maisie said. "One more item on the agenda. We haven't talked specifics about the ring. The right ring can make or break the proposal."

"And you know this because . . ."

She scoffed. "Because I watch *The Bachelor*." Obviously. "You gotta go big with the ring. Break the bank."

Oliver laughed. "Thanks. I'll keep that in mind. I'll talk to you soon."

"Okay, bye!" Maisie said cheerfully, but he'd already ended the call.

She had barely put her phone back in her pocket when Frankie flopped down on the bench beside her, his eyes narrowing with suspicion. "What are you up to?"

"I shouldn't really say . . . but . . . promise you won't tell Kate?"

"Tell her what?"

She scooted over a few inches on the bench. "Kate's boyfriend is planning an epic surprise marriage proposal. He's heading to the Grand Tetons today!" She expected Frankie to look pleased, but a scowl darkened his expression.

"What makes you think Kate wants him to come here?"

"Um"—she tried not to sound too know-it-all-ish—"because he's her boyfriend. Of course she wants him here."

Frankie shook his head. "I've spent a lot of time with Kate these last few days. A lot. And she's never once mentioned a boyfriend to me."

Huh. Actually, Kate had never mentioned Oliver to Maisie, either.

Frankie raised an eyebrow. "What do you even know about this guy? Where does he live? Where does he work?"

Maisie's enthusiasm faltered. "Um . . . I'm not sure."

"How long have they been dating?"

Maisie hesitated. "Sounds like . . . for a while?"

Frankie whistled two notes, one up, one down. "Clearly, you know a lot."

Maisie felt a bit deflated.

"Kate told me it took her months and months to save enough money for this trip."

"Yeah, but—"

"But nothing. She's working really hard to break into the wildlife photography world. This guy will do nothing but distract her."

"She can get back to her picture taking after she's engaged. Trust me. Girls *dream* of a proposal like this."

"You should give Kate a heads-up about this."

"No way! And don't you dare tell her. You promised me."

"No, I didn't."

Shoot. He was right. She should have exacted a promise out of him before she spilled the beans. "Well, I made a promise to Oliver that I'd help him with the surprise proposal."

Frankie made a *tsk tsk* sound.

"What?"

"You're making a big mistake."

"I'm not! Oliver asked me for his help and I said yes."

"Right. You just want to feel important."

Maisie opened her mouth to object . . . but there was some truth in that. Not entirely, though. "Frankie, you don't realize how significant this moment will be for Kate and Oliver. Someday they'll tell their children and grandchildren all about it. Imagine . . . getting engaged at Grand Teton National Park!"

"Seems to me," Frankie said, "you're meddling in something you have no business with." He leaned back, crossing his arms. "You know what they say about meddling, right? 'To force nature is to do her harm.'"

Bleh! Why couldn't he just talk normal? "Um . . . meaning . . ."

"When you try to control everything, it can totally backfire and mess things up big-time."

Frankie got up and walked away, leaving Maisie sputtering

218

with outrage. "Control everything? Me? I'm just trying to help people with love!"

Without turning back, Frankie lifted his shoulders in a shrug.

What was *his* problem? Why was he so upset?

Hold it. A thought came out of nowhere, like a sudden storm cloud, casting a shadow of doubt over her excitement. Could it be that Frankie had more than a schoolboy's crush on Kate? Was he . . . in *love* with her?

This was a tragic discovery! Maisie had set her own heart on Frankie, but now, after he practically made a declaration of his devotion to Kate, her hopes felt like fragile glass, ready to shatter at any moment.

She sighed, leaning back against the bench. Love was so complicated.

Wade had *told* Feldmann to make sure the hotel staff did not enter his room, not for any purposes. But today, when he returned from archery practice, he found his room had been cleaned, vacuumed, sheets changed, and worst of all, his highly valuable papers—topographic maps, satellite imagery, bear anatomy charts, aerial photographs—had been tidied up and stacked, like they were today's junk mail.

Topping that off, Feldmann was calling to tell him that he saw a bear near Mormon Row. "I thought you might want to try some target practice with the new bow."

"Feldmann," Wade said, his voice tight and sharp, "who else might be sighted near Mormon Row?"

There was a very long pause. "Oh. Right. Rangers."

"Exactly." Mormon Row was one of the most visited sights in Grand Teton National Park. Wade had driven by it nearly each day. He wasn't all that surprised that a bear might be roaming the area, as there was vegetation and fast-flowing streams—all things bears sought.

Wade was *this* close to firing Feldmann and calling off the hunt. If he weren't so deeply invested in it, if he hadn't promised his mother that this would be the last one, he'd do just that. Hiring Feldmann had been the worst decision he'd ever made.

Feldmann had been highly recommended by a big game hunter, Jack Miller, whom Wade had known for a couple of years. Jack and Wade shared a similar philosophy about hunting and were some of the few who didn't use apps on their smartphones, like onX Hunt, to provide GPS, satellite imagery, or to track movement. Using technology was cheating. Wade scoffed at it. And so did Jack.

So when Wade put out word that he was looking for a seasoned scout (frontman) for an inside job (inside the park), he took Jack at his word when he vouched for Feldmann. Not just vouched. He sang the guy's praises.

Something occurred to Wade. A hunch.

"Feldmann, by any chance . . . are you related to Jack Miller?"

"Uh . . . well, I, uh, I married his little sister."

Bull's-eye.

SEVENTEEN

Look deep into nature, and then you will
understand everything better.
—*Albert Einstein*

Two hours later, after hiking what felt like a never-ending vertical ascent, Kate was struggling again to keep pace with Coop. Just as she was about to voice her exhaustion, he came to a sudden halt, his gaze fixed ahead. Peering through his binoculars, he scanned the landscape before dropping them.

He pointed to a hillside. "There is 399's lair. At least, it was last year's den. I saw her coming in and out last spring. Bears usually reuse their dens, or they den in the same area."

Shielding her eyes from the glare of the sun, Kate strained to see. "I see nothing but trees and thick brush and granite."

Coop handed her his binoculars. "About halfway up, there's a big hole under a huge Douglas fir tree. It's an earthen den."

It took Kate a long moment before she spotted exactly what he had described. "Is this as close as we can get?"

"Yeah, I don't want to risk getting any closer. She'd catch our scent in the wind. A hungry bear coming out of hibernation is not one you want to tangle with." Coop scanned the surroundings. "Can you set up your camera from here?"

"I think so." It was farther away than she had hoped to the cave's opening, but it would have to do.

"While you set up, I'm going to explore a little and see if I can find any evidence that she's been out of the den. I won't be far. I'll be in sight at all times. But if you need help, blow on your world's loudest whistle."

As he ventured off to explore the area below the den, Kate settled on the ground, getting her equipment ready, all the while sneaking glances at Coop. The way he looked at her! His gray eyes held such concern and steady reassurance, making her feel like she was nailing it—even though she was struggling to keep pace with him. Coop had this knack for making her believe she could conquer the world.

Here she was, perched atop a freezing mountain, setting up her beloved camera to capture that elusive bear. It was a task she never imagined, but Coop's faith in her abilities made her feel brave. The sheer joy and excitement bubbling inside her were intoxicating. It was amazing what a difference having someone in your corner could make.

Unzipping her backpack, she retrieved her camera bag and carefully attached her 200–600 mm lens. Peering through the viewfinder, she aimed at the den's entrance. Not ideal, but it was her best chance for a shot.

Setting the motion detection functionality for still photography, Kate hoped her battery would hold up. Tonight's cold temperatures might deplete it. She didn't let on to Coop, but it did worry her to leave her precious camera unattended overnight. Any wild animal could easily destroy it, even if just out of curiosity. If a rainstorm hit tonight, it would ruin it. If a gust of wind knocked it over, it could shatter.

She'd spent months saving to buy this specialized equipment. This was a significant risk, both financially and professionally. She placed the front leg of the tripod firmly into a deep crevice in a boulder, thinking that might keep it from toppling in the wind. Wiping down every inch of her camera and tripod with unscented wet wipes, once, then twice, Kate ensured it was as inconspicuous as possible, just as Coop returned to her. "All set?"

"Did you find any sign of her?"

"I'll tell you on the way down. We should get going before the weather changes and the wind picks up." He pointed to the low and overcast sky. "Are you ready to head back?"

Inhaling, she felt a burst of energy. "I'm ready." She hoisted her backpack on and glanced one more time at her camera, saying a prayer that she knew was the right one to pray. *Lord, thy will be done here.*

This might not even work.

But it might.

And if it did, this could be the one-in-a-million shot Kate came to the park to get.

Maisie's anticipation bubbled as she waited outside the Jenny Lake Visitor Center, her phone clutched tightly in one hand, a dozen red roses in the other. It was actually *happening*! Oliver decided to take Maisie's advice and propose to Kate at Oxbow Bend at sunset. Maisie planned to film the whole event on her iPhone. She couldn't wait to see the look on Kate's face when Oliver popped the question.

The only glitch in the plan was that Maisie had no idea where Kate had gone all day. Or when she'd be back. It was a sizable glitch.

As Maisie paced in front of the visitor center, she spotted Frankie and ran over to him. "Hey, Frankie! Do you know where Kate is?"

"No."

"Do you know where Coop went?"

"No. Why should I? No one tells me anything."

"But Coop is your roommate. You're his intern. You must have some idea where he went. He's been gone all afternoon."

"All I know is that Coop said he's doing ranger work and I should butt out."

"Oh."

"What's the big deal? Why are you looking for Coop and Kate?"

Maisie felt as if she might burst with excitement. "It's happening! Tonight! Oliver's coming to the park to propose to Kate tonight!"

Frankie raised an eyebrow. "No way."

"Yes! I've been helping him plan the whole thing." She held up a bouquet of roses that were wilting. She should've put them in water hours ago. "The proposal is going to take place at Oxbow Bend, if, y'know, you want to come."

"Ha! You couldn't drag me there."

Frankie's lackluster response was a disappointment. "Why not?"

"I told you. Because it's a terrible idea to meddle in people's lives."

Before Maisie could respond, she caught sight of a drop-dead gorgeous man heading toward her. This man *had* to be Oliver. He looked like a tall Tom Cruise in *Mission Impossible*. Of course it was him! He was as handsome as Kate was beautiful. They were a perfect couple.

So odd that Kate had never mentioned him. If Maisie had a boyfriend who looked like Oliver, she would tell the whole world.

"You must be Miranda," Oliver said, grinning, as he drew close.

Maisie returned his greeting with a beaming smile of her own, her heart fluttering with excitement. "Maisie, not Miranda," she said. "So, Oliver, you made it!"

"Wouldn't miss it for the world," he said. "Where's my Katie-Kat?"

Katie-Kat. Sooo cute! But then Maisie's smile faltered. "Um, actually, at the moment, I'm not quite sure where Kate is. I haven't seen her today."

Oliver's expression fell, disappointment clouding his beautiful features. "She hasn't answered my texts or calls, either. Where could she have gone?"

Frankie gave Maisie a nudge and she looked to see him tip his head toward the parking lot. Coop's truck had just come rumbling in and Kate was in the passenger seat. *Perfect timing.* This was meant to be! "Oh look—there she is." Maisie tugged on Oliver's jacket. "Let's go! She'll be *so* excited to see you."

Kate had climbed out of the truck and hoisted her backpack over her shoulder when she caught sight of Oliver and Maisie approaching the truck. Kate froze, looking stunned. Dirty and tired, too. Not a great look for a wedding proposal moment. Maybe Maisie should've given her a heads-up.

"Oliver," Kate said in a flat voice. "*What* are you doing here?"

Uh-oh. Maisie thought Kate's tone sounded . . . irritated. *Yep.* She definitely should've given her a heads-up.

Oliver's gorgeous smile faltered, but he quickly composed himself. "I came to see you, of course."

Maisie watched as Kate's expression softened slightly. Okay, there was hope.

Oliver eyed Coop. "And you are . . ."

"Ranger Grant Cooper," Coop said.

"Kate," Oliver said, eyes on Coop, "is this who you said you had to meet up with? The two of you spent all afternoon together?"

Frankie elbowed Maisie and mouthed, "See? I told you."

Coop hoisted his backpack over one shoulder. "I think I'll

just head over to the visitor center. Maisie and Frankie, why don't you come with me?"

"I can't," Maisie said, holding up her smartphone. "I'm needed here."

"Why?" Kate looked at her in confusion. "What's going on?"

"Something wonderful!" Maisie clapped her hands. "I've been in cahoots with Oliver!"

"What do you mean?" Kate looked from Maisie to Oliver and back to Maisie. "How do you know each other?"

Maisie glanced at Oliver. "There's a special surprise waiting for you! We need to go to Oxbow Bend." She glanced at the sun, already worrisomely low in the horizon. Almost disappearing. "Right now!"

"Yes," Oliver said. "We should hurry. My rental car's over there."

Kate squinted in confusion. "Oliver, this isn't a good time," she said, her tone apologetic but firm. "In fact, it's a terrible time."

"Kate, I came a long, long way . . . to see Oxbow Bend at sunset. To be with you."

"But I told you that I was here to work." Kate sounded like she was upset. Really upset. "You just don't listen to me, Oliver."

"But I do! You've made Oxbow Bend sound magical. You said it was the most beautiful sight in the world."

"For *photography*. For viewing wildlife." Now Kate's voice had a sharp edge.

Maisie exchanged a worried glance with Oliver, unsure of how to proceed. He seemed baffled too. What was going wrong? She had wanted today to be so perfect. The sun was already setting behind the mountains. Now it would be too late for the perfect Oxbow Bend videography she had planned.

She felt Coop's hand on her shoulder as he steered her away from Oliver and Kate and toward the visitor center.

Maisie kept looking over her shoulder. She stopped when she saw Oliver bend down on one knee and hold out a little jewelry box to her. The ring! Maisie hadn't had a chance to see it. To give it her approval.

Coop and Frankie stopped and turned around. All three watched the wedding proposal in the parking lot of the visitor center. Kate had her arms crossed against her chest. She didn't look at all happy.

Coop squeezed Maisie's shoulder. "Let's let the two of them sort things out."

Frankie snorted. "You mean, let's let them break up without an audience."

Maisie blew out a puff of air. "This isn't going the way I planned."

"Kiddo," Coop said, "sometimes life has turns of its own."

She glanced up at him, confused by the lighthearted smile in his voice. Coop was never lighthearted. The expression on his face was a mixture of emotions. Sheepish yet hopeful.

Frankie caught it all. Laughing, he gave Maisie another elbow jab. "Told ya."

What? What had she missed?

Kate plopped down on the edge of her bed in her Jackson Lake Lodge hotel room, fuming. The scenic beauty of the Grand Tetons out her window, usually a balm, might as well have been a blank wall for all the peace it offered her now.

The audacity of that man, thinking a surprise visit—and a proposal, no less—was a good idea. How dare Oliver just show up here, especially after she'd spelled it out that she didn't want him to come? Hadn't she been clear? Apparently not clear enough for Oliver, who seemed to operate in a world of his own, where "no" was just a hurdle on the way to "yes."

Kate could still see the bewildered look on Oliver's face when she let loose her fury, a mix of hurt and confusion that made her feel like the villain in a bad romance novel.

But no, she reminded herself, she was not the villain here. She had every right to be angry. Oliver had crossed a line, ignoring her wishes and invading her space, all under the guise of a grand romantic gesture. It was suffocating, presumptuous, and . . . and just plain wrong.

Oliver, for his part, seemed stunned by her reaction. Then crushed. As if the thought had never crossed his mind that she wouldn't be overjoyed by his unannounced appearance and proposal while she was on a work trip. There he was, bent on one knee in the parking lot, looking like a lost puppy that had just been kicked, not understanding what he'd done to deserve such treatment.

"Kate, I . . . I thought you'd be happy," he had stammered, still down on one knee, the ring box in his hand. "I thought this was what you wanted."

"What I wanted?" Kate's voice had risen, incredulous. "When did I ever say I wanted this? Oliver, I've been trying to find the right moment to talk about us . . . about how things aren't working. And instead of giving me space, you show up here . . . with a ring! You involve a very overly enthusiastic, overly talkative thirteen-year-old girl with your plans to propose to me. Everyone in the park is going to hear about this!"

At that, Oliver rose to stand. He turned to look at Maisie in front of the visitor center, watching them with her hands held tight against her heart. Next to her were Frankie and Coop. And next to them was a semicircle of at least twenty strangers, all staring at Oliver and Kate, curious to observe the proposal-gone-sour.

Great, just great. They'd all witnessed the whole cringeworthy episode.

Kate had to pause her rant for a moment, take in a deep breath, as she struggled to untangle her thoughts from her feelings, to find a little calm amid the storm of emotions. "You just don't listen to me, Oliver."

"Don't listen?" Oliver looked incredulous. "What do you mean I don't listen? When you said you thought it was time for a change, I thought this was what you meant."

"I'm sorry." Kate softened slightly, despite herself. "But you thought wrong."

There was a heavy silence, filled with words unsaid. Oliver finally nodded, a sad acceptance in his eyes. He closed the jewelry box and tucked it in his coat pocket. "I think I'd better just head home," he said. "Goodbye, Katie-Kat." On that note, he turned and walked to his car.

She stood there, watching his car disappear into the distance. At last, he had heard what she'd been trying to tell him. They weren't meant to be.

Kate collapsed back onto the bed, a mix of relief and sadness washing over her. The hurt in Oliver's eyes was hard to see. She'd never wanted to hurt him . . . which was probably why she'd let their dating relationship continue too long. This was for the best, she told herself. It was time to move on, to find her own path. Without Oliver.

But first, she had to straighten things out with Maisie. Sweet, meddling Maisie, who somehow got caught up in this mess, turning it into an exhibition for all to see! Kate pinched the bridge of her nose, trying to ward off the headache brewing from the whole debacle. Maisie had only been trying to help, in her own chaotic way, but goodness, did she have to turn it into such a public spectacle? Did she have to make it happen in front of Coop?

Coop. She wanted to spend more time with him. Because throughout the afternoon, as they hiked along Pilgrim Creek, she'd seen something in Coop's eyes that suggested maybe she wasn't the only one feeling something more than friendship.

Coop couldn't have been more pleased with this day.

First, having the entire afternoon with Kate was . . . *awesome*. Talking with her was so easy, so natural. They discovered they had a lot in common, even their embarrassingly vast knowledge of Lord of the Rings trivia. It had been a long time since he'd met anyone he liked half as much as Kate.

Second, the bothered look on Kate's face when she first spotted Oliver was no small thing. To Coop—well, to everyone within earshot at the visitor center—it was clear that their relationship was over.

Which meant that he had a shot with Kate.

And then there was 399. He had found convincing evidence that she was alive and well—the remains of an elk calf carcass below the lair. Fresh scat, to boot. The bear, he was pretty sure, was just taking her own sweet time to leave the cozy den. He called Sally and told her. After he hung up, he decided to call Tim. He repeated everything that he'd just told Sally—the evidence she was alive, the coordinates of the den. It took him off guard that Tim had sounded alarmed that he'd given the coordinates of the den to Sally, but what else should he have done? She was the boss. The NPS was a vertical chain of command.

Let Tim do the worrying about Sally. Coop had other things on his mind.

It was a great day.

He reached over to check his phone. Was it too late to text Emma? Why not? Well, if so, he hoped she had her silent notification on.

He texted her:

Still up?

A few minutes later, she texted back.

Yes. What's up?

I owe you an apology.

For what?

For not really listening to you. I'm sorry.

Long, long pause. So long that Coop started to think he should've called instead of texted. Finally, he saw three dots start dancing.

I'm sorry too.

He smiled, relieved. Then he added:

And I hope you can forgive me.

Another long pause. Then, finally, three dots appeared.

Of course! I hope you can forgive me too.

I do. And I hope . . . your wedding day is everything you wanted.

Another long pause. And then . . .

Thank you, Coop.

A wave of relief washed over Coop as he set his phone aside. It felt right, finally addressing the rift between them. Tim was right. He should have done it long ago. Closing his eyes, he welcomed the peace that settled over him and drifted off to sleep.

Wade's day had turned out even better than he thought it would, especially when he got the update that the bear was still cozy in her den. But his mood almost hit the roof when he found out the turncoat refused to cough up the coordinates. She was adamant about leading the expedition herself. According to her, the lair was way up there, trickier and more dangerous than expected, what with high altitudes, treacherous water crossings, and plenty of bears roaming around. She claimed to know the terrain like her own fingerprints, boasted of her marksmanship, and promised she could bring them back in one piece.

That's when it clicked for Wade. Why not play along? Let her think Feldmann *was* the client. They could scout ahead, handle the rough patches, and keep the bears at bay. Meanwhile, he'd trail behind, out of sight. Once they made it to the lair, Feldmann could throw a curveball—fake a twisted ankle or play up some altitude sickness, anything to get her to focus on him and head back down the trail.

And just like that, Wade would have his chance to swoop in and finish the hunt.

As the sky hung on to that twilight glow, Wade drove around the park restlessly. His car's headlights sliced through the gloaming, spotlighting elk and moose grazing on meadow edges, oblivious to how easily he could take them down. So tempting, he thought, eyeing them.

But Wade wasn't here for them.

As darkness started to take over, that thrill—the hunter's buzz—started pumping through his veins. He knew he was on the verge of something epic, a showdown that was months in the making. He imagined the bear, out there somewhere, totally unaware that tomorrow would be its last day.

Gripping the steering wheel a bit tighter, he peered into the growing shadows, half expecting to see those telltale eyes staring back. The big moment was almost here. No more rehearsals, no more planning. It was game time.

Bring on the morning, bring on the hunt.

EIGHTEEN

The message is simple: love and conserve our wildlife.
—Steve Irwin, Australian wildlife conservationist

Tim tossed and turned all night, his mind consumed by troubling thoughts. Sally, the ultimate parkie, seemed to be entangled in a scheme to aid and abet a poacher. He felt sick to his stomach. How could this have happened? Why?

Money, he guessed. She'd always been concerned about her finances. Their line of work had its perks, but striking it rich wasn't one of them. As the saying went, park rangers were paid in sunsets.

Had Sally come to the conclusion that sunsets weren't enough?

He recalled a conversation they'd had in April after submitting tax returns. Sally had complained bitterly about the financial strain of being a federal worker. "It's outrageous," she said, "to endure government shutdowns without pay, only to have the IRS come knocking for more."

And then there was a time when Sally returned from a meeting with a financial planner in Jackson, disheartened and discouraged. "I got a cold dose of reality about what my upcoming retirement will look like. I'll never see the Eiffel Tower or Big Ben or the Great Wall in China."

He rubbed his face. *What to do, what to do?* If he went to the park superintendent with his suspicions, it would put Sally's job at risk. All her benefits would be lost. Worse, she may face charges. He wanted to help her, not hurt her.

But if he did nothing, he couldn't live with himself.

His eyes popped open.

He had to stop her before she went too far, that's what.

Coop stood at Pilgrim Creek, the predawn light casting long shadows around him as he surveyed the scene. Frankie tagged along beside him. A group of discouraged photographers huddled together, their frustration palpable in the chilly morning air. "Coop, any signs?"

"I haven't seen her," he said truthfully. He heard murmurings among them that the bear must be dead. "Don't give up hope yet."

He saw Kate up ahead, so he sent Frankie back to the truck to get his coat. As soon as Frankie was on his way, he hurried up the line of photographers to join her. "Morning."

"Morning," she said, smiling.

Man, that smile did him in. "Spare camera?"

"Yes. Not as good as the Sony Alpha, but it'll do."

How to word this? "Did, uh, everything turn out for the best last night?"

"With Oliver, you mean? Yes. Let's just say that chapter has closed."

Awesome. Just the outcome he had hoped for. He leaned in to whisper, "I'll go up and get your camera this morning."

"Really?" Her eyes went wide. "Can I come?"

"To be honest," he said, his tone apologetic, "I need to get up and down again really fast. I only have a few hours to spare. Another ranger is covering for me."

She frowned. "And I would slow you down."

She wasn't wrong. Reluctantly, Coop nodded. "I'm sorry."

"But what if I just stay in the truck?" Kate said, her eyes bright with anticipation. "The least I could do is to keep you company on the drive."

A grin tugged at the corners of Coop's lips. "I'll need to leave by six a.m. If you're at my truck at the Jackson Park Lodge parking lot, then, I . . . wouldn't mind the company."

"I'll be there."

Frankie popped up between them. "Where are we going?"

The sun was barely up when Tim arrived at Sally's office and knocked on the door. "Got a minute?" he asked, trying to keep his tone casual.

Sally glanced up from her desk, a distracted look on her face. "If it's quick, darlin'. There's someplace I have to be."

He chose his words carefully. "Rangers are getting a lot of visitor complaints about the additional closures you've added to the list. Seems like half the park is fenced off."

"Just temporary," Sally said, her attention divided as she rummaged through a lower desk drawer. "Standard procedure for springtime. Sensitive habitats. Trying to minimize human-wildlife interactions." She closed that drawer and opened another.

Tim nodded, sensing her evasiveness. "And what's with the extra attention to 399?"

Sally's brow furrowed as she continued her search, seemingly unfazed by Tim's questions. "Just protective measures. Nothing out of the ordinary."

Tim pressed on. "Unless something out of the ordinary is going on?"

She gave him a sharp look. "Like what?"

Tim took a deep breath, steeling himself for what he was about to say. "Like, what's this about a Yellowstone ranger on loan to us?"

Sally's gaze flicked to him briefly before returning to her rummaging. "He's on temporary assignment, doing some cross-park collaboration."

"First of all, I've never heard of Yellowstone having surplus staff to spare a ranger. Second, just a few weeks ago, it seems like we would've talked about that kind of thing."

"Oh, I get it." She paused. "Look, I know I haven't had much time for"—she waved her hand back and forth between them—"us lately. But that'll change soon." She gave him a benign smile. "You have nothing to worry about, dear."

Tim frowned. "But I do. I'm worried about you."

Sally's smile faltered, her eyes flickering with uncertainty. "I appreciate your concern, Tim, but this conversation will have to wait. There's someplace I need to be." She pulled open another drawer and riffled through it.

Tim knew to go slowly here. "You know what I've always admired about you, Sally? You've had a guiding principle to take care of the park, its wildlife and its visitors, above anything else. 'Make the trails a little bit better for park visitors and you'll be making the world a better place.' I've heard you tell rangers that very thing hundreds of times. In the parks, it's not about profits or investors. It's simply making someone's experience a good one."

"Mm-hmm." Riffling through her desk, she hardly paid any attention to him.

"It's a good life, this ranger work. We might be paid in sunsets, but a nest egg would be nice too."

Growing increasingly annoyed by her dismissiveness, Tim couldn't hold back any longer. He pushed himself off the wall. "Sally, I wish you'd have come to me first about your money troubles. Before . . ."

Sally froze. She looked at Tim, eyes narrowed.

"Before you got yourself involved with a poacher." Tim

reached into his pocket and pulled out an envelope. "Is this what you're looking for?"

The air between them practically vibrated before she reached out to snatch the envelope from his hand. "You've made me late," she said, her tone sharp with resentment. She marched out of the office, leaving Tim more troubled than ever.

Hands on his hips, out of the corner of his eye, he noticed that her rifle was not in the case. Out the window, he saw her jeep make a fast turn out of the parking lot.

He had a feeling he knew just where she was headed. He bolted out the door and down the hall to follow her.

The morning sun cast a warm glow over the parking lot as Kate stood beside Coop's truck, her fingers tapping impatiently against her thigh. She glanced at her watch for what felt like the hundredth time, anxiously waiting for Coop to arrive. Finally, she saw him heading toward her, Frankie following behind.

Frankie's face lit up when he spotted Kate. "Aww, yeah!"

"I couldn't get rid of him," Coop said.

"Kate! Coop! Frankie! Wait! Wait for me!"

They turned to see Maisie, easy to spot in her big yellow coat, running from the park shuttle bus. "Pops left a note that I should spend the day with Kate."

Kate and Coop exchanged a look. He sighed and opened the passenger door to the truck to let Frankie and Maisie get in the back.

Immediately, Maisie started to ask about Oliver, but Kate shut her down fast. "You do not mention his name today, got it?" She gave her a don't-mess-with-me look.

Chastened, Maisie nodded. She recovered quickly, and soon her steady chatter filled the truck. Frankie cross-examined every one of her fun facts. Now and then Coop would glance over at

Kate, his eyes crinkling at the corners as he smiled at her, as if to say, *Can you believe those two?*

So much for having some time alone with Coop. On the upside, Kate was glad Maisie was preoccupied with Frankie and didn't press her to explain what happened with Oliver. Because she was still sorting it out herself.

Whatever it was between them, it wasn't the real deal. Ending things had absolutely been the right decision, long overdue. But the look on his face! Devastated. Shattered. She wobbled, nearly caving in.

She didn't, though. Not this time.

Too soon, they reached the Pilgrim Creek Road turnoff. After parking the truck, Coop went through his backpack in the truck's bed, ensuring he had all the essentials for the hike. "I'll try to be back within two hours. Three at the most. You all stay put."

"Two to three hours?" Frankie sounded horrified. "I'm coming with you."

Coop zipped up the top of his backpack, shaking his head. "No. You stay here with the girls."

"Coop," Kate said, "maybe you should reconsider. Buddy system, you know?"

"I can't afford to be slowed down," Coop said. "Or distracted."

"Me?" Frankie scoffed, obviously itching to join the trek. "You think I would slow you down, old man?"

Coop looked him up and down. "No backpack, no water bottle, no bear spray, no whistle, no mosquito repellant."

Frankie held up a foot. "Got my boots on. That's all a real man needs in the wilderness."

Kate could see Coop's patience waning. As annoying as Frankie could be, she wanted him to go along with Coop for safety's sake. "Frankie, take this." She tossed her bottle of water to him.

He caught it with a look of gratitude as if she had handed him a treasure. "Kate, if that slick Oliver dude is out of your life for good, will you marry me?"

Frankie's cheekiness earned him a playful smack on the back of his head from Coop. "Let's go, Romeo." He pointed to Kate. "You two stay in the truck."

Kate settled back into the truck, watching the two disappear up the trail until they were out of sight.

Maisie leaned over the front seat, her chin resting on her folded hands. "Three men are in love with you, and I can't attract even one."

Kate shifted in her seat, meeting Maisie's gaze. Her little friend looked dejected. She felt a pang of sympathy. "When I was thirteen, I wore big thick glasses and my hair was in pigtails."

Maisie squinted, trying to picture it. "Oh, that's bad."

Kate chuckled. "Don't be in a rush to grow up. It's not all it's cracked up to be."

"Are you going to tell me what happened with Oliver?" Maisie asked.

"I'm not," Kate said firmly. "And I'm not sure what your role was in his arrival to the park last night, but I've decided I don't want to know anything more."

Maisie sighed.

Kate reached for her spare camera, intending to use the time to review the morning's pictures and delete any that weren't worth keeping.

Five minutes later, Maisie popped her head over the seat again. "Kate?"

"What?" Kate looked up, meeting Maisie's slightly panicked eyes.

"I have to go to the bathroom. Really, really bad. Pops was gone this morning so I had a giant Coke for breakfast."

Kate rummaged in her backpack, pulling out some tissues. "Here you go."

Maisie's eyes widened. "You mean . . . out there? Where someone might see me?"

Kate nearly laughed out loud. "Well, I'm the only one around here . . . and we're miles from any kind of convenience. You don't have much of a choice. Go behind the truck. I won't look."

"No way! I need privacy."

"You've got to be kidding me. Haven't you gone outside before?"

"Never." She peered out the window. "I'll just go over to those trees." She squeezed her face. "Please, Kate. I really need to go bad."

"Fine. But I'm coming with you." Kate shut off her camera and slung her backpack over her shoulder, ready to accompany Maisie. She didn't think there was much harm in the two of them getting out of the truck and walking around a little, stretching their legs while they waited. After all, with Maisie's constant chatter, there was no chance of surprising any bear.

Maisie had never, ever, in all her life, gone to the bathroom outside. It was mortifying. She needed to find the perfect spot—totally private—and it took a while. Following the sign for the Middle Pilgrim Creek Trail, they went up a hill and quickly reached a flat, widened area of the rushing creek.

"Maisie, this is as far as we should go," Kate said. "I promise to keep my back turned."

"You might hear me . . . you know . . . tinkling."

"Not over the sound of this creek!" Kate looked like she was trying to swallow a smile. "Stay close to the trail. I'll wait for you here." She lifted her hand in a wave and turned around to face the rocky creek bed.

Maisie wandered in the opposite direction and looked for a narrow spot to jump across the creek to an area that was full of bushes. She finally found a suitable, private spot, completely hidden. *Imagine if Frankie came along right now. I would curl up and die.*

But he didn't. And she survived the moment of mortification. As she zipped up her jeans and tucked in her shirt, she went back to the narrow part of the creek to cross it. She noticed something moving on top of a fallen tree and realized it was a bear cub, trying to climb over it. She stopped to watch. *Soooo cute!*

Long before dawn, Wade had Feldmann drop him off at the trailhead that led to Middle Pilgrim Creek. Feldmann planned to meet the turncoat at the parking area right at seven o'clock, and Wade wanted time to scope out the area and stake out a position to wait, watching for them, so he could trail them, unseen. He smiled to himself. Another form of glassing.

He had time to spare, and he was too amped up to sit still, so he left his hiding spot to follow the creek for a distance, looking, listening, vigilant for the slightest hint of life. His heart thrummed a rapid beat against his ribs. Adrenaline flooded his veins, sharpening his senses to a razor's edge. Every whisper of leaves, every crackle of a branch underfoot sent a jolt of alertness coursing through him.

Periodically, he'd halt to scan the surroundings through his binoculars, then check his watch impatiently. Feldmann and the turncoat should be heading up the trail soon, so he turned around to head back to his hiding spot.

Suddenly, a subtle movement snagged his attention. He stilled, every muscle tensed in electric anticipation. Among the shadows, a dark silhouette stirred. Could it be the bear? Could it really be this easy? Scarcely an hour into the hunt and he'd found this elusive creature. He could've laughed out loud, almost giddy.

His heart hammered with a fierce intensity as he crouched lower, every sense homed on the large rumbling figure as it moved along the creek bed. Cautiously, he followed it. The air vibrated with tension, the hunt was nearing its crescendo, the final act about to unfold.

With the target in sight, Wade silently withdrew an arrow from his quiver.

NINETEEN

An animal's eyes have the power to speak a great language.
—*Martin Buber, philosopher*

Kate wandered slowly along the rocky creek bed, camera in hand, trying to capture the light as it danced on the rushing water, filtered by the quaking aspen leaves, creating a mesmerizing play of shadows and reflections. As she adjusted the focus on her lens, a deep and guttural huffing sound echoed through the forest, reverberating off trees, filling the woods with an ominous presence. It sent a shiver down Kate's spine. Slowly, she turned around to discover that Maisie was standing on a long, rocky creek island between a grizzly bear on one side of the water and her curious cub on the other.

Maisie, eyes wide, frozen with fear, had realized what danger she was in. Kate lifted her hands like a stop sign to indicate that Maisie should stay put and not run.

A scream built in Kate's throat. Why had they left the truck without bear spray? Why had she let Maisie rush her? She was responsible for this girl! *Stay calm*, she told herself. *Think, think, think.*

But she couldn't think what to do. She couldn't think at all. How was that possible? A person had to think.

No. She didn't. Hadn't Coop just told her about the importance of paying attention to your gut instinct?

So what was it telling her?

That the sow only wanted to protect her cub. Bluffing. Please, please, please, be bluffing.

Think, think, think.

Kate scanned the area, her mind racing as she assessed the situation. She needed to create a clear path for the cub, now standing up on the log, to reunite with its mother. Her eyes fell on a large boulder on the creek island, about ten to fifteen yards behind Maisie. That's where she needed to get herself. Kate gestured toward it with an urgency, just as the bear let out a loud huff, heavy with warning.

"Kate, I'm scared!" Maisie's loud voice had a quiver.

Kate slowly made her way into the water toward the creek island, all the while trying not to think about Coop's warning that bears were excellent swimmers. She kept one eye on Maisie and the other eye on the grizzly—who was watching her cub. Maisie still hadn't budged.

When Kate made it behind the boulder, she called out to Maisie. "Take slow steps to back up."

With cautious steps, Maisie began to inch her way down toward safety. When she was just a yard or two from the boulder where Kate now stood, the bear huffed again. Startled, Maisie slipped over a rock and fell, prompting Kate to act swiftly. She picked up a big rock and threw it about two feet beyond the bear cub on the log, startling it so that it darted into the water toward its waiting mother. *Don't look*, Kate thought. *Don't look a bear in the eyes!* But she couldn't help herself. She did look, just as the mother bear looked over at her. Their eyes met and held, just for an instant. But in that look, there was some kind of communication between them, some understanding. It was the strangest thing, yet it was real.

Then the bear lifted its nose, as if catching a scent. Kate looked down the creek and saw something large moving along the creek bed. She squinted. It was a man, holding a bow and arrow. He paused to draw the string, aiming straight at the bear. Kate grabbed the world's loudest whistle, brought it to her lips, closed her eyes, and blew with all her might, as long as she could, until she ran out of breath.

When she opened her eyes, the bear and its cub were gone. So was the hunter.

Tim Rivers raced down the winding roads of Grand Teton National Park, his heart pounding with urgency. He was trying to catch up with Sally before she made it to Pilgrim Creek Road, desperate to stop her from making contact with the poacher, to talk some sense into her before it was too late. Before the poacher found 399. For the hundredth time since yesterday, he'd wished Coop hadn't told Sally the bear was out of her den—even more so, he wished he hadn't given her the lair's coordinates. Unintentionally, Coop sealed the bear's fate.

Just as Tim turned onto the main road, a silver Camry whizzed by, driven by none other than that tall Yellowstone ranger. Without a moment's hesitation, Tim grabbed the microphone to radio in to law enforcement. "This is Ranger Tim Rivers," he said. "There's a silver Camry heading out of the east end of the park within the next few minutes. Stop him. The driver is a white male, in his thirties, tall. Extremely tall. Possibly wearing a Yellowstone ranger uniform."

"Copy that." The LE ranger on the other end took down the information. "So he's a ranger?"

"No. He's an imposter. Detain him. Don't let him go."

"Understood, we'll intercept the vehicle. What's the charge?"

Tim's grip on the steering wheel tightened. "Um . . . speeding. Just hold him 'til I get there. Got that? Do *not* release him."

"Copy that. We'll take care of it," the ranger said before signing off.

His phone buzzed with Sally's name on the screen. He'd barely answered when she snapped at him. "Tim, I heard you over the radio. Stay out of this. That's an order." She hung up.

Ignoring her, Tim accelerated. He had never disobeyed a direct order in his life, but today was different.

Arriving at the parking area off Pilgrim Creek Road, he saw Sally's car, as well as an official game warden car. Panic surged through him. He parked and sprinted up the trail, his mind racing with worst-case scenarios, praying he wasn't too late.

Kate continued to blow on the world's loudest whistle, as Maisie, shaking like a leaf, cowered behind the boulder. "Are you okay?"

"No! I'm terrified." Maisie's voice quivered with raw emotion.

Kate's own fear mirrored Maisie's. An eerie silence filled the forest, even louder than the rushing creek. Huddled together behind the safety of the boulder, Kate prayed for help.

Maisie's breathing had grown erratic and her face was flushed. "I think I'm having an asthma attack. I forgot my inhaler."

Oh man. Kate had no idea what to do next. Except . . . to pray. *Oh God, please, please, please.* The words ran through her head, a silent plea repeated over and over.

"Kate," Maisie said, wheezing, "I need help." She was breathing with difficulty, and her face, now pale, had drained of the flushed color. It even had a bluish tinge. Her eyes filled with tears. "I want my mom."

Kate's mind swirled—what options did they have? The mother bear and her cub had gone in one direction, the hunter in another. But which direction had they gone? She had no idea. Danger from the bear, she understood. Danger from this hunter, she was unsure of.

Oh-God-help-me. Please-please-please. I don't know what to do.

Help came sooner than Kate expected. She'd barely finished her desperate prayer when she heard Coop shout her name.

Kate poked her head around the boulder to see Coop and Frankie cresting the hill on the narrow trail that led to the creek. She waved to them. "Coop, over here! We need help!"

Coop rushed over to them, scrambling down to the creek, splashing through the water to reach them, concern etched on his face. "What's going on? What's happened?" Frankie followed right behind him.

Kate couldn't believe they'd come back down the mountain so soon. "Maisie's having an asthma attack."

Frankie's attention homed in on Maisie. "No, she's hyperventilating. Maisie, take a seat." He gently guided her to sit on the ground, surprising Kate with a tenderness she hadn't expected from him. Placing a comforting hand on Maisie's back, he began rubbing it in soothing circles. "Keep your back straight. Breathe in slowly and steadily. Breathe in, hold, breathe out, hold." He said it over and over.

Following his instructions, Maisie complied, and gradually, her breathing started to improve. A normal color started to return to her face.

Relief trickled through Kate. "Thank God you came when you did." She looked up at Coop. "How did you know to come?"

"Frankie forgot his phone and insisted we return to the truck so he could listen to music. We weren't far from here when we heard the whistle." His gaze kept returning to Maisie. "What brought this on? Why'd you leave the truck?"

"Bear!" Maisie wheezed. "Hunter!"

Coop's head swiveled. "What bear? What do you mean . . . a hunter?"

"Look." Kate pointed across the creek to a tree with an arrow sticking out of its trunk. "Someone out there is trying to kill a bear."

Listening, even Frankie appeared shaken, his usual bravado replaced by genuine concern. "How close were you to the bear?"

Kate cleared her throat. "Not exactly a football field." More like, fifty heart-stopping feet.

Coop's gaze swept the creek. "Did you see which way the hunter went?"

"No," Kate said. "We were hiding behind the boulder."

Through his binoculars, Coop looked up and down the creek, then crossed the water to pull the arrow out of the tree.

A shrill voice pierced the air. "Cooper!"

Kate peeked out from behind the boulder to see Sally far up the creek, clutching a hefty rifle.

"Coop, hon, is everyone alright?"

"Sally!" Coop said, stepping a few feet away from the boulder. He cupped his hands around his mouth. "What are you doing here?"

Sally raised her rifle, aiming it upstream. "We got him!"

Kate shielded her eyes to see three people coming around a bend in the creek to reach Sally.

Frankie stood up to see. "Who are they?"

"I think . . . they're state game wardens," Coop said.

"Who's between them?" Frankie said.

"Must be the poacher who shot the arrow," Coop said.

By now Maisie, fully recovered and fully curious, had stood to join them, watching carefully as Sally and the others drew near. She let out a loud gasp. "But that's . . . he's Oliver!"

No way. Kate squinted. It was! It *was* him.

248

Sally, close enough now to hear, let out a loud snort. "Oliver? Is that the name he told you?"

As they walked past the creek island, Oliver tried to break loose from the agents. "I came to protect Kate and the kid! The bear was coming for them! Kate, tell them!"

"You're a liar!" Maisie shouted. "And I am NOT a KID!"

"Kate!" Oliver was pleading. "Tell them about us! Tell them how I came here to propose to you!"

Kate's mind struggled to absorb the sight of Oliver, held firmly between two game wardens. "I don't . . . I don't get it. What is going on?"

"They've got me mixed up with someone else. Kate, tell them! This is all a terrible misunderstanding."

"Is that so?" Sally said, hands on her hips. "Cuz Tony Feldmann's been singing like a canary ever since he was nabbed trying to leave the park just a bit ago."

At that, the change in Oliver's countenance was immediate, from sputtering protests to utterly silent, mouth drawn in a straight line, a look on his face like he could murder someone. And then it was gone, and he was back to claiming innocence.

Who was Tony Feldmann? Kate couldn't keep up.

She wasn't the only one.

A red-faced Tim Rivers appeared out of nowhere, looking just as confused as Kate felt. "What," Tim said, huffing and puffing as he reached them on the creek island, "the Sam Hill is going on?"

"Pops!" Maisie hurried down the hill into her grandfather's arms. "That man tried to kill the bear! And then he was going to kill us too!"

"Don't listen to the kid!" Oliver yelled.

"I AM NOT A KID," Maisie yelled back.

Oliver ignored her. "Kate! Sweetheart! You're the only one who can clear this up. Tell them who I am! Tell them about us!"

Ignoring his protests, the agents kept pushing him along the creek bank toward the trailhead that would lead down the hill to the parked cars. Coop motioned to the rest of them to follow along.

"Hold up!" Sally hurried over to the game wardens. She took off her ranger hat and pulled a thick envelope from it to hand to a warden. Then she reached into her shirt and pulled a small tape recorder to hand over. "Take good care of this. You'll be needing all of it for evidence." She turned to give Tim a *look*.

"Oh boy," Tim said.

"Sally," Coop said, "who is that guy?"

Sally turned to face Coop. "Hon, have you ever heard of Wade Schmidt?"

Frankie whistled. "Aww, yeah! My dad's talked about him! Big-time poacher. Stealth hunter!"

"He's what?" Kate said. "He's a . . . stealth hunter?" How could she have missed so much?

"Wade Schmidt," Coop said, "is one of the most wanted poachers in the national parks. No one's been able to catch him. They've never even gotten an image of him. He uses all kinds of disguises. All kinds of aliases. All kinds of ways to keep from being identified."

Like Oliver, the churchgoing, straightlaced boyfriend. It was all a facade. A sickening nausea flooded over Kate.

Coop turned back to Sally. "So this was a sting?" Hands on his hips, he said, "You've been working a sting?" He sounded impressed.

She grinned, ear to ear. "Sure was, darlin'. Wade Schmidt offered up thousands of dollars for the pleasure of hunting the world's most famous bear."

"Kate!" Oliver said, turning his head back to shout as the

agents led him down the trail. "Katie-Kat! Tell them! This is all a big mistake!"

But it wasn't. Somewhere, deep inside Kate, she knew it was true. Slowly, her mind started to piece things together. Meeting Oliver at the zoo, right in front of the bear exhibit. His keen interest in bears. His fascination with 399. His evasiveness whenever she asked him about his work.

How relentlessly he pursued her. He was a hunter. She was his prey.

She squeezed her eyes shut. What a *fool* she'd been.

Still at a distance, Sally put her hands on her hips. "Zoo Girl, I hope you got yourself that picture you wanted."

It took a moment for Kate to realize Sally was talking to her. Her eyes popped open. "What do you mean?"

"Hon, that's the bear you came for."

Kate gasped. "*That* bear was 399? Really and truly? You're sure? You're absolutely sure?"

"Darlin', I know my bears," Sally said. She narrowed her eyes at Tim and jabbed a finger in his direction. "I know a lot more than some people might think."

"Oh boy," Tim said.

"But I have to give you props for tipping off LE to detain Feldmann. That ended up being helpful." Sally spun around and hurried to catch up with the game wardens.

Frankie gave a light punch to Maisie's arm. "You okay? You aren't talking nonstop like you usually do."

Maisie managed a shaky smile. "I think I'm still in shock."

"Let's get you two back to the lodge," Coop said.

Wait. Kate couldn't leave Pilgrim Creek without her camera. She just couldn't. She looked at Coop. "I really need to retrieve my camera. It's my only chance." Her only chance to redeem this disaster.

"You've got to be kidding," Coop said. "After all this?"

"*Because* of all this. I can get it myself. I don't have to involve anyone." She'd done enough of that with Oliver.

"No, Kate," Coop said, "I'm not going to let you go alone up there. You've already had one bear encounter for the day." He looked at Tim. "Would you mind dropping Kate at Jackson Lake Lodge? Frankie and I have an errand."

"Aww, yeah!" Frankie said, pumping his fists. "Let's race to the top."

"Hold it, cowboy," Coop said. "First let's get everyone to the jeep."

Tim and Frankie helped Maisie cross the creek.

"You're really alright?" Coop said.

"I really am," Kate said. "I've never felt such a stone-cold fear before, but I'm fine."

He held out a hand to help Kate, then didn't let her hand go until they reached the vehicles. As they parted, he gently pulled her a few feet away from Maisie's listening ears. "I'll come looking for you as soon as we're back in the valley."

"Coop, I feel like such a fool. I can't believe how deceived I was."

"Well, as bad as you might be feeling, rest assured that Wade Schmidt is probably feeling a whole lot worse."

Thank God for *that*, Kate thought. "Coop, why didn't the bear attack us? Maisie was right in between the bear and her cub."

"You handled it well by not panicking. But I know what Tim would say in situations like this. Someone," he said, pointing upward, "was looking after you."

Thank you, thank you, thank you, God.

Tim bellowed for him to hurry up. At the last second, Coop leaned forward, placed a light kiss on Kate's forehead, and squeezed her arms. "I'm glad you're okay." Then he and Frankie started up the trail for the second time.

Kate watched them go, still feeling dazed, but this time in a good way. Her heart lifted like it was light as air.

Before Tim started the car, he turned in his seat to check on Maisie. "Breathing easier now?"

Maisie nodded, still subdued.

Turning his attention to Kate, Tim said, "And you? Feeling alright?"

Kate hesitated, then shook her head. "I feel foolish, embarrassed, even angry. But also strangely grateful." And happy.

"Grateful is a good place to be." Tim gave her a reassuring smile before starting the ignition.

Sitting in the back of the game wardens' SUV, the cuffs digging into his wrists, Wade simmered with a mix of anger and disbelief. How in the world could this have happened to him? He shot a glare at the metal mesh separating him from the front seat. For years, he had prided himself on staying ahead of the game. Always a step ahead. Always.

How had he made so many mistakes?

Feldmann. It was all Feldmann's fault. That fool fell for the act of a pint-sized ranger, who'd been playing him like a puppet from the start.

Then there was Kate. Her betrayal stung like a thousand beestings, sharper than the cuffs on his wrists. He had underestimated her.

Wade had approached Kate with the same precision and confidence he brought to his hunts. Meeting her at the zoo, wooing her, dangling *that* particular bear in front of her so carefully that she thought she had been the one to discover it, and then to come up with the notion of photographing it. Hunting 399 had been Wade's plan all along. Kate was always meant to be a decoy, a clever distraction. Even the marriage proposal was a ploy. It didn't matter to him if she said yes or no; the goal was to divert attention, like a magician captivating the audience's gaze while executing a hidden trick. The public proposal was insurance. Plenty of witnesses to attest to his identity as Oliver, the boyfriend. Kate was his guarantor.

But then, as he pleaded with her to identify him, she said nothing. *Nothing.* That kid, Maryanne, was more helpful than Kate. At least the kid admitted she recognized him. Called him Oliver.

Wade had been so confident that he had Kate firmly under his control. She'd always bent to him, accommodated him. Yet today she betrayed him with her silence.

The small ranger peered into the SUV, her smug expression infuriating him even more. "Now you know how an animal feels when it's been trapped. One thing I will promise you, Schmidt. That was your last hunt." She stepped back from the vehicle and clapped her hands. "Take him away, boys."

TWENTY

The earth has music for those who listen.
— *Reginald Holmes*

Kate stood in her room at Jackson Lake Lodge, a towel wrapped around her body after a long, hot shower. She sank onto the edge of the bed, her thoughts swirling with confusion and regret. The events of the morning buzzed in her mind, over and over.

It all seemed so clear now. She was able to see all the blinking red lights she'd either missed or ignored, like gentle but persistent warning signs from God. She knew she'd never felt totally comfortable with Oliver, never totally herself, but she blamed herself for that. Her insecurities.

As she sat there, the pieces started to click into place. She thought back to their first meeting, at the zoo, how he'd commented on the T-shirt she'd worn with her church's logo. He told her that he attended the same church, and sure enough, there he was at the next Sunday morning service. Stalking his prey. Could she have made herself any more of an easy target? She'd been set up from the start.

Such an idiot. She felt like such a fool.

It was unsettling to think how easily Oliver had managed to overpower her, both mentally and emotionally. He had a way of confusing her, clouding her judgment with his charm and charisma and persistence. Especially his persistence.

Imagine if everything had gone the way Oliver intended.

Imagine if she had wavered last night when he surprised her with a proposal. Imagine if she had caved in as Oliver pressed and pressed. She usually did cave in to his persistence. He was a master manipulator. Imagine if he had taken down that magnificent bear with his bow and arrow. If she and Maisie had stayed in the truck, Oliver might have killed the bear. Imagine if he had gotten away with it.

Everything could have gone wrong—but it actually went right instead. So many things went right. The bear was safe. Oliver/Wade was in jail. Kate *had* said no to him. Before she had any idea of his true identity, she had said no. Relief washed over her.

Thank you, thank you, thank you, God. But how do I get over this?

She hadn't been listening for an answer, but one came.

Forget the former things; do not dwell on the past. See, I am doing a new thing! Do you not perceive it?

The Bible verse she'd once memorized as a child came to her full-blown, startling her with its intensity.

Forget the former things; do not dwell on the past. See, I am doing a new thing! Do you not perceive it?

Over and over, she repeated those words. And, on their heels, *Thank you, thank you, thank you, God.*

She changed into fresh clothes and combed out her wet hair, drying it with the blow dryer, and her mind bounced to the bear. She couldn't believe she had actually seen Grizzly Bear 399, up close and personal. If only she'd had her camera for that astonishing moment when the bear locked eyes with her. Kate would never, ever forget it. She felt an amazing connection—almost like there'd been some kind of understanding between them.

Today she understood what the other photographers had been telling her—there was a critical difference between zoo photography and wildlife photography. A bear in a zoo was stunning to behold, but its power and majesty faded away. Seeing that beautiful grizzly bear in her natural habitat was . . . thoroughly terrifying. And thoroughly thrilling.

She could hardly wait to download her memory card from her Sony Alpha, assuming it was still in one piece. Hoping Coop and Frankie were able to retrieve it.

And then her restless mind landed and settled on Coop. She was counting the minutes until she saw him again.

Huddled behind a stack of empty bear-proof garbage cans, Maisie couldn't resist eavesdropping on Frankie's conversation with his dad. It was a side of Frankie she hadn't seen before. He talked about his dad like they were strangers, like Frankie didn't care about him at all. Clearly, it was an act. He did care. She peeked over the top to see the expression on his face. The scowl was gone. He looked . . . uncool. Happy. Maisie dipped down again before he saw her.

"It was incredible, Dad!" she heard him say. "We nabbed Wade Schmidt! Yeah, you heard me right. *Wade Schmidt!* Remember when you found his wallet in Denali? You knew back then that this guy was trouble, but no one listened to you. Man, Dad, you had him nailed."

Frankie paused for a moment to listen. "Well, yeah, I guess you didn't actually nail Wade Schmidt, but you were onto something. It took a whole sting operation to catch him. And get this—no feds. All local law enforcement. It was like being in a movie, seriously." Frankie listened intently for a long while, then a pleased look came over him. "Me? Yeah, I had a big role in it. Really big."

Maisie had to bite on her lip to keep from laughing. She didn't want to alert Frankie to her presence. This was way too fun.

"Dad, you wouldn't believe it," Frankie said. "There's this acting chief ranger, a super short woman with fuzzy blond hair and she calls everyone hon or darlin'—" He paused to listen. "Yeah. Sally Janus. I guess I should've figured you would know her. You know everybody." He listened a little longer. "Well, anyway, Sally set the whole thing up. This incredible sting operation. Wade Schmidt was using this ridiculously tall guy as his frontman. He was pretending to be a Yellowstone ranger." Pause. "How'd you know his name was Tony Feldmann? Man, Dad, you know everybody."

Frankie said it in a tone of admiration, not his usual sarcasm. So uncool. So sweet. Maisie felt warm from head to toe.

"Coop said he knew something was fishy when he first met Feldmann and shook his hand." Frankie chuckled. "He said it was like shaking an accountant's hand." Pause. "Coop? Oh, he's the seasonal ranger I got stuck with. We're roommates too. Yeah, he's not so bad. A little fussy as a roommate, but he's a good guy."

It occurred to Maisie that, up to now, Frankie hadn't told his dad anything about his summer. Nothing. But that had just changed.

"Hey, Dad, you remember Tim Rivers, right? The ranger who's always got that serious, drill sergeant vibe? Yeah, him. Well, turns out he's the one who caught Feldmann. Crazy, right? Tim can be kinda intimidating, but he's not too bad once you get to know him. Anyway, Feldmann got spooked when Sally Janus didn't show up to guide him into the backcountry. She was supposed to lead him to the bear's den, with Wade Schmidt trailing behind all stealthy-like. Apparently, that's Schmidt's thing, staying invisible and all . . . Oh, you knew that? Yeah, figures.

"So, Sally had this plan brewing to meet up and have the wardens close the net, but then Tim slowed her down and she was late to the rendezvous. When Feldmann saw the game wardens drive up, he freaked out and bolted. Tim Rivers spotted his car and called the LE rangers to nab him at the gate."

Pause.

"Hold on, Dad. There's more. It gets even better. Then the game wardens—they caught Wade Schmidt red-handed, bow in his hands, arrows in his quiver. Schmidt started wailing like a baby. It was so awesome. Like a scene from a movie!"

Pause.

Maisie could hear the admiration in Frankie's voice for Sally, for Coop, for Tim.

"Man, Dad," Frankie said, "I've been hearing about Wade Schmidt from you for as long as I can remember, but he was always one step ahead of the law. Then, *bam!* The trap was sprung, and he fell right into it."

This was too much! Maisie couldn't help herself. She popped up and peered over the garbage bin. "Tell him about Kate! About the marriage proposal! About me!"

Frankie spun around, eyes wide. "I'll call you later, Dad. I gotta go." Frowning, he walked over to the garbage bin. "Aww, Maisie, are you going all Nancy Drew on me? Seriously lame. Haven't I told you that you need to get your cool on?"

"I didn't mean to eavesdrop." Maisie came around to the front to meet him. "Not at first. I didn't want to interrupt your call . . . and then, listening was so much fun." She grinned. "Frankie, you called your dad to tell him all about the capture of Wade Schmidt!"

She watched in surprise as his face first turned pink, then

bright red. He started scuffing his boots uncomfortably. "Yeah, yeah, whatever," he muttered, trying to recover his typical aloofness, but she knew better.

"I bet your dad must've been thrilled to hear about it from you first. Pops said it's going to make national news. Bet you'll get your name mentioned."

Frankie rolled his eyes but couldn't suppress a small smirk. "Don't make a big deal out of it."

"It was a big deal! The whole thing was a big, huge deal!" Maisie bounced on her toes, undeterred by Frankie's attempt to downplay the situation. "A big-time poacher caught in a trap set by a miniature-sized chief ranger. And then Kate and I, we helped too."

Frankie scoffed. "You helped?"

Maisie placed her hands on her hips. "The whistle. *That* was a game changer."

He grew serious. "Maisie, you could've been lunch for a very hungry bear."

At first, she thought he was making fun of her, like he usually did. But when she looked up at him, concern covered his face. It almost made Maisie think that he'd been worried about her. The thought filled her with happiness, from her toes to her nose.

"Why'd you leave the truck, anyway?"

Maisie's happiness dimmed. "Well, um, because I needed a private moment in nature."

His eyebrows furrowed in confusion at first, but then a chuckle burst out. Soon, it turned into a full-blown laugh. He laughed so hard that he doubled over, guffawing until he was out of breath.

And just like that, the sweet moment between them was over.

Tim waited in his office until he knew Sally had returned to headquarters after providing formal statements at the Jackson

Police Department. Then he waited a while longer. Finally, he made himself go to her office, but he hesitated for a long moment before knocking on the door. He poked his head around the threshold, bracing himself, confident he wouldn't receive a warm welcome.

Sally barely spared him a glance. "Not now, Tim," she said, her tone curt. "I have a lot of work to catch up on."

"This won't take long. I'd like to explain a few things." Taking a deep breath, Tim stepped farther into her office. "Sally, I owe you an apology."

She leaned back in her chair, her expression guarded. "Go on."

"I knew something was going on with you, but I didn't have any idea what—until I saw that picture."

"What picture?"

"Kate Cunningham, the photographer—"

Sally squinted. "Who?"

"The Zoo Girl."

"The same woman who was up at Pilgrim Creek today?"

"Yeah, her. She was at Willow Flats when you and that tall Yellowstone—"

"Tony Feldmann. Frontman for Wade Schmidt."

"Right. The Zoo Girl took some pictures, and you and Tony Feldmann were in the background. You had a rifle."

Sally raised an eyebrow. "That Zoo Girl really gets herself into tight spots with bears."

"I think she's learned some valuable lessons about wildlife photography this week." Tim paused, gathering his thoughts. "Anyway, Kate thought you were aiming for the bear—"

"I fired a warning shot."

"Right, right, of course." Tim felt foolish for not realizing it sooner. Sally Janus would never have missed her target. "I just wish you would've told me."

"Tim, this has been in the works for weeks. When I went to the Yellowstone conference, Tony Feldmann approached me. Offered me a bundle of cash if I'd help his client out."

"Why didn't you tell me about it?" That's what he just couldn't get his head around.

Sally sighed, resting her elbows on the desk. "The more people who knew, the greater the risk for a slipup."

"I didn't think I was just . . . anybody."

"Maybe not." Sally leaned back and crossed her arms against her chest. "But it sure didn't take much for you to assume I'd gone to the dark side."

"Sally, you sacrificed a gray wolf for this . . . this scheme."

She held his eyes. "That wolf had already been identified to be culled. It had been harassing a rancher's livestock. I knew what I was doing." She leaned forward in her chair. "And that's the problem, right there. All along, I knew what I was doing."

"Sally—"

"Look, Tim. Right now I need to get back to work."

From the expression on her face, she was in no mood to see his side of the story. And maybe she never would. She turned her attention back to her work, the conversation already a distant memory, leaving Tim to wonder if they'd ever truly known each other at all.

Kate sat at the small desk in her room at Jackson Lake Lodge, carefully examining her Sony Alpha camera, which had spent the night in the high country, its motion detection capability activated. She'd never actually used the motion detection capability. Now, she prayed for it to yield something useful.

"Lord, let there be something. Anything," she murmured as she inserted the memory card into her computer. "Please, please, please."

Hours passed as Kate scrolled slowly through the footage,

her anticipation building with each passing moment. A chipmunk examined the camera up close, its curious eyes staring directly into the lens. A family of raccoons shuffled by. A deer cautiously approached, its ears perked up, before darting away, startled by something.

But so far, everything was useless. It was during the dark of the night when the motion detection had been activated, as the animals moved about in their nocturnal activities. Then, as dawn began to break, she saw something that caught her eye. She slowed down the speed of the footage and watched it again and again, using the still photography feature to extract shots from the video. She examined every frame meticulously, searching for that one perfect shot. And then she found it.

Her camera marked it at four thirty in the morning. The sky was starting to lighten, though the sun wouldn't be up for a while. In the soft light of dawn, a bear emerged from her den and sniffed the air. Slowly, she ventured out a few more steps. Standing on her hind legs, she lifted her paws in the air.

Freeze the frame.

Kate stared at the shot for the longest while, transfixed, a mixture of exhilaration and satisfaction coursing through her veins. She had the shot. The one that could change everything.

This was it. The one-in-a-million shot that she had come to get. Stunning.

She knew just what to call it: "Morning Stretch."

On her computer, she searched for the *Nat Geo* editor's email address. Back home, she had meticulously studied their strict guidelines: no fabrication, minimal post-processing (all she had done was to crop the photograph), no staging, complete transparency, and respect for the wildlife. Check, check, check.

She crafted an email to the editor, explaining the picture, the circumstances, and the famous subject. Hands shaking, she attached the photograph.

She breathed another prayer—this time, it was "Thank you, thank you, thank you, Lord."

And just like that, her email bounced back with the message: *"Undeliverable."*

She went to the *National Geographic* website, to the staff directory, and searched for the woman's name. Nothing.

She dropped her chin against her chest.

Oliver. Another setup.

~

In a bleak room at the Jackson Police Department, Wade Schmidt sat defiantly, a cold metal chair beneath him and stark fluorescent lights buzzing above. The game warden seated across the table kept asking him questions, but Wade didn't answer a single one. He folded his hands together on the surface of the table and stared down at them.

"You know, cooperation could really simplify things for you," the game warden said, trying to sound casual, like two pals having a chat.

Wade was unmoved. His instincts were honed. He wasn't about to walk into a trap. "I'm not saying a word without my lawyer present."

My lawyer. That was a lie. Wade had always been a step ahead of the law and never needed a lawyer. In fact, he'd always been a little pleased that he didn't even know any. In retrospect, he should have thought that through.

He accepted the game warden's offer to make a phone call, stepping toward the station phone. Dialing the one number he knew by heart, he listened to the rings, each one echoing his rising anxiety. A cold spark sizzled down his spine, a real bone-chiller. Fear hit him like a ton of bricks—it was a first for him. Then, relief flooded in as a familiar voice picked up on the other end and said a casual "hello." He quickly checked to make sure the game warden was out of earshot before he whispered into the phone.

"Hey, Mom. Yeah, it's me. Do you know any good lawyers?"

TWENTY-ONE

I took a walk in the woods and came out taller than the trees.
—*Anonymous*

As the day wound down, Maisie and Pops sat on the worn-out bench on his cabin porch, soaking in the serene beauty that surrounded them. Maisie's mind still buzzed from the whirlwind of events from this morning. Pops seemed quieter than usual, lost in his own thoughts.

Just as Maisie was on the brink of asking Pops his thoughts on whether Wade Schmidt might end up spending the rest of his life in jail, a car came into view, pulling into the driveway. Her eyes widened in surprise. "Is that Mom?"

Pops followed her gaze, squinting against the bright afternoon sunlight. "Well, I'll be," he said, a smile spreading across his weathered face. "Sure looks like her."

Maisie bolted across the patio and threw herself into her mom's open arms. "You're back! Mom, we have so much to tell you!"

Mom hugged her back. "I have a lot to tell you too." She stepped back and did a double take. "You're wearing makeup?"

Pops had joined them by now. "Tim, did you encourage her to . . . experiment . . . with makeup? So much of it?"

He laughed. "Don't look at me. It's all your daughter's doing."

Mom put her hands on Maisie's shoulders and examined her face with a puzzled look. "Well, I suppose it was inevitable. But maybe we can tone it down a little."

Not a chance. If anything, Maisie would like to tone it up. She *loved* wearing makeup. It made her feel grown-up, like she was fifteen.

She hooked her hand through her mom's elbow. "You won't *believe* what's been happening here." She launched into the entire story, starting at the beginning, on the day her mom dropped her off. Mom listened, eyes wide, glancing at Pops now and then as if she couldn't believe her ears.

"All true," Pops said, when Maisie finally finished the tale.

"A notorious poacher?" Mom said. "Here?"

"The worst one of all!" Maisie couldn't stop smiling over the thought that Wade Schmidt was behind bars, far away from bears. From Kate.

After Coop had given Kate a big smooch, right in front of everyone, Maisie realized she had completely missed their budding romance. It was a happy discovery for her, because Frankie had witnessed the kiss too. She saw the look on his face, like his crush on Kate had been doused by a big bucket of cold water. A delightful moment for Maisie. *Too bad, Frankie*, she wanted to shout. *You should be crushing on* me, *not on a woman old enough to be your . . . big sister.*

"Thea, you must be hungry," Pops said. "Let's get inside and I'll whip up my World-Famous Spaghetti."

Mom and Maisie exchanged an amused look. Pop's World-Famous Spaghetti consisted of a jar of spaghetti sauce, a package of dried pasta noodles, and sliced hot dogs.

Later that evening, sitting around Pops's little kitchen table, twirling her spaghetti around her fork, Maisie's eyes fixed on her mom. She looked different somehow—calmer, settled, like a weight had been lifted off her shoulders.

"So how was the retreat?" Pops said. "Was it everything you hoped it would be?"

"It was . . . unexpected," Mom said. "In a good way."

Pops raised an eyebrow. "Unexpected? What do you mean?"

Mom took a deep breath. "Well, at first, I didn't realize it was a Christian retreat. I thought Rebecca had roped me into something and I gave some serious thought to . . ."

"Bolting," Maisie said, filling in the pause.

"Yes. I admit it. To bolting." Mom cast a side glance in Pops's direction. "It even crossed my mind that Ranger Tim Rivers might have been in cahoots with my friend who encouraged me to go."

Pops let out a small chuckle. "Not guilty."

"During the retreat, we were encouraged to reflect on the main emotion in our lives. There was even a shrink to talk to—"

"Uh, counselor?" Pops said.

"Well, she called herself a spiritual director, but I thought she sounded more like a shrink. Anyway, Maisie convinced me to stay and give it a chance—"

Lifting his eyebrows, Pops looked at Maisie. She beamed back.

"—so I signed up for time to talk to this shr—uh, spiritual director, and she asked me some pretty intense questions. You know, about the main emotion that drives everything."

"Like what?" Pops said.

"Like, decisions. Coping with change. How well I work with others."

"Oh boy." Pops muttered it under his breath, but Mom noticed and gave him a look.

"Anyway," Mom said, "after some serious soul searching, I realized that for me, my main emotion was anger."

"Anger?" Maisie repeated, surprised. Her mom never got angry. Silent. Moody. So tired she needed to sleep a lot. But not angry.

Mom nodded. "Anger can affect people in different ways. Especially if it's buried."

"Go on, Thea," Pops said.

"I think I've been angry at God for taking my mom when she was still young, when she had so much to look forward to in life." She paused. "Most of all, taking her when I needed her the most."

Maisie's heart twinged. She knew her mom and grandmother had been super close. And Mom had already lost her dad when she was around thirteen, Maisie's age.

"The shr—uh, spiritual director told me to have a long talk with God, and to not be afraid to tell him exactly what I thought. About everything. She also said I might be surprised by what he might say back to me. So that's what I did." Mom put down her fork, her eyes brightening. "And something remarkable happened. I did just what she said to do. I told God everything that made me so mad at him. I really let him have it. I almost expected a lightning bolt to hit me. But you know what? I didn't feel anger in return. Instead, I felt this overwhelming sense of love. From the top of my head down to my toes. I've never felt anything like that before. It was as if God was saying it's okay to be angry. He can take it. But he wanted me to know that he still loves me. He's still there."

Pops had been watching Mom with a soft expression in his eyes. "Sounds like something your mother always wanted you to know."

"I feel . . . different. I can't quite explain it. But I think everything's going to be better from now on." She glanced at Maisie. "Really, truly better. Not just Band-Aid better."

Maisie felt a surge of emotions. Relief, mostly. "I believe it too."

"Thank you, sweetheart," her mom said, reaching across the table to squeeze Maisie's hand. "And thank you for being so patient with me." She glanced at Pops. "Both of you."

Pops cleared his throat, a hint of emotion in his voice. "Well, there's a reason your mother named you Calathea."

Mom laughed at that. She pointed her fork in his direction. "Are you absolutely sure you didn't have something to do with sending me to that retreat?"

He shook his head. "Only if you consider consistent prayer on your behalf as a tool of coercion." He rose. "Thea, would you like some moose drool?"

Her mom looked grossed out. "Moose drool?"

"It's park-speak for coffee, Mom," Maisie said. "You got to keep your cool on."

"Keep my cool on?"

Pops grinned. "She's quoting Frankie, the park hottie."

"Pops!"

Mom's eyebrow lifted. "Is Frankie someone I should meet?"

"Oh, you'll definitely cross paths with him," Pops said. "He's always fluttering around this kid."

"I am NOT a kid!"

Pops laughed, and Mom laughed, and soon Maisie loosened up and joined in.

Later, as Maisie brushed her teeth, she had a revelation: for the first time in a long while, as she got ready for bed and her mind settled into quietness, she didn't feel worried about her mom.

Less than two weeks had passed since Kate had arrived in Grand Teton National Park, yet she felt like a different person. Being here had taught her so much about herself. For the first time in her life, she realized that seeing things differently was a gift, not a burden. So maybe God hadn't made a mistake in wiring her brain the way it was. *She* wasn't a mistake.

And she definitely sensed God's protection over her with Oliver's treachery. Everyone at the park congratulated her, as if she'd played an important role in catching the notorious Wade Schmidt. She still felt like a fool for believing him. No—actually, she felt like a fool for not trusting her instincts about him. She'd always had a hitch in her gut. Always felt a need to slow things down with him. Why hadn't she listened to it? That hitch in her gut was from God. She knew that now.

When she told Coop that the *Nat Geo* editor was a complete fake, he put his hands on her shoulders and smiled at her. That smile said *Believe in yourself.* "You know what I admire most about you? Your resiliency."

Wasn't that something else? He saw resiliency in her.

She might just love that man.

Later that day, back in her hotel room, she examined her photograph again. It truly was a one-in-a-million shot. So she took in a deep breath and sent it to *National Geographic*, to a vague depository that everyone submitted their pictures to, with the subject: "First and best photograph taken this year of Grizzly Bear 399 from Grand Teton National Park." She held out little hope that it would even get noticed.

On a notepad, she wrote down other sites to send the picture to, even local newspapers. They weren't *Nat Geo*, but they were something. Like Coop said, everybody has to start somewhere.

A few hours later, she heard a ping on her phone that an email had come in. She glanced at the sender, then blinked and read it again. Kate felt a jolt of adrenaline. This email was from *National Geographic*.

This is the real deal? The first glimpse of 399 this year?

Yes, she typed back. *It can be confirmed by multiple park rangers, including the director of the park. It was taken in the last twenty-four hours.*

A few minutes later, another email came in.

And you didn't do any post-processing? You'll sign off on that? This is a critical point. We had to yank the cover for the next issue because the photographer had done more post-processing than he had led us to believe. He will never work for us again.

No *post-processing*, she typed, *other than cropping.*
A long time elapsed and Kate sat back down on her bed. She was just about to set her phone down when another email came in.

Well, it's been decided. Your photo is going to be on the next cover. It's quite a remarkable shot. Timing is perfect because we're running a feature on grizzly bears.

Kate stared at her phone for the longest while. Hands trembling, she typed back. *I'm honored. Thank you.*

Look for an email with documents to sign and return. And . . . congratulations.

Kate fell back on her bed, gobsmacked. The first thought that ran through her head was, *Thank you, thank you, thank you, God.*

Her second thought, as soon as her heart stopped pounding, was to call Coop to share her news.

~

The next afternoon Coop found himself smack-dab in the middle of the road, playing traffic cop. As he directed cars around a bear jam near Mormon Row, Sally's voice crackled through the radio. "Where are you?"

"Bear jam near Mormon Row," Coop replied, keeping his eyes on some overzealous amateur photographers. He'd warned them twice already to stay one hundred yards away from the bear, but as the bear moved closer, they didn't budge. He wasn't sure which park visitors annoyed him more—this type, or the kind that jumped out of their car to snap a picture and took off again. "Which bear?"

"Blondie and her cub."

"Is Frankie with you?"

Coop couldn't help but scoff. He glanced over to where Frankie stood, happily accepting a Tupperware container filled with cookies from a well-meaning park visitor. How many times had Coop told that kid not to take food from strangers?

"Is he ever not with me?" Coop muttered into the radio.

"Good. I've sent two other rangers over to relieve you. As soon as they arrive, bring Frankie to my office. And find Zoo Girl and bring her too."

"Kate? Why?" Coop questioned, but Sally had already signed off.

Coop tucked the radio back onto his belt and dialed Kate's number. "Hello there," he said, smiling. "Still walking on air from last night's news?" Kate had woken him out of a sound sleep with her news about making the cover of *National Geographic*, and he couldn't have been more pleased. For her, for him, for 399, for the park. He felt kind of proud that he had helped her get that shot too. But the credit belonged to her. It was a phenomenal photograph and he couldn't be happier for Kate.

"Honestly, I haven't come back to earth yet."

"Where are you now?" he asked as he scanned the horizon for any sign of Blondie or her cub.

"I'm over by Jenny Lake. There's a bald eagle's nest that's as big as a small house." Her voice sounded alive with excitement.

Coop grinned. He knew that nest well and could imagine the

awe in Kate's eyes as she marveled at it. "Can you break away soon? The chief ranger wants you in her office."

"Me? Why?" Kate sounded puzzled.

"No idea. She wants me there too," Coop said. And Frankie, which was really odd.

"Okay. You've got my curiosity piqued. I'll head over."

As Coop ended the call, Frankie sauntered up to him with a mischievous grin. "Bet you ten bucks that you were talking to Kate. You had a goofy look on your face."

Coop scowled and adjusted his binoculars to check on Blondie, who had vanished behind the tree line. "Bear jam is breaking up. Hop in the truck and I'll be there in a minute."

Twenty minutes later, Coop knocked on Sally's door and entered to find a distinguished man seated across from her desk. His presence commanded attention, and his sharp gaze swept over Coop before moving on.

"Ranger Cooper," Sally began, her tone formal, "let me introduce you to Deputy Director Donald Franklin."

Deputy director? Of the National Park Service? Coop felt a surge of nervousness in the presence of such a high-ranking official. Unsure whether to extend his hand for a shake, he hesitated.

"Where's my son?" Franklin's voice cut through the air.

Coop's mind raced. "Your son? What . . . you mean . . . Frankie?" It dawned on him suddenly that the deputy director was Frankie's dad. "He's . . . well, he saw Maisie—she's a granddaughter of a ranger—and they're talking. I'm sure he'll join us in a minute or two."

Franklin relaxed slightly. "Sounds pretty typical for Frankie to be distracted by a pretty girl."

Feeling a bit starstruck, Coop stumbled over his words. "I can, um, well, I can go get him."

"No need." Franklin reached out to shake Coop's hand. "Sit

down, Ranger Cooper. I understand you're the one to thank for the changes in my son."

Coop slapped a hand against his chest. "Me?"

"I'm sure it's no secret that Frankie's been having trouble. He's been in three boarding schools in less than two years. I can count on one hand the times he's called me in the last few years. But yesterday, he called me with excitement in his voice. He called *me*. He went on and on about the poacher and 399 and hiking in the backcountry and, well, you. He sounded like the boy I remember, the one who loved the great outdoors. I thank you for that."

"Me?"

"Sounds like you've reignited his love of nature."

"Honestly, sir, he's always had it. I think he's just been burying it to hurt you."

"Cooper!" Sally shot him a warning look.

Coop glanced at Sally. "My apologies. I've said too much. During the school year, I'm a high school teacher. I should keep my ranger hat on."

"No need to apologize. Frankie and I, we've had to weather a lot of changes in the last few years."

"So he's told me."

Sally shot Coop a sharp look, then refocused on the deputy director. "Perhaps we should go. The other rangers are gathering out in front of the visitor center."

"Hold it." Franklin waved her off. "Go ahead, Ranger. Say what's on your mind."

"I think there's been too much change for Frankie. He likes to sound like a man, but he's pretty immature."

"Cooper! That's enough."

Why? Should Coop not have said that? Wasn't it obvious to everyone? "Kids like Frankie, I see them all the time at my school. They're starved for their parents' attention."

Sally groaned and dropped her chin to her chest.

"It's okay, Ranger Janus." Franklin lifted a hand to reassure Sally. "I don't disagree. I just haven't known what to do about him. He's been so . . . angry."

Coop cast a glance at Sally to see if she was trying to warn him, but she seemed to have calmed down from high alert. "Sounds like he's had a lot to deal with. First his mother's death, followed closely by your DC appointment. Honestly, I think he feels like he's lost both parents."

The professional facade of Donald Franklin dropped, and he looked like just another confused dad. Coop saw a lot of them in high school. "Hey, but you're here now, and that says a lot." Why was he here, anyway?

The door burst open, Frankie's usual style of entry, but then he froze when he saw his father. "Dad? You came."

"Hello, Frankie," his dad said.

"I didn't expect you to drop everything. I didn't expect you to come all this way."

"You should expect that," Franklin said, his voice cracking. "You're my son." He rose from his chair and opened his arms. "You've helped to nail Wade Schmidt. That's a pretty big deal to me." For a long awkward moment, Frankie seemed puzzled, like he didn't know quite what to do. Then it clicked and he took a step forward, just enough encouragement for his dad to reach out and pull him into his arms. Awkward, but a start.

Coop motioned to Sally that they should leave the room. On the walk down the hallway, Sally said, "I had no idea you were a child psychologist."

Coop laughed. "That situation didn't exactly take rocket science."

"Neither did the photograph at Willow Flats." Sally stopped to look at him. "I wish you had come to me with your suspicions."

Coop turned to face her. "I'm sorry, Sally. I just didn't know what to do. So I went to Tim."

"That was the right thing to do. Even though you both had it all wrong." She waved it off, like it was ancient history. "The deputy director has some announcements he wants to make. The off-duty rangers are meeting out in front of the visitor center. The Zoo Girl is coming, right?"

"Kate. Her name is Kate Cunningham. And yes, she's on her way."

Sally turned and went briskly down the hall, leaving Coop with an uncomfortable feeling in his gut.

Tim Rivers and Maisie stood in front of headquarters, along with a few off-duty rangers, after receiving a cryptic message from Sally: *There's going to be special announcements, so get on over here.* He watched as Sally emerged from the front door, followed by Coop, and then a man strolled out with his arm around Frankie—just enough familial resemblance for Tim to know who this man was. He grinned at the sight of a father and son acting like fathers and sons should.

Without waiting for introductions, the man addressed the small gathering of rangers. "Good afternoon," he began, his voice exuding authority. "My name is Donald Franklin, deputy director of the NPS."

Tim fought back a smile as he noticed how every ranger straightened up at Franklin's words, a subtle sign of respect.

"I want to personally thank each one of you for your dedication to preserving the integrity of our national parks. It's a job that demands the utmost vigilance, and I'm proud to see such commitment." He clasped his hands together. "But that's not the reason I've come. There's been an impressive collaboration here between rangers, law enforcement, and even a wildlife photographer. Caught the poacher, saved the bear."

Give Sally credit, Tim thought. *She deserves full credit.*

"We've got a lot to celebrate today. Is Kate Cunningham here?"

Kate, standing next to Coop, raised her hand.

"My son told me about your quick thinking. Impressive stuff. In fact, I've been talking with Sally here about your photography skills. She shared some of your work with me, and I must say, your photos are impressive. However, what really caught my attention were your captions. Nowadays, many parks are utilizing social media to connect with younger audiences, active on platforms like Intergram—"

"Aww, Dad," Frankie said, groaning. "Instagram." Under his breath he muttered, "He's gotta get his cool on."

"Right. Instagram." Franklin cleared his throat. "Ranger Janus thinks you're the ideal candidate for this new social media role for the park."

Nice, Tim thought. *Really nice.* He had to smile at the stunned look on Kate's face. Her eyes widened in astonishment, then she sputtered, "I'm . . . speechless! Thank you so much."

Smiling, Franklin said, "Just keep coming up with those captions." He turned to Coop, standing next to Kate. "And we've got a seasonal ranger who deserves some recognition."

Sally, Tim thought. *Talk about Sally.*

"Ranger Grant Cooper, I understand that you've gone above and beyond the call of duty to keep 399 safe during this poacher threat."

Coop shook his head. "I didn't do anything that other rangers wouldn't have done."

"Not according to Sally Janus. She mentioned how you never hesitated to follow her lead, even when you had doubts. She credited you as a crucial player in nabbing Wade Schmidt. The NPS would like to offer you a full-time position as a Jenny Lake Ranger."

Stunned, Coop exchanged a look with Kate that spoke volumes to Tim. His young friend had finally healed from the Emma Dilemma. At last.

But there's still Sally, Tim thought. *Don't forget her.*

"And Frankie," Don said. "I will give parental consent for you to be part of the Wildlife Brigade."

"Aww, cool," Frankie said, trying to keep his cool on. Not too successfully, either. He broke out with a big grin.

And now for Sally, Tim thought. *Give her the credit she deserves.*

Finally, Don addressed Sally. "Ranger Janus, you've done an outstanding job managing this park, especially during this recent challenge. You're to be commended for your role in aiding federal agents to apprehend a notorious poacher. The National Park Service would like to reward you with a promotion from acting chief ranger to chief ranger. Effective immediately. Congratulations."

Everyone erupted into cheers. Good, Tim thought, clapping loudly. She deserved that promotion. She had a mildly pleased look on her face. Not quite as pleased as Tim would've thought.

Tim hung around after the meeting dispersed. He peeked into Sally's office, noticing the flurry of activity as boxes were stacked against the wall. "Hey," he said, stepping inside. "I was happy to hear about your promotion. You deserve it." He looked around. "Are they making you move offices?"

"I'll say," Sally said, motioning for Tim to take a seat amidst the chaos of packing. She moved a box to make room for him. Leaning against her desk, she exhaled deeply. "The deputy director didn't announce it, but my assignment is not Grand Teton. It's Isle Royale in Michigan."

Tim needed a minute to absorb this bombshell. Sally's expression remained composed, but his mind raced with what he knew of Isle Royale. Situated in the middle of Lake

Superior, it was hard to get to, hard to get out of. "Well," he said, clearing his throat. "I guess I can see why Don didn't make that piece of information public."

"You know how things roll with the NPS. To move forward, you have to go sideways."

"I've never been to Isle Royale."

"No. Not many have. Less than twenty-five thousand visitors each summer."

"Hardy souls, I would imagine."

Sally snorted. "I'll say."

"I'm a hardy soul. I'll visit. If you'd like me to, that is."

Sally's arms crossed, a thoughtful expression crossing her face. "I don't think so, Tim."

No, he didn't think so, either. This last week had shown him something he hadn't wanted to see. He'd always focused on what they had in common—a shared passion to protect and preserve the national parks. But in doing that, he'd missed the deeper differences between them. "I wish you well, Sally."

"As do I you."

The weight of their words hung between them, final and heavy. It was really over between them. Tim noticed the shimmer in Sally's eyes and was just about to say something, when she shifted the focus away from their personal turmoil. "So, Don asked me to recommend someone to replace me as acting chief ranger, just until they make their final choice," she said, her gaze unwavering. "I told him you'd be the best one for the job."

Tim dropped his chin, overcome.

⁓

The deputy director worked some magic and snagged a special preseason dinner at Jenny Lake Lodge for Coop, Kate, Sally, Frankie, Tim, Maisie, and even Maisie's mother, who had just arrived. Kate had been inside the lodge a couple of times, but dining there seemed like a dream. According to Maisie's fun facts, the lodge was a product of the 1930s Civilian Conservation Corps, starting as simple cabins and growing into a luxury wilderness destination.

Kate had read the hype about Jenny Lake Lodge's dining experience from guidebooks. People booked tables months ahead, the gourmet menu boasted locally sourced ingredients, and the food was rumored to be exquisite—and it lived up to the hype. The meal was beyond anything she could have imagined—leisurely, elegant, and absolutely delicious.

But the real showstopper was the view. As the only patrons, they were seated at a table by the massive windows showcasing the breathtaking Grand Tetons. It was a sight that left everyone at the table in awe.

Everyone hung around, staying way longer than they probably should have. It was getting late by the time they finally left the lodge. They all ambled to their cars, dragging out their goodbyes. Finally, only Kate and Coop remained.

"Was it just me," she said, "or did it seem like there might've been sparks between Frankie's dad and Maisie's mom?"

"I had the exact same thought. They never stopped talking." Coop leaned his back against Kate's car, as if he was in no hurry to leave. "I think Frankie had a very uncool ear-to-ear grin on his face tonight."

Kate burst out with a laugh. "Seems like there's been a turning point for Frankie and his dad."

"Yeah," Coop said. "A turning point for Tim and Sally too, but not in a good way. He told me her promotion is in Isle Royale in Michigan." Coop tipped his head. "I guess this was a pivotal week for you too."

Kate's eyes widened. "You mean because of Oliver? I would call it more than a pivot." She let out a puff of air. "I feel foolish. So naive."

"Innocent," Coop said. "Trusting."

"I can see now how I basically dangled 399 right in front of him."

"So he didn't know of her until you brought her up?"

"Yes. No. I'm not sure." Kate let out a huff. "I keep thinking about this. I thought I was the one who told him about 399—but now I'm not sure who brought her up first. Honestly, I'm not sure about a lot of our conversations. But I do know that she's all I talked about these last few months. A man like that—how could he not see it as a dare? Because of me, he tried to kill that wonderful bear."

"Because of you, she was protected. Because of you, one of the most elusive, notorious poachers has been caught and will face justice."

Kate looked at him. How kind. "Thank you for not blaming me."

"You did nothing wrong, Kate. In fact, you did a lot of things right." His eyes met hers. Met and stayed.

She tried to keep her cool on, but she felt a sizzle of attraction run through her entire body. He was beautiful to her, inside and out. His looks—those even features, the seawater-gray eyes with crinkles at the corners. But also his heart—calm strength under fire, protective and caring.

Tenderness was written on his face. "What would you say about heading over to Oxbow Bend? Full moon tonight."

What would Kate say? Yes, yes, yes! But, to quote Frankie, she kept her cool on. "Sounds like a plan."

They left Kate's car in the Jenny Lake Lodge parking lot and drove over in Coop's truck. A small detail but significant for Kate, because her camera was in her car's trunk. No photograph-taking tonight. No distractions.

The full moon came out from behind a cloud, casting a bright glow over Oxbow Bend. Kate and Coop walked along the riverbank. Everything felt serene, almost magical. The Tetons stood tall in the distance, their snowy tops glistening in the moonlight and doubling themselves in the calm Snake River below. "I can't get over how different this area seems in the moonlight compared to the day. It's always changing." Across the water, something darted out from a bush and dove into the water.

"Nocturnal wildlife is different too."

"God is so interesting," she whispered softly.

He smiled. "That, and God is so . . . vast."

"These last few days . . . God was in all of it. I've never felt his presence quite like I did. Or maybe a better way to say it, I've never seen God's presence quite like I can see him now. All those just-in-the-knick-of-time moments. Like, Frankie forgetting his phone and making you return for it."

Coop nodded. "Or Tim passing by Feldmann's car and recognizing him."

"So what do you think?"

"About . . . all that went on in the last few days?"

"Do you think God was in it?" It was important for Kate to know what he thought.

"I'll be honest that if you'd asked me a week ago about those coincidences, I might've chalked them up to just that—coincidences. But now . . . I have no doubt there's more to them." He gazed over the river. "The same God who made this incredible park in the first place, who takes care of all the wild creatures in it, is more than capable of delivering hunches at just the right time."

She smiled, appreciating his candor, his openness. She believed he was telling her the truth, sharing genuine conviction. "It's the listening to the hunches part I need to get good at. There's a verse in the Old Testament about how God speaks not in a fire, not in an earthquake, but in a whisper."

Coop scoffed a laugh. "No wonder we miss it so much."

They walked a while longer until Coop pointed up the bank

to where someone had left a plastic bench. He brushed the dirt off with his hand and they sat, soaking in the tranquil scenery together.

"I wish this day wouldn't come to an end," Kate said softly. "I think it'll always be the best day of my life."

"Me too. It's been quite a day." Coop's gaze was warm as he turned to her. "What do you think? Are you considering accepting the social-media-slash-photographer-in-residence position?"

"I'd like to. I really, really would. It combines everything I love. There's just one thing that I wish would happen first."

Coop shifted on the bench to face her directly. "What's that?"

"I wish . . . "

He waited, but she couldn't voice the words aloud.

"What do you wish?"

I wish I could be fearless, she thought. *Bold and brave. What's the worst that can happen if I put myself out there?* She took in a deep breath and blurted out, "I wish you would accept the full-time Jenny Lake Ranger job and stay here." There, she said it.

And in return, he said nothing.

This didn't seem promising.

He just looked at her with those steady seawater-gray eyes of his, like they could see right through to her very core. And what would he see? Someone who wished she could rewind the last thirty seconds. Take back her bold and brave declaration. Slide back into her safe turtle shell.

And then, a smile tugged at the corners of his lips. "Full disclosure." A full smile emerged. "Before dinner tonight, I sent in my resignation to the principal."

He did . . . *what*? Any more happiness and Kate felt as if she might fly away like a helium balloon. She smiled, big and wide. So much for keeping her cool on.

"This week, well, it's been an eye-opener for me. I think I've been needing a change for a while now. Meeting you has pretty much sealed the deal for me."

In her head, she heard a sound very similar to the triumphant crescendo of a symphony's grand finale. "So then . . . it looks like we'll both be here at Grand Teton National Park for the foreseeable future."

"Kate," he said, his tone softening as he reached one arm around her, "this might be the best day of your life so far . . ."

She turned to face him. In his gaze, she saw everything. Respect. Caring. Love.

". . . but I think there are more best days to come."

And with that promise hanging in the air, Coop leaned over to seal it with a kiss. *And what a kiss.* The kind of kiss that swept a girl away from the here and now, making time and space fade into the background. The kind of kiss that made tomorrow seem like a blank canvas, full of hope and endless opportunities.

A perfect note, Kate thought, *to end on.*

DISCUSSION QUESTIONS

1. So, hunting's a big deal in this story, right? We've got Wade Schmidt's prowl for a grizzly bear, Oliver's chase of Kate, and even Kate's pursuit for the perfect bear shot. How do you think all these hunts tie together?

2. What about the surprise elements in the story? Did a few twists and turns catch you off guard? Was there a moment that had you do a double take?

3. Let's get into the nitty-gritty of the characters' development. Who do you think had the most growth by the end of the novel? Was there a character who really surprised you with their choices?

4. Coop's introspection about his past mistakes with Emma and the parallels he sees in Oliver offer some food for thought. How does this self-awareness indicate that he's finally ready to move on from Emma and have a successful new relationship?

5. And speaking of Kate, it was a bold move when she rejected Oliver's proposal, even before the full truth comes to light. Did you think that moment marked a

crucial point when she found her own voice? Or do you think it was inevitable?

6. Did you see any similarities between Wade Schmidt and Oliver? Or did they strike you as completely different characters? After you finished the book, did you go back and notice a few things that you might have missed the first time? Like that moment when Wade was thinking about his girlfriend and whether she'd fit into his life. Maybe she would work for him, he thought. Maybe not. Any other catches?

7. Tim and Sally are quite the pair, aren't they? Super passionate about their work, but it's like they're dancing to different tunes. What do you think—will they figure out a way to sync up, or has that little gap between them turned into a canyon too big to cross?

8. And then there's Frankie and Maisie. Do you think Maisie's feelings are entirely one-sided? What's your take on how the relationship between them might develop over time? Any moments that made you cheer or want to give one of them a gentle nudge in the right direction?

9. And then there's the majestic national park setting, almost a character in its own right. The wild, untamed landscapes they find themselves in seem to parallel their own journeys toward authenticity and maturity. Maybe even understanding God in a bigger, wider way. How does this backdrop reflect or contrast with the characters' struggles and growth?

AUTHOR'S NOTE

There's just something about that bear. I first learned about Grizzly Bear 399 when I was planning a trip to Grand Teton National Park. She's a pretty big deal.

This remarkable bear is not just a symbol of the park's wild essence, but she's also become somewhat of a celebrity in her own right. Nearly three decades old, 399 has successfully raised several generations of cubs, teaching them to navigate the complex interplay of wilderness and human presence. Her resilience and maternal instincts have made her a subject of fascination for wildlife enthusiasts and researchers alike. Her story is a powerful reminder of the delicate balance we must maintain in our national parks and the profound connections between their inhabitants and visitors.

Like Kate Cunningham, I'd like to meet her . . . from a distance. But 399 wasn't the reason I pitched the Summer in the Park series to my editor. That was sparked by a serendipitous encounter in the rustic yet charming Jackson Lake Lodge gift shop when I struck up a conversation with a young college girl working behind the counter. She was from Alabama and told me, with a mix of excitement and nervousness, that this was her first time out of her home state. Her mom had just dropped her off for the summer. That simple revelation hit me profoundly. Here was this young woman, stepping way out of her comfort zone, ready to take on an adventure far from everything familiar. It was her first step into a much larger world, a wild one at that.

That one conversation planted the seed for the Summer in the Park series. I started thinking about all the people who come to our national parks, each with their own stories and backgrounds, and how these majestic places play a part in their personal growth and adventures. The more I thought about it, the more I wanted to explore the rich tapestry of lives intertwined with the natural beauty and historical depth of our national parks.

Speaking of history, did you know that there are over sixty-three national parks across the United States? Each one, from the most visited like Yellowstone and the Grand Canyon to lesser-known gems like Crater Lake or Badlands, offers a unique glimpse into the natural and cultural heritage that shapes our country. These parks aren't just plots of land preserved for their scenic views or wildlife; they are places where Americans come together, where we find common ground, and where the spirit of exploration and preservation is alive and well.

This fascination with our national parks has turned into a personal goal of mine—to visit as many as I can. Maybe not all sixty-three, but I'm going to give it a good try! Each visit teaches me something new, not just about the park, but also about the people who visit and work there. They are truly our country's treasures, these slices of wilderness and history, and they remind us of our duty to protect and cherish these spaces.

As you dive into this series, I hope you find a little bit of that wonder and connection that I felt during my visit to Grand Teton. Whether it's the allure of new experiences, the beauty of untouched landscapes, or the stories of those who travel far from home to find something new, these stories are a celebration of the spirit that national parks inspire in all of us.

Enjoy your journey through the pages, and maybe it'll inspire your own adventure into America's vast, beautiful backyard and find a national park to love. Happy reading!

P.S. As I was finishing the final edits on *Capture the Moment*, heartbreaking news broke: the beloved #399 had been hit by a car and killed. Like so many others, I felt heartsick. Though I knew she wouldn't live forever, I had hoped for a more fitting and majestic end. She brought the world so much wonder and joy in her wild, natural home, and she will be deeply missed. Rest in peace, dear bear.

ACKNOWLEDGMENTS

I'd like to extend a heartfelt thank-you to Joy and Jeff Kreps for generously sharing their experiences as volunteers in national parks. Their insights were invaluable, and they also introduced me to Jeff Lahr, a seasonal ranger at Yosemite, whose knowledge added depth to my research. You couldn't have been more helpful. Your contributions went beyond what I could have imagined, and I'm truly grateful.

A special shout-out to Mary Dietler for pointing me toward a few special rangers, which became instrumental in shaping this novel. While I try to capture the important work of rangers accurately, this is a work of fiction. Any and all blunders are mine!

Of course, none of this would be possible without the support of readers like you. Your enthusiasm and engagement drive these novels forward, and I am deeply grateful for you.

As I wrap up this first installment of the Summer in the Park series, I am filled with awe at the wonders of creation, especially in the context of the Creator. God is so interesting. We are all truly blessed to experience the beauty and majesty of nature, and I hope this novel brings a piece of that joy to your lives.

RESOURCES

If you might be interested in delving deeper into the story of our national parks, past and present, apart from the usual up-to-date travel guides, here are some recommended sources:

Anderson, Joel, and Nathan Anderson, *63 Illustrated National Parks: Celebrating Our Heritage of Wilderness and Wonder* (Nashville: Anderson Design Group, Inc., 2021).

Bryant, Kathleen, *Western National Parks' Lodges Cookbook* (Arizona: Northland Publishing, 2007).

Bryson, Bill, *A Walk in the Woods: Rediscovering America on the Appalachian Trail* (New York: Anchor Books, 1998).

Duncan, Dayton, and Ken Burns, *The National Parks: America's Best Idea* (New York: Alfred A. Knopf, 2009). (Also a PBS series.)

Grizzly 399: Queen of the Tetons, nature documentary on PBS *Nature* (2024).

Knighton, Conor, *Leave Only Footprints: My Acadia-to-Zion Journey through Every National Park* (New York: Crown, 2020).

Smith, Matt and Karen, *Dear Bob and Sue: One Couple's Journey through the National Park* (self-pub., 2012).

Whittlesey, Lee E., *Death in Yellowstone: Accidents and Foolhardiness in the First National Park* (Boulder, CO: Roberts Rinehart, 2014).

Williams, Terry Tempest, *The Hour of Land: A Personal Topography of America's National Parks* (New York: Sarah Crichton Books, 2016).

TURN THE PAGE TO
READ A SAMPLE FROM

a YEAR of

FLOWERS

one

You're only here for a short visit. Don't hurry, don't worry.
And be sure to smell the flowers along the way.
—*Walter Hagen*

Jaime Harper stepped back to examine the bridal bouquet she'd created for the Zimmerman-Blau wedding. She had to get this bouquet right today. Did it seem balanced? Was anything sticking out? A bridal bouquet was the most photographed floral piece of an entire wedding. Nail it down and everything else would fall into place.

This was the sixth mock-up. All previous ones had been shot down by the mother of the bride. These mock-up meetings were critical steps in the planning process. And Mrs. Zimmerman was a critical customer. She had a way of making Jaime feel like a rooster one day and a feather duster the next.

The Zimmerman-Blau wedding was going to be the highest-profile wedding yet for Epic Events. Sloane, the project manager, reminded her that it was such an important wedding that Epic's owner Liam McMillan was leaving an initial design consultation with a prospective client to be at this flower mock-up with

Mrs. Zimmerman. "Liam asked me to make lunch reservations at his favorite restaurant," Sloane said. "A congratulations lunch," she added, crossing her fingers. "Today's the day." Final approval from Mrs. Z, she meant.

"Let's hope so," Jaime said, but she wondered. She'd been tinkering with the arrangement all morning. Her mind kept wandering, and she had to keep tugging herself back to the here and now. When she was distracted, she missed things. When she missed things, bad things happened. She knew that for a fact. "Do you think it's too, too . . ." Too much? Too little?

Sloane rolled her eyes. "Stop sounding so pathetic."

"I can't help it," Jaime said. She had a better sense of the terrible things that could happen in the world than most people did.

"Hurry and finish and clean up your workshop!"

Jaime looked at her and sighed. "I don't know why y'all are always in a rush."

Sloane turned from the door and winked. "My little Southern belle, have you still not realized we have only one speed? Express."

Jaime listened to the sound of Sloane's staccato heels doing their fast-walk down the hallway. Why did New Yorkers go through life like their hair was on fire? And for what? She got the same results by taking her time.

In the mirror, she examined the bouquet one more time. Was it as good as Sloane said? She hated that her first thought was no, that she never thought her work was good enough. She didn't know what took a greater toll on her sense of well-being—her own self-deprecating thoughts or high-maintenance clients with way too much money. Something was still cattywampus with the bouquet, and Mrs. Zimmerman would notice that indescribable *something* and reject, yet again, the design.

For most weddings, flowers took about 10 to 15 percent of

the total budget. Clients were delighted to cut down on costs and waste by letting the ceremony flowers do double duty at the reception space. The welcome arrangement from the ceremony could be reused at the table seating display. Or the bridal bouquet could be put in a vase and used as the sweetheart table arrangement. But there was no such skimping for the Zimmerman wedding.

Flowers, Mrs. Zimmerman insisted, were to be the main décor for her daughter's wedding. She loved flowers and wanted lavish displays to fill every space in the venue, the New York Botanical Garden—a beautiful oasis in the middle of the Bronx. All in all, the flower budget for the Zimmerman wedding came to a staggering sum. That was the reason there was such heightened concern at Epic Events to get Mrs. Zimmerman's approval on the flowers. Sloane couldn't start billing until Mrs. Z signed off, and Jaime couldn't order the flowers without paying a sizable deposit up front. So today was the day. She had to get the mock-up bouquet right today.

She took a picture on her phone of the bouquet and sent it to Liam. A minute or two later, Liam texted back *Subtract*, and of course he was right. He was always right. Jaime had a tendency to jam-pack so that blooms competed for space as they expanded in the heat of the day. What looked to be a perfectly balanced floral arrangement in the cool of the morning would look stuffed and tight by evening. So she subtracted by pulling stems and removing materials, until she thought it thoroughly resembled Liam's recipe.

That man had some kind of superpower in how he could read his clients' minds. He was able to visualize and articulate what the clients wanted even if they didn't seem to know themselves. This was the sticky-floral-tape thought for Jaime: How to put into reality the creation Liam had imagined. That was the secret sauce for everyone at Epic Events—to think like

Liam McMillan thinks and execute like he executes. He *was* the brand.

She went over to the mirror again to hold the bouquet low against her belly, the way a bride would. She rotated the bouquet to see it at every angle, examining different viewpoints to make sure it looked balanced. Photographs exaggerated the depth of field, so it was wise to note whatever might jut out.

Everything looked good. Better than good. Jaime exhaled a sigh of relief. Time to stop. Knowing when to stop was critical.

Jaime taped the stems and set the bouquet in water in the walk-in cooler to keep it as fresh as possible for the meeting.

Before closing the cooler, she breathed in deeply the perfume of fresh flowers, letting their scent calm her nerves. Whenever she paused to soak up the fragrance of flowers, she was instantly transported to the sweetest, happiest time of her life. Back in high school, working afternoons and weekends in Rose's Flower Shop in a tiny town in North Carolina with her two best friends, Claire and Tessa. Mentored in the art of flower arranging by Rose Reid, the shop owner, who had the patience and kindness and generous nature to teach the three girls everything she knew. Flowers were the business of happiness, Rose had often reminded them. They brought joy and comfort to people.

Rose Reid had been on her mind all morning. She was the reason Jaime felt as if tears kept threatening. The reason she felt emotionally wobbly. It was hard to squeeze shame back into its box. Even harder to keep it from spilling out again.

When Jaime had arrived at work this morning, a registered letter was waiting for her. Instantly, she recognized the elegant handwriting, the pale pink stationery. She hurried to the workshop and sat right down on a stool, her chest stinging with pain. How had Rose found her? It was the first time there'd been contact between them since that terrible August day. She cringed at the memory she'd tried so hard to forget. Hands trembling,

Jaime skimmed the letter once, twice, then read it again more thoroughly. *All is forgiven,* Rose wrote. *It's time to come home.* And then she outlined a plan for Jaime to return to live in North Carolina, to run Rose's Flower Shop.

Run a little flower shop in that off-the-beaten-track Southern town? Was Rose serious? After all that had happened between them, that offer took gumption. But did she really think Jaime would give up all *this* . . . for *that*?

Because *this* included quite a bit. A floral dream job led by a remarkably creative boss. And when it came to Liam, there was potential for romance written all over their relationship. Well, sometimes it seemed to be written all over it. Scribbles, maybe. They had "moments" now and then that made her think something was brewing. She hoped so. Oh boy, did she ever hope so.

Then again, so did most every female who worked at Epic Events. So did every female client.

Jaime closed the cooler door—pushing with two hands because it had a tendency to stick—and grabbed a broom to clean up the stems and leaves and petals strewn over the floor. As she gathered the excess flowers to return to the cooler, she glanced at the large wall clock. An idea had been tickling in the back of her mind for a unique bouquet—a contemporary take on a cascade style. Why not? She had time. Sitting in the cooler were leftover Zimmerman flowers, plus some unusual flowers she'd picked up on a whim this morning at the New York City Flower Market.

First, she began with a dense center: clusters of color for focus. The showstoppers. Café Latte roses, Cappuccino roses, Café au Lait Ranunculus as big as roses. She built intensity by adding pops of color: Black Parrot tulips and Hot Chocolate calla lilies. The black tulips were the color of an eggplant (Mother Nature doesn't make truly black flowers), petals glossy with a dark luster, tops fringed like feathers—hence the name parrot tulips. The calla lilies were a deep chocolate burgundy bloom.

She brought in texture with trailers of creeping fig woven in through the roses. Next came gradients, accent flowers to bridge the colors—mini Epidendrum orchids, ruffly Lisianthus. Then foliage to fill the gaps. A light hand, though.

She stood back to assess. It felt like it still needed more, but she hesitated, thinking of Liam's text: *Subtract!* A phrase from Rose popped into her mind: *"Let the flowers speak."* So Jaime added layer upon layer, letting the flowers do the talking. She stood in front of the mirror, just as she had done with the Zimmerman bouquet, and felt a deep sense of satisfaction.

The door opened and Sloane stuck her head in. Her mouth opened, closed, opened again, then stopped. Her eyes and attention were on the bouquet. "Jaime, it's an absolute stunner." She took a step into the workshop. "It's like an oil painting." Adding in a warning tone, "But . . . that's *not* the bouquet that Liam wanted—"

"No, no. Don't worry. This isn't the Zimmerman bouquet. That's in the cooler."

Sloane crossed the room to examine the bouquet in Jaime's hands.

"Sometimes . . ."

"What?"

"Sometimes . . . I wish I had your job."

Jaime's eyes narrowed in surprise. Sloane was a phenomenal project manager. So smart, so capable. She kept the team on a strict timeline. "I thought you liked doing what you do."

"I do. Sure I do. I mean, if I want my own company one day, this is the best path. But there's just something about flowers."

Sloane bent over to inhale deeply from the bouquet and

Jaime understood. There *was* just something about flowers. "I'll tell you *what*! After the Zimmerman wedding, maybe I can teach you some flower basics."

Sloane smiled. "I'll tell *you* what." She liked to mock Jaime's Southernness. "You're on." She tipped her head. "Are those black tulips?"

Jaime nodded. "Tulips symbolize eternal love."

"Get a picture of that one. I want it for my wedding." Sloane rolled her eyes upward. "If Charlie will ever get over his allergy to commitment." They'd been engaged for seven years. She pointed to the large clock on the wall. "I just heard from Liam. They're on their way."

More than on their way. Through the large warehouse window, Jaime could see an Uber pull into the parking lot, followed by Mrs. Zimmerman's white Tesla. She took a few steps over to the large window, watching Liam, her heart humming like a contented cat. She enjoyed observing him unawares. Stolen moments, she thought of them.

"Checking out Mrs. Z's latest ensemble?"

Not hardly. Jaime's eyes were on Liam. He hurried over to open the door on the Tesla for Mrs. Zimmerman. *Such a gentleman.*

Sloane came up behind her to join her at the window. "What's she got on today?"

Mrs. Zimmerman, somewhere in her late sixties, had memorable taste in clothing. Today, she wore an orange pantsuit—radiation, glow-in-the-dark orange—and her hair was hidden under a yellow and purple scarf, its tail resting on her shoulder. Sloane whistled, long and low. "I'm still amazed that the flowers for the wedding are subdued colors."

"She wanted everything in pink, all shades, especially hot pink, until Liam told her that pink was requested all year long."

Sloane coughed a laugh. "He's got her figured out. Mrs. Z wants nothing more than to stand out from the crowd." She gave Jaime a pat on her shoulder and started toward the door.

Jaime was barely aware of Sloane's departure. Her eyes were still glued on Liam. Mrs. Zimmerman was giggling at something he was telling her. Mothers of the brides seemed especially vulnerable to Liam's charms. Maybe it was his thick Scottish brogue. There was definitely something mesmerizing about it. Or maybe it had to do with the way he looked at you when he spoke, as if you were exactly the person he was hoping to see and he just couldn't believe how fortunate he was to find you. She wondered if that characteristic might be true of all Scotsmen . . . or if it was just part of the Liam McMillan magic.

Add to that musical accent his good looks—finely chiseled features, his deceptively casual appearance—and females became captivated. Jaime, especially. If he were tall, he might have been an imposing figure, but his below-average height for a man only added to his appeal. He was so approachable, so inviting. Today, Liam was dressed in a black merino sweater and olive trousers, Ferragamo loafers. Jaime caught herself calculating how much money his outfit cost—easily between one and two thousand dollars. Right in the range of hers, though everything she was wearing today had been purchased at an upscale consignment store for a fraction of its original cost. It was one of the perks of living in New York City—lots of one-season-wear castoffs.

With that thought, her stomach started turning again. This, she knew, was the core of her insecurity. Pretending to be someone she wasn't.

With a start, she hurried over to the walk-in cooler to switch the bouquets. She pulled at the door with her free hand, but it wouldn't open. "Stupid cooler!" She rued the day she'd bought this cooler. It was a smoke screen—it looked new but broke down regularly. She yanked and yanked, but she'd need two hands to open the stuck door. She spun around to find a place to set the cascading bouquet and there were Mrs. Zimmerman and Liam, staring at her with wide eyes.

Suzanne Woods Fisher is the award-winning, bestselling author of more than forty books, including *The Sweet Life*, *The Secret to Happiness*, and *Love on a Whim*, as well as many beloved contemporary romance, historical, and Amish romance series. She is also the author of several nonfiction books about the Amish, including *Amish Peace* and *Amish Proverbs*. She lives in California with her very big family. Learn more at SuzanneWoodsFisher.com and follow Suzanne on Facebook @SuzanneWoodsFisherAuthor and X @SuzanneWFisher.

Connect with SUZANNE

SuzanneWoodsFisher.com